THE ARK FILES

AN EDEN BLACK THRILLER

LUKE RICHARDSON

THE KEY TO THE NILE

The Key to the Nile is a symbol representing eternal life in
Ancient Egypt.

PROLOGUE

Al Mina Quay. Tripoli, Lebanon. 1876.

GEORGE GODSPEED LOOKED out across the inky surface of the
Mediterranean. Today of all days, the usually flat sea
churned and broiled. A mammoth wave slammed into the
quay, shaking the ground beneath him, and flinging spray
into the air like venom from a viper.

He muttered to himself, questioning why the storm had
to come today. He shuffled from foot to foot in a vain
attempt to stay warm.

He narrowed his eyes to slits and examined the dark
water. Other than the occasional flicker of a white-crested
wave in the scant moonlight, the darkness was absolute.

Another stream of barbed, salty water slapped across his
face.

For a moment, Godspeed wondered whether they would
even be able to sail in weather like this. He shook the
thought from his mind. These men were as hard as the
weather herself. They had lived their entire lives on the sea,
he supposed. Plus, he had communicated the urgency of his

mission. Come hell or high water, he and his precious cargo needed to leave these shores tonight. The Almighty had certainly delivered on the latter of those, George thought, as another fist of water spray slammed into his cheek.

George pulled his ill-fitting coat even more tightly around him. He doubled it up across his chest and used the thick piece of rope to secure it closed. He had been forced to buy the ragged garment from the hotelier in whose care he had been staying for the last two weeks. Unable to leave the hotel, his shopping options were limited, so when the man dug the old moth-eaten thing from a dusty box, George had no option but to accept it. George thought about the fistful of oily notes he had exchanged for the garment. It wasn't worth one tenth of that, really, but he needed it. He had a long crossing ahead of him. First across the Mediterranean, and then the Atlantic. The crossing would take anywhere upwards of two weeks. If tonight's weather was anything to go by, every bit of warmth would be essential.

Again, George squinted out to sea. Breakers the size and color of wild horses rushed toward him and flung themselves against the harbor arm. Was that some other movement out there amid the waves? The hull of a ship, maybe? At this distance George couldn't be sure.

He turned and looked around the dockyard. Further down the quay, two large iron-hulled freighters sat at anchor. Even in the protected waters of the harbor, they rose and fell on each swell, tugging at their shackles as though attempting to break free. The nearest one, a vessel of some fifty feet in length, sat low and heavy in the water. Perhaps she was fully laden and ready to go, just waiting for a break in the weather. Waiting was a luxury George wished he had.

Several buildings reared up like cliffs somewhere behind him. Packing facilities, George assumed. This port was one of the country's arterial routes, exporting produce grown in Lebanon's fertile soil, all over the Mediterranean.

A gas lamp on the back of the nearest building flickered under a fresh attack from the wind. The lamp's inept flame shrunk in size, retracting the island of light to little more than a puddle. You wouldn't get that problem with electric lights, George pondered, turning back toward the great black expanse of the water.

"If it isn't the dead man walking." A voice echoed from somewhere behind him, barely a whisper against Poseidon's roar.

George whipped around, searching for movement. His heart beat at twice it's normal pace.

"It's alright old boy," came the voice again. "Don't worry, it's only me. I'm the one who should look like I've seen a ghost."

"Rassam." George breathed a sigh of relief. His friend's lithe figure moved through the gloom. George had always thought there was something feline about the man. He moved as though in a state of constant relaxation.

"That's right. Who else would it be? Nobody knows you're here." Rassam materialized and stood beside George. "How are you holding up?" Rassam's Persian accent purred, deep and smooth.

"Well, you know. It's not been easy, but needs must," George said, scrutinizing the man beside him. As usual Rassam was impeccably dressed. His long camel colored coat whipped around his ankles, alternately exposing and hiding a pair of handmade, tan leather boots. The son of a wealthy statesman, Rassam lived life governed by his own agenda, rather than the simple need of money. Godspeed was well aware that without Rassam's funding, many of their more eccentric expeditions would never have been possible.

"Where are the documents?" George hissed in a moment of panic. "You said you would bring them."

"Relax, brother." Rassam smiled at Godspeed. "They are waiting in the carriage. My man will bring them to us when the ship arrives. We don't want them out here getting soaked through. In fact, look... I think that's the Martha Ann now." Rassam pointed out into the void.

Squinting hard, Godspeed could just about make out a shape slipping through the waves on the other side of the harbor arm. A dull lamp mounted on the bridge offered a pinprick of light by which to recognize the vessel.

Rassam produced an oil lamp from beneath his coat and set about lighting it. He dug out a box of matches and struck one to life. He turned on the gas and slid the burning match inside. The lamp flickered as though deciding whether to obey, then rose into a steady orange glow.

In the light, Godspeed recognized the box of matches. Brighton seafront in colorful oils was printed on the front. The image seemed incongruous on the stormy shores of the Mediterranean.

"How many of those have you got?" Godspeed asked. They were far from an ordinary box of matches, Godspeed knew.

"Several," Rassam answered, his voice laced with amusement. Rassam held the box out toward his friend. "You have this one. A memento. Besides, you never know when you might need it."

Godspeed accepted the box of matches and then looked up at his friend. A sudden wave of finality broke across him. "This is it, isn't it? We will never see each other again."

"Not in this life, no," Rassam said. Neither man uttered a word for several seconds. Around them the wind howled, and the sea churned and dragged. "She's in the harbor, look." Rassam pointed with the lamp. The Martha Ann slid inside the protective harbor wall. The thud of her engine thronged through the turbulent air.

Rassam gestured into the darkness. Two men appeared, struggling under the weight of a trunk. They half-dragged, half-carried the trunk along the quay. By the time they reached Godspeed and Rassam they were out of breath. The men placed the trunk by their masters' feet and slunk back into the shadows.

The pounding of the Martha Ann's engine grew louder now. Godspeed looked up at the vessel. She was about sixty feet in length and sat high in the water. A pair of stocky funnels coughed out streams of black smoke.

"She'll be fine out in this," Rassam said, looking up at the ship. "I bet she's beaten many worse storms that this."

Godspeed nodded wordlessly.

The Martha Ann's engine sunk into its lowest register and with a series of slow movements, the skipper brought her alongside the quay. A hatch on the side of the ship swung open and two men jumped out. They quickly lashed the Martha Ann to the quay. The engine continued to rumble and hiss far beneath them.

"How long will it take you to make sense of this?" Rassam said, looking down at the trunk.

"Two years, maybe three," Godspeed replied.

Rassam beckoned for his men. They emerged from the gloom and carried the trunk up onto the ship.

"And the original tablets?" Godspeed asked.

"They'll be moved soon. I know where they're going. I've got the rest of my life to figure out how to get them there."

Godspeed nodded. "This is it then. I'll see you —"

"In the next life," Rassam interrupted. The men merged into a hug. "Inshallah. If God wills it."

A lump forming in his throat, Godspeed hurried up the gangplank and into the belly of the Martha Ann. Beneath his feet the engine that would take him halfway around the world rumbled hungrily.

The sailors unleashed the ship from her bindings and hurried back inside. The engine roared, sending power to the twin propellers, which churned the harbor waters anew.

Godspeed bustled up a set of metal stairs and out onto the deck. He looked down at the quayside, but his friend had already disappeared.

"In the next life it is," Godspeed whispered, his voice lost between the howling wind and the pounding engines.

1

Sarajevo, Bosnia and Herzegovina. Present day.

Paavak Mahmud pushed between the crowds which thronged through the streets of old town Sarajevo. Laid out in the same medieval blueprint, this part of the city had been serving traders, drinkers, smokers, and socialites for over four hundred years. The tightly twisting cobbled streets had withstood the fall of empires, the ravages of war, and perhaps most surprisingly, the insidious rise of the motorcar.

Paavak cut through the central market square, glancing up at the iconic wooden fountain which had stood in the center for nearly two centuries. He paused for a moment and regarded the forest-covered hills surrounding the city on all sides. The minarets of countless mosques bristled from the suburbs, the muezzins within ready to call the faithful to midday prayer. Pavaak glanced at his watch, then pushed on. He didn't want to be late.

He skirted around two hijab-wearing women walking with children and then ducked into the narrow alleyway leading to his favorite of the city's cafes. Despite being tucked away, Café Nafaka was always busy. From ten in the morning until long after midnight, its dedicated staff served Bosnian coffee, fruit juices, and the flavored hookah pipes which were common throughout the Arabic world. Today Paavak would have an iced tea, he decided. Maybe two. Crisp, luscious, and cool, and exactly what he needed on a hot summer afternoon.

Paavak shuffled past a man on a bike, then another dragging a large cart of canned drinks, and emerged into the small square. He scanned the brightly colored seats of green and purple. The person he was due to meet had yet to arrive. *Good*, Paavak thought. He wanted to be first.

He found an empty table — no mean feat in the busy café — and slumped down into the shade. This was perfect. From here he could watch the comings and goings of the café, without even breaking a sweat.

The bubbling sound of a shisha pipe drifted across the café, pursued by a cloud of apple-scented smoke.

Paavak ordered his iced tea from the waiter and relaxed, allowing his pulse to slow and his breathing to normalize after the rushed journey across Sarajevo. Today, Paavak was meeting his friend Giulia. He and Giulia had been working in the same field for well over a decade. The relatively small size of their specialty, and the money available, meant everyone knew each other. When he and Giulia had first met on a dig in Lebanon back in 1998, a roaring friendship had begun. There were times during that three week dig, glimpsing Giulia's ice-blue eyes, that Paavak wondered whether their relationship could be something more. But it never was. The world of archaeology was fast-paced, frantic, and involved traveling all over the world on a moment's notice. Relationships barely lasted more than a few weeks. It was wise to stay out of the whole thing altogether, especially with other members of the fraternity.

The out-of-the-blue message from Giulia this morning had surprised Paavak. When he had told Giulia of his secondment to the University of Sarajevo, and suggested she visit whenever she was passing, he had never actually expected it to happen. Of all the researchers Paavak knew, Giulia was the most in demand. She always seemed to be traveling.

As it turned out, she was passing through Sarajevo on her way to a dig near Mostar, meaning that today they would get to spend the entire afternoon and evening together.

The server delivered Paavak's iced tea in a tall glass with plenty of ice. Paavak nodded in thanks.

He took a sip from the drink and let himself relax further. He leaned back into the couch and placed one arm across the seat beside him. A moment later he placed both hands awkwardly in his lap. He didn't want Giulia to think he was being inappropriate.

The chaotic noise of downtown Sarajevo floated across the rooftops. Somewhere nearby an ancient tram rumbled across an intersection. The clamor of negotiations jumbled with the distant groove of Arabic music, all backed by the ubiquitous grunt of traffic.

Paavak put his glass down and scanned the café. His eyes rested on the access passageway just in time to see a figure barge from the gloom. The figure was Giulia's exact opposite; a large, muscular man, his long hair tied into a ponytail, and an expression as hard as steel. A second, perhaps even larger man who looked strangely similar to the first, joined him a moment later. Two teenage boys jumped out of the way just in time.

Paavak didn't pay the men any attention. He turned and watched the square's other access route. At any moment he would see Giulia's radiant smile, highlighted by the glittering eyes he remembered so well.

In his peripheral vision, Paavak noticed the two men barge across the café. The leading man shoved the waiter out of the way. The men stopped in their tracks, standing side by side.

Paavak turned slowly. The two mountains of muscle and bone looked down at him. At first, Paavak wasn't sure that he was the focus of the brutes' attention. He glanced over his shoulder. They couldn't be looking at anyone else. Paavak scrutinized the men. They looked almost identical, except one of them had a jagged scar across one eye, the eyeball within it pale and unseeing.

The men scowled back, watching Paavak in the way a predator would examine its prey.

The men took a step forward, their formidable shapes casting shadows across Paavak. Muscles bulged in places Paavak didn't even realize muscles should be. The men wore casual shirts and tan-colored shorts. It was as though they were trying, yet failing, to blend in with the tourist crowd. Their postures were far too straight and their attention far too focused to be bumbling tourists.

Ice-cold fingers of fear ran slowly up and down Paavak's spine. He tried to swallow, but his tongue sat in his mouth like a dried-up slug. Paavak shot up straight, as though an electric current had gripped his spine. His hands groped at the cushions beside him. All of his senses tuned in to the men as his fight-or-flight instincts raged. Paavak swallowed hard and made another realization. This one struck him like a physical fist to the jaw, but in an instant, he knew it to be true.

Giulia was dead.

That morning they had communicated by text message. Giulia never communicated by text message.

"Keep my thoughts to a few hundred characters? You must be joking. Talking like that is for idiots," Giulia often joked. Paavak even remembered her using one of those basic phones that could only make calls. Even that she barely used. Spending weeks on end in some of the world's most remote locations effectively shut her off from the advance of technology.

The thugs took another step forward. Paavak snapped back into the present.

People in the café continued to chatter, smoke, and drink, unaware of Paavak's unfolding nightmare.

Paavak tried to speak, tried to breathe, tried to shout, but nothing seemed to work. Whatever these men had planned, carrying it out in public wasn't a concern.

The men stepped forward in unison again. Their bulging forearms hung at their sides. The man with one eye drew a tiny syringe from the pocket of his shorts. The whole device was no longer than an inch. He pulled off the lid with his teeth and spat it to the floor.

Paavak's heart beat like a jackhammer. His pulse raged like the hooves of wild horses. That's how they would do it. They would inject him with that thing and then just melt into the crowd. By the time anyone noticed his corpse, the killers would be long gone.

"But, but," Paavak tried to say, tried to question, to even understand. He was a researcher on a pretty average project — why would anyone want him dead? He wasn't handling any secrets. He knew nothing important or dangerous.

The one-eyed brute slipped the syringe into the palm of his hand and closed his fist around it, making the deadly device invisible. The men edged forward again. They were just six feet from Paavak now. Just two small coffee tables sat between Paavak and the killers.

The two-eyed man raised a finger to his lips as if telling Paavak not to make a scene.

Paavak looked wildly from one man to the next and back again.

A flurry of laugher echoed from a large group of tourists on the far side of the café. Sipping colorful drinks and working their way through a well-stoked hookah pipe, their world was a million miles removed from Paavak's.

The thugs lunged forward, stepping around the tables to surround Paavak. At the last possible moment, Paavak shot to his feet and leaped backward over the chair.

Both men swung their giant hands in Paavak's direction, missing him by mere inches.

Without pausing for a moment, Paavak half ran, half crawled in the direction of the passage at the other end of the café. The one-eyed thug yelled something and the men, now not caring who saw them, charged after him.

Silence descended on the café as the half-dozen customers looked toward the action.

Paavak struggled upright and ran full pelt. He leapt across a table, scattering drinks and smashing glasses to the cobbles. He sent one of the hookah pipes flying too. Hot coals and tobacco skipped across the stones. Angry orange sparks flew into a pile of cushions, instantly smoking in the dry heat.

A group of customers screamed and jumped out of the way just in time to avoid Paavak's flailing arms.

Paavak's shoes crunched over the detritus now littering the café's floor. Paavak didn't care. He was running now. He was running for everything he had; life, freedom. and Giulia.

Paavak swallowed. A sandstorm of Saharan proportions whirled in his stomach. He reached the far side of the café and turned into the passageway which led back into the old city. He risked a glance over his shoulder. Forgetting all subtlety, the men charged his way. Tendons bulged from their necks like Amazonian vines.

Paavak sped up, scattering a group of teenage girls eating ice cream, then swerved into the metalworking alley.

In the Sarajevo of ancient times, all merchants and makers of a particular product lined the same street, allowing buyers to browse all the products on offer in just a few minutes. In many cases, this tradition had disappeared, except in the metalworking alley. Here, a dozen men or more who worked in bronze, zinc, and steel, occupied the same one-hundred-foot section of the narrow passage.

Paavak accelerated down the constricted street as hard as his worn-out loafers would allow. Shooting past a stall of ornaments constructed from old bullets, he breathed hard. Each exhalation sounded like a charging stallion, and yet didn't seem to pull in enough air to sustain his movement.

Still running in single file, the men bowled after their quarry, thick arms pounding like the pistons of a steam train.

Paavak glanced over his shoulder. His eyes bulged in shock and fear. The men were almost upon him. The far end of the metalworking alley was still sixty feet up ahead. By that time, the men would be on top of him. Paavak's eyes darted around for a closer route of escape, or at the very least, a weapon. Inches to his right, dozens of pots and pans in bronze and copper covered a small table. Without a second thought, Paavak flipped the table, sending the entire display clattering across the cobbles. A discordant clang echoed through the alleyway, causing the merchants to rush forward.

The brutes slowed their stride and picked their way through the bouncing metalwork.

Paavak charged on, increasing the gap between him and the men. His heart climbed its way up inside his throat, feeling as if at any moment it might slip right out of his mouth.

Paavak reached the next shop. A collection of teapots alongside war time memorabilia — soldiers' hats and replica rifles — sat in piles at the door. With a grunt, Paavak heaved the table over. He spun around and charged on. Reaching the end of the alley, Paavak swung to the right. He knew that this narrow passage connected with a wider street lined by a few dozen restaurants and cafes. This street would be busy too. Maybe, just maybe, he could blend in amongst the crowd enough to make his way to safety.

Paavak turned right, doubling back toward the center of the old city. Sure enough, a mixture of lunching locals and tourists strolled from one restaurant to another. Paavak weaved around two families, then between a pair of long-haired European men, then ducked into a restaurant's entrance.

His pursuers paused at the mouth of the metalworking alleyway, their thick necks twisting this way and that. For the first time, a flurry of hope rose in Paavak's gut. They had lost sight of him. He might just get away after all.

Hunched over, Paavak scurried between a group of older women wearing bright headscarves. The women, absorbed in their lunchtime chatter, barely noticed the strange man scuttling in their midst. After twenty or so feet, he tucked in behind a couple eating outside a restaurant.

He glanced back at his pursuers. The men appeared to have separated. Paavak saw the scarred face of the leading man pushing his way. His partner was nowhere to be seen. That had to be good news. Escaping from one man was bound to be easier than losing both. Paavak let the hope bulge in his stomach a little further. He would get out of this, and he would find out what had happened to Giulia.

Paavak turned and scurried on. He pushed in haste across the market square, weaving around people eating ice cream, tourists taking photos, and ducked into another alleyway on the far side. Jewelry shops, their displays glinting, lined the passage. Paavak ducked into the doorway of one and examined the scene behind him. It didn't look as though anyone was following. Perhaps he had lost them altogether. There was no time to rest now. He needed to get somewhere safe.

His senses still on full alert, Paavak slowed to a fast walk. He didn't want to draw unnecessary attention to himself, and it already felt as though his heart was about to leap out of his chest. He resisted the temptation to stop and hyperventilate.

In his mind, Paavak pictured an aerial view of the old city's streets. He had been here several weeks already and knew many of the thoroughfares and cut throughs. Too thin to be detailed on any map, these passages only existed in the memory of the people who walked them frequently. To the untrained eye, many of them appeared as nothing more than a shadowy gap between shops. Paavak would arrive at one such alleyway in a few moments time. If he had his calculations correct — which he usually did — this would lead him straight to a tram stop on the north side of the old city.

Paavak glanced behind him. A group of hijab-wearing

women examined glittering jewels in a shop window. A European couple dressed in tie-dye vests lumbered under the weight of heavy packs. His pursuers were nowhere to be seen.

Another flutter of hope grew in Paavak's chest as he rounded the corner into the tiny alleyway. Still looking behind him, Paavak collided with something hard. He stopped, his feet skidding across the uneven stones. His head whipped round at such speed it threatened to decapitate him.

Paavak tried to swallow, but the Sahara had returned to his gullet. He tried to back out of the gloomy passageway, but his feet only tapped uselessly at the stones. He tried to speak, to shout, to bellow, but his lungs felt as though all the air had been sucked from the surrounding space and there was none left for him.

All Paavak could do was stare into the one small, pig-like eye of the man in front of him.

The second man stepped into the passage behind Paavak, almost blocking out the light. Paavak looked from one man to the other and back again, like a deer caught in the lights of an oncoming train.

Paavak tried to back away again, to push out into the sunlight, but a meaty hand reached out and grabbed him. The hand, and then the arm, closed around his neck, bending him double.

The thugs dragged Paavak through the passageway, his feet half walking, half slipping across the uneven floor.

Paavak tried to take a breath, but the powerful muscles squeezed against his neck. He tried uselessly to pull the meaty arms away, but his strength was nothing compared to that of the thugs.

Paavak heard the distant sound of voices, maybe echoing

from a nearby café. He tried again to speak, tried again to shout, but his voice only came out in short, sharp, throaty bursts.

Hearing his protests, Paavak's captor tightened his grip even further. The passage spun around him now. Paavak's lungs stung, begging for air.

The scar-faced man dragged Paavak to the far end of the passageway and then paused. The other man peered out at the traffic on the road beyond. He spoke to his colleague in a series of short, guttural grunts.

Then another noise filled Paavak's ears. The medieval bricks of the marketplace started to rumble and vibrate. Paavak used his last threads of consciousness to glance up. As he'd remembered, the trams ran within feet of the rear wall here.

The leading man grunted again. Paavak's captor gripped him hard, almost hard enough to crack bones. The leading man grunted twice more and then Paavak was shoved forward. Paavak stumbled clear of the passage, out into the city, out into the sunlight, and out into the way of the speeding tram.

On shaking feet, Paavak turned. Brakes squealed. A horn roared. Paavak locked eyes with the tram driver, attempting to stop the vehicle. In a moment that lasted less than a heartbeat, Paavak realized what was about to happen. He looked away from the speeding tram and somewhere in the ether he saw Giulia. Maybe she was even smiling at him. Paavak couldn't be sure.

Then, a great whooshing sound roared in Paavak's ears, followed by a crack, and a thump that shook the ground. Then all went quiet. Dark and quiet.

2

Gatwick Airport Air Freight Facility, near London, England. Present Day.

EDEN BLACK GRIPPED Milo's waist tightly as the motorbike accelerated. Milo was fast and accurate. Should they get into a sticky spot later, he would be their best chance to get away. After almost two decades racing motorbikes professionally, and then several years turning his skills to less scrupulous means, he was the best in the business. That's why Eden had hired him.

Milo turned hard, the bike leaning at an impossible angle. Eden flashed back to her many hair-raising training rides with Milo. Resisting the urge to stay upright, she latched onto the grab handles that had been installed for this very purpose and leaned in sync with him. The airport's perimeter fence loomed up ahead, a twenty-foot-high wire chain-link barrier that ran in both directions. Spirals of razor wire looped along the top. Every fifty feet, a floodlight illuminated the fence, beside a camera, which was monitored back in the airport's security center almost two miles away. Eden knew all of this. She was prepared for it. She glanced down at her watch. 2:15am.

"Put it in behind those trees," Eden said. With the speakers and microphones installed in the helmet, she didn't even need to shout.

Milo heard her and immediately geared down, slowing the bike to a crawl. The engine's deep rumble sunk into a murmur. Twenty feet from the fence, shadows hung about the clump of trees.

Milo kicked down the stand and killed the engine. The 200-horsepower turbo injection engine grumbled and then died.

Eden scrambled off the bike. She steadied herself, then pulled off the helmet and shook out her jet-black hair.

The distant high-pitched whine of an Ivchenko turbofan jet engine pierced the night air. Eden turned to face the airport. The bright light of an incoming aircraft twinkled in the sky, like a star on steroids. Eden removed her backpack and pulled out a set of binoculars. The aircraft lined up for landing, revealing the markings on the side of its fuselage.

"Right on time," Eden said, turning to face Milo. "When you get my signal, you know what to do?"

Milo nodded.

Eden dug a smartphone from her pocket, and her fingers flew across the screen in a practiced pattern.

Milo stepped away from the bike and plucked a packet of cigarettes from the inside pocket of his leather jacket. He offered Eden one, but she didn't even notice.

The ground shook and the howling engines grew louder as the hulking aircraft thumped down onto the tarmac. The Anatov AN-225 was the largest transport plane in the world.

Usually, it drew a crowd wherever it landed, but not tonight. Tonight's flight was off the books. It wasn't supposed to be happening at all.

Eden glanced up at the monster aircraft. She didn't care about planes. She just wanted to get on there and get what she needed before her time ran out.

The blue glow from the phone washed Eden's pale skin in an eerie light. She fired off a message to one of her support team in Turkey. Based out of Istanbul, the guy was one of the best she'd ever worked with. Calling himself the Guardian of Truth, he seemed loyal to her cause. Eden only worked with people who understood that cause. While she paid them well, people who understood why she put herself in danger like this were more thorough and dedicated. When her life was on the line, attention to detail was everything.

Eden's phone buzzed.

All set.

The Guardian of Truth would, on Eden's command, delay the feed from the airport's security cameras. Once Eden broke cover, she would have five minutes before the feed caught up to the screens in the control center, and all hell broke loose. Three hundred seconds. Any more than that and suspicions would be raised.

Eden set the timer on her watch. Three hundred seconds to find what she needed and get out. She turned toward the fence.

The rumble of the colossal AN-225 aircraft filled the air. Thirty two thick tires carried the payload of over 200 tons toward this gloomy end of the airport.

Eden shoved noise cancelling plugs into her ears. The blast of those engines up close could do some real damage.

Eden pulled a deep breath of the cool night air. The tang

of jet fuel played on her tongue. A thrill of excitement moved through her body like a shiver. She clenched her hands into fists and then dropped into the position of a sprinter on the blocks. She looked down at her hands. This was the last chance to turn back before she did anything that couldn't be undone. Eden steeled herself against the growing doubts and scanned the airport beyond the fence. She knew what she was doing.

Without a backward glance, Eden charged from the cover of the trees.

Keeping low, she scurried toward the fence. With the security cameras temporarily out of action, eyes on the ground were now the real threat. Her black clothing would protect her some of the way, but to be noticed now would mean failure in the extreme.

Ten feet from the fence, Eden dropped into a crawl. She glanced up. Beyond the chain-link, the hulking plane turned toward her. The air was alive with the humming of the six jet engines.

Eden wondered for a moment how a machine of that size could ever get airborne. She shook the thought from her mind and scurried up to the wire. Reaching the fence, she pulled a laser cutter from her belt and fired it up. The wire zinged as the laser cutter got to work, quickly slicing through it.

Eden peered up at the nearest camera, just twenty feet away. In less than four and a half minutes that feed would reach the control center and a whole team of police would head this way. No, forget the police. With what she suspected was transported in the Anatov's loading bay, they would go straight for the military. The airport was on high alert tonight.

Eden clipped the laser cutter back to her belt, pulled open the wire, and scurried beneath.

The colossal plane was just sixty feet away now. In a few seconds, it would pass Eden on the way to its designated unloading area. Eden lay flat on her belly and crawled forward.

She glanced to the right. Several hundred feet away, three vehicles pulled out of a hangar to meet the Anatov on the tarmac. Their headlights cut through the darkness. Eden pushed herself flat against the ground and waited. The regular beating of her heart intensified.

The whine of jet engines filled her ears, even with the top of the range plugs. The ground beneath her flattened body rumbled. Her bones shook.

Eden scurried on. She reached the edge of the taxiway and pulled in close to a yellow sign, instructing pilots on the routes to use around the airport. From here she should be invisible to the pilots of the Anatov, sitting high above the tarmac.

The noise rose further. The Anatov turned on to the final stretch. Eden peered up over the sign. The nose of the aircraft towered above her now, its aluminum skin glistening in the damp night.

Eden tucked in tight and waited. She pulled a deep breath. The air seemed to throng with noise. She glanced down at her wrist. Four minutes and fifteen seconds remaining.

The Anatov rolled on, blocking out the glare of the airport's floodlights. Eden counted out another few seconds as the first of the heavy tires rumbled past. Through the windows of the cockpit above, Eden saw the pilots, lit by a ghostly glow from the flight consoles. As the plane rolled past her position, Eden scurried around to the other side of the sign.

She slid out her phone and hit send on a message waiting to go.

Kill the power.

A second later, the airport's power cut out. Eden stood from her hiding place. The strobing lights of the aircraft and the headlights of the waiting vehicles were now the only illumination in this corner of the airport.

"Fifteen seconds," Eden muttered to herself. That's how long it would take for the back-up generators to kick in. Fifteen should be enough. It would have to be.

Eden's trainers dug into the soft earth as she sprinted across to the tarmac.

The jet engines dropped to a whisper, and the plane slowed to a crawl.

Eden ducked into a crouch and scuttled behind the giant craft. The noise thumped in her solar plexus, threatening to disorientate her. Warm air pounded across her skin. She struggled to remain on her feet behind the dying engines. She placed her hands on the tarmac and darted toward the fuselage. Now, just inches from the tires, the plane's movement thundered in her chest.

With a high-pitched whine, the engines died completely.

Eden ran up behind the fuselage.

The floodlights snapped back on.

The aircraft decelerated further and then, brakes hissing, crunched to a stop. Eden dropped to the tarmac and crawled beneath the belly of the Anatov. Despite the size of the aircraft, it sat very low to the ground. She shimmied further out of sight between the two sets of wheels.

The engines sunk into silence, and the great beast sat

still. Eden pulled out her earplugs and stashed them away. She shook off her rucksack.

Distant diesel engines groaned into life. Something hissed from deep inside the aircraft. Eden glanced at her watch. She had one hundred and seventy seconds remaining.

3

Just outside Byblos, Lebanon. 1998.

"GET CLOSER EVERYONE. Come on, shuffle in!" The photographer gesticulated wildly, indicating that they should all move together.

Eden did what she was told, stepping in close beside her father. His two colleagues shuffled in beside them, too. Eden knew them by name, Paavak and Giulia. She had met them back in England several weeks ago. It seemed like a lifetime ago now. Back then, Eden had known nothing of Lebanon, of the ancient civilization they were investigating, or who Paavak and Giulia really were.

Eden smiled up at Giulia, and the woman returned the gesture. Since Eden had joined their team, they had all become friends. Or so Giulia said — even as a child, Eden knew that she probably wasn't particularly helpful to have around and doubted that she was really their friend. Eden enjoyed being around adults, though, and she enjoyed being part of the team. When she was older, Eden thought she might like to be like Giulia when she grew up, maybe.

Giulia was so clever, so funny, and could clearly get Paavak to do anything she wanted him to. Eden suspected that Paavak fancied Giulia, although she wasn't totally sure what that meant.

Looking up at the adults, Eden realized that she really enjoyed being in Lebanon. Here they treated her like an adult, which was so much better than being at school in England. Although Eden was very good at school, she didn't really like it. There were two things she especially didn't like about school — doing what she was told, and respecting her teachers. Other than that, she had it down to an art. She didn't especially like the other children either; they were all far too babyish for her. So other than the teachers, the things she had to do, and the other children, school was okay. Needless to say, she much preferred it in Lebanon.

Eden bustled in close to her father, standing in the center of the group, pushed up high on her tiptoes, and gave her most heart-melting smile. The photographer peered through the camera, adjusted one of the settings, and then took several photos.

"Just a few more," he shouted, forcing the group to hold the pose far longer than was comfortable. Finally, he checked a dial on the camera, nodded, and shot a thumbs-up high in the air. Relieved, the team swiftly dispersed.

"Take one of me and my daughter, please," said Alexander Winslow, Eden's father, his arm still around her slender shoulders. "This is a special day. I want to remember it."

Eden looked up at her father. He hadn't shaved for several days, and his stubble was now turning soft, lightened by the Mediterranean sun.

The photographer nodded, raising the camera again.

Eden smiled toward the lens and heard the faint clicking of the camera.

"Thank you," her father said to the photographer. "You head up there. We will be with you shortly."

Eden turned to look at the scene behind them. She knew that they were in a country called Lebanon, and that the sea she was looking at was called the Mediterranean. Somewhere over the glittering water to the right was Cyprus, and beyond that, Turkey. Somewhere to the left, although quite a long way, the excitement of Africa gnawed at her. Eden knew all this because she had studied it carefully in her atlas. It was always important to know where you were, Eden thought, just in case you needed to get home again. Although home was a long way from here.

"Eden, listen," Alexander said, sinking to his knees and looking deep into Eden's eyes. The early morning sun washed him in a pink glow. He swept a hand across her face, moving the hair from her eyes. Eden felt herself smile, naturally, instinctively this time. "Today is a very big day for us and the team."

"I know, Daddy, I know." Eden had been here almost two weeks already. She lived with her aunt while Alexander was away, which was often and for long periods of time. Sometimes though, very occasionally, he would ask her to join him. Those times were always the best, Eden thought.

"But I mean, *really* important. What we hope to discover today will change the way people think about the past. We've been living and teaching a lie for hundreds of years, and today we will prove that."

"Does that mean I'll have to relearn all the history we do at school?" Eden remembered the topics they'd been studying for as long as she could remember. It wasn't that she found the topics themselves boring — when her father

talked about history, Eden would hang on his every word —
but learning about it inside, from books, made Eden's eyes
feel heavy and her mind wander.

Alexander smiled. "I'm afraid so."

Eden thought, a finger to her lips. "Even the bit about
the Beatles and the Yellow Submarine?"

"The Beatles aren't history; I can still remember them,"
Alexander Winslow said, defiantly.

Eden shrugged.

"Well, okay, I suppose they are history to a ten-year-old.
But listen, I have something I want you to have, to help
remember this day." Alexander slipped a hand in the pocket
of his jacket and pulled out a slim silver chain. "Open your
hand."

Eden did as he asked. Alexander laid the chain across
her tiny palm. Eden noticed that there was a symbol
attached to the chain. She held it up and examined it
closely. She smiled, her eyes opening wide in awe and
excitement. She'd seen people wearing jewelry, mostly
women, but didn't have any of her own.

"Look at this symbol," Alexander said, picking up the
pendant between his thumb and forefinger. The fine metal
looked impossibly slender against his fingers.

Eden concentrated on the pendant. It looked like a cross,
but the top, instead of being a stick, was looped.

"This is called The Key to the Nile," Alexander
explained. "The symbol stands for eternal life. It's the
symbol used by the woman whose tomb we're opening
today."

"A tomb?" Eden said, confused. "We're going to see a
dead person?"

"She's been dead a very, very long time, so her body
won't be there anymore. There's something else in the tomb

that we want to find. But listen Eden, this is important. I know I may not always be with you, having to go away a lot, but I am always there for you. That's why I've bought this for you. If ever you miss me, you can look at this and know that I'm watching over you." Alexander slipped the chain over Eden's head and tucked it inside her shirt.

"Like a guardian angel."

"Like a guardian angel," Alexander agreed. "And look, I have one too." He pulled a matching chain and symbol from another pocket and slipped it around his neck.

"I'll be your guardian angel too then," Eden said, hugging her father.

"That would be perfect," Winslow said, wrapping his arms around his daughter. "That would be just perfect. Now, come on, we have history to rewrite. Although this has nothing to do with the Beatles."

4

Gatwick Airport Air Freight Facility, near London.
Present day.

SEVERAL VEHICLES CRUNCHED to a stop around the rear of the aircraft. Eden couldn't see them from beneath the plane's broad stomach. Boots thumped to the floor. A man barked into a radio. From Eden's position, his voice was unintelligible.

The aircraft whirred and then hissed and, suddenly, the huge sheet of aluminum which made up the beast's stomach sunk toward her. Eden's hands shot to the concrete. She looked left and right. The heavy wheels blocked her path either side. The plane lowered itself inch by inch.

Eden's feet scraped against the ground as she pushed herself toward the aircraft's nose. She scurried twenty feet backward as the towering plane sunk into a crouch. The tail end was now just inches from the ground. With the hiss of hydraulics and the whine of motors, the ramp at the rear of the aircraft lowered. To Eden, in the tiny space beneath the machine, it felt as though the thing was alive. The ramp thumped to the tarmac. Boots pounded around the fuselage to the rear.

Eden checked her watch: 2:22. In less than two and a half minutes her presence here would be discovered. She'd hoped to have more time. It could take her several minutes to find what she needed in the cavernous cargo hold. She peered at the distant airport buildings. She estimated it would take security forces a few minutes to get to her, anyway.

Eden opened the rucksack and pulled out the tools she needed for the next part of her mission. She laid them on the ground before her. A gas mask and three capsules, approximately the same size as golf balls. She pulled the gas mask down over her face. It covered her nose, mouth, and eyes. The device restricted her view, but she wouldn't need to wear it for long.

Lowering her face to the ground, she peered beneath the Anatov's belly. About two hundred feet away, boots thumped up the ramp and into the aircraft.

Eden grabbed one of the capsules. The metal surface was smooth. She moved her hand up and down, instinctively judging the power she would need to reach the tail of the aircraft. Beneath the gas mask, her tongue poked from the corner of her mouth in concentration.

She flung the capsule across the tarmac as though she were skipping stones at the lake. Eden lowered her face to the ground and watched the capsule slide easily beneath the plane. When it emerged from the shadow, she thumbed a button on her watch. The capsule dissolved into a cloud of smoke. Seconds later, Eden counted three dull thuds.

She scampered out from under the aircraft and covered the two hundred feet in mere seconds. Sure enough, three men, all dressed in nondescript black clothes, lay comatose on the ground.

Although Eden was fit, and could run long distances with ease, each inhalation sounded freakishly labored from within the thick rubber gas mask.

Eden glanced up the ramp and into the hold. Rows and rows of crates ran the length of the plane. Access passages ran down either side. Moving on the balls of her feet, Eden darted up the ramp.

She listened carefully. Two voices echoed from somewhere inside. It sounded as though the men were inspecting cargo at the far end of the hold. Eden glanced up at the ceiling, high above her. She was now in the belly of the beast with only one way in or out.

She took the second of the capsules and crouched in preparation. She couldn't roll it accurately here, though, as the floor rutted with fastening tracks and loops. The capsule would skip and bounce. She stood and peered into the depths of the plane. Throwing these things was never as accurate, but this time it would have to do. Reluctantly, she moved further into the hold. Placing each foot carefully, she listened to the rising thump of her heart. Somewhere deep inside the plane, one voice spoke, and another answered. They were louder now.

Eden crept forward. She paused, looking over her shoulder. She was now deep within the vast cargo hold, the ramp and the fresh night air almost a hundred feet behind her.

The voices came again. Close by this time.

Eden stopped and listened intently, trying to work out the exact location of her quarry. She drew her arm back in preparation for the throw.

A man appeared from behind a stack of crates beside

her. The man's face contracted like a disturbed sea urchin. Confusion gave way to anger and then to fear.

"Who are you?" the man grunted, his hand hovering beside his weapon. He spoke with a thick accent which Eden thought was from somewhere in Eastern Europe.

Eden reacted first, throwing the capsule in a high arc over the man.

The man watched the capsule and then examined Eden closely. The man paused, confused by the strange gas mask-wearing woman. Eden used the momentary pause to her advantage and prepared the next capsule.

Now sensing the threat, the man pulled his weapon from the holster at his hip.

"This is a restricted area. You shouldn't be here," he barked.

Eden knew that using the weapon would be the man's last resort. Firing in the aircraft's belly would cause expensive damage to the cargo or the plane itself. Even so, it wasn't a risk she wanted to take.

She swiped out with one hand, knocking the man's gun to the side, and then threw the third capsule. Eden leapt in between two crates, falling hard against the rutted floor. The impact knocked the air from her lungs.

The man looked around in panic. His finger tightened around the trigger as he struggled to bring the gun back around to bear on Eden.

The space where Eden had been a moment ago was now empty. She crawled in between two crates and thumbed her watch.

The capsules dissolved into noxious smoke. Two voices rose in confusion. No shots rang out.

Eden's vision clouded as the smoke filled the hold. She scurried into a crouch, breathing heavily through the mask.

A thud echoed through the fuselage as the man fell to the ground. Another thud followed.

Eden glanced at her watch. Her anonymity would remain intact for another fifty five seconds. She clambered to her feet. Using the stacked crates to orientate herself, she staggered on.

Her foot struck something on the path before her. Eden paused. Through the swirling mist she could make out the comatose figure of the man lying on the floor where he had fallen. His body curled up as though he were a child.

Eden smiled to herself. Within a few minutes he would be awake, with nothing more than a sore head. Maybe a bruised ego too.

5

Just outside Byblos, Lebanon. 1998.

"LADIES AND GENTLEMEN, ARE WE READY?" Alexander Winslow said, reaching the site of the dig. It was a steep ten-minute walk from the road where they'd taken the photos. Even though the sun was only just rising, the temperature was on the climb.

Winslow pulled a handkerchief from his pocket and dabbed at his forehead. He glanced across at Eden, sitting a few feet away on a rock in the shade. It wasn't just the temperature that was causing him to sweat, though. Today's dig was the result of years of work. Hundreds of thousands of hours of research.

Winslow looked at his team. Paavak and Giulia grinned widely, waiting for Winslow's say so, tools at the ready. The photographer paced around snapping photos of the archeologists and the dig site. Winslow just hoped what they found could be used for the good he'd envisioned, not misused in the greedy power struggles of the ruling classes.

Winslow turned and looked around the hillside dig site.

Several miles away, at the base of the hill, the ancient town of Byblos squatted in close to the glimmering sea. He could make out the muscular, blocky outline of the town's citadel, surrounded by a few concrete buildings. In the next few decades, Winslow supposed, once the locals realized there was good money to be made in tourism, there would be villas and hotels all over here. Boats that were once used for fishing would be repurposed for day trips, ancestral family homes would be flattened in favor of chain hotels, and the winding mountain roads would be widened for air-conditioned buses. He'd seen the same thing happen all over Europe — in Greece, in Spain, and more recently in Croatia. The unstoppable march of capitalism, trampling over archaeological wonders in an effort to make a profit. It was extremely lucky they found this one in time, Winslow thought.

Winslow shook the worries and doubts from his mind. If you started doubting the world, he knew, then nothing would get done. He planted a smile on his face and turned back to his team. As usual, the first gaze he met was Eden's. He nodded almost imperceptibly at his daughter and then turned to Paavak and Giulia.

"There she is," Winslow said, walking up to the symbol they'd discovered just before sundown the previous day. A large Key to the Nile was carved into the stone. It had already taken four days work to excavate the site to this level. But now they were here, Winslow didn't feel the rush. He wanted to savor in this excitement. Winslow often thought that being an archeologist involved thousands of hours reading, working stuff out, and planning, for just a few minutes of pure thrilling excitement. He planned to revel in the excitement as much as possible.

"Do you want to do the honors?" Paavak said, offering Winslow a shovel.

Winslow looked from the shovel to the man. He reached out a hand to accept it and then withdrew it. "Absolutely not. You have done most of the heavy lifting here. It's only right you're the ones to break through."

Paavak and Giulia nodded, sharing a glint of excitement. Winslow recognized the pair's excitement of their first real dig. He stepped back and watched as they set about pulling down the rocks. For a moment Winslow thought about his own first dig, over fifteen years ago now, deep in the Cambodian mountains. Then Winslow shuddered at the thought. Although they'd found what they were looking for, the excavation hadn't ended well.

Ten minutes later, Giulia and Paavak's efforts revealed a hole in the mountainside.

Winslow peered in with excitement. The smell of damp rock and stale air rushed out to meet him. Winslow inhaled a deep breath of it. To a man like Winslow, that was the scent of excitement. His senses tingled at the smell.

Paavak pulled the final rocks aside to make the hole large enough to climb through. Winslow leaned in close and examined the indentations of the laborer's tools; even after several thousand years they were still clearly visible. The entrance was roughly hewn into the hillside.

The photographer continued buzzing around, snapping photographs of everything.

Winslow slid a light from his bag and stepped toward the opening. Whilst he would offer to let the team go first, many superstitions surrounded opening tombs like this. If a plague of locusts, or a nest of giant vipers, or whatever curse Hollywood films were touting this season, should actually come true, it was only fair that he should go first and give the others a fair chance to escape. Winslow smiled at the thought. Curses be dammed. Buzzing with excitement, Winslow couldn't wait to get inside.

From her sitting position fifteen feet away, Eden watched her father duck and disappear inside the cave. The light of his torch swept through the darkness. The team stood at attention, waiting, their tools by their feet.

The only sound that disturbed the silence of the hillside was the snapping of the camera and the distant grumbling of a car as it strained its way up the road.

Not two minutes later, Winslow appeared again at the opening. The color had drained from his face. His mouth hung agape. He looked from Paavak, to Giulia, to Eden, and then shook his head.

6

___

Gatwick Airport Air Freight Facility. Present Day.

MILO PULLED the final drag of his cigarette and flicked the butt down to the gravel. He crushed the butt beneath the toe of his boot, then picked it up and slid it into a pocket. It wasn't a good idea to start leaving evidence around the place. Whatever Eden was up to, it was definitely illegal.

Milo exhaled a lung full of smoke and peered out at the airport through the covering of trees. He checked his watch for the sixth time. Eden had gone in nearly five minutes ago. In three minutes, he would get out of here, whether she was back or not. That was what they'd agreed.

Beyond the fence, a giant aircraft squatted in the gloom. Milo shuffled another cigarette from the packet and lit it.

Although he knew the basics of Eden's business, she never told him the specifics of the job. He was happy not to know. Full deniability. He was paid to get her here and get her out again. No more. No less. Whatever it was on the plane that she wanted, that was not his concern. That's what he told himself, anyway, suppressing a small flame of curiosity as it tried to rise inside him.

He took a drag of the freshly lit cigarette and glanced back at the bike. His body itched to be on the machine and riding away already. He could deal with the running part; it was all this waiting around that felt impossible. He checked his watch again, knowing the time had only incrementally advanced.

In two and a half minutes he would be out of here, speeding to safety. He ran through the various escape routes he had planned. Some were simple, others more complex. It all depended on whether they were discovered, and if they were, how much firepower gave chase.

A high-pitched shriek filled the air. Milo spun back toward the airport so quickly that he almost lost his balance. He exhaled, nearly choking on the smoke.

Alarms rung somewhere beyond the fence. Milo scrutinized the scene; somewhere in the distance, multiple vehicles moved across the tarmac. Eden's time had run out.

Milo muttered to himself. He stubbed out the cigarette and pushed down the visor of his helmet. He slid Eden's helmet on to his arm, then jumped on to the bike and started the engine. The powerful machine thronged to life. He tore back the throttle and swung the bike around, cutting a thick arc in the soft ground. Mud and grass sprayed up behind the tires.

Then he heard something. A muffled voice on the breeze. Milo paused and turned. The vehicles were getting closer now. Their headlights cut strange angular shadows around the fence. Milo recognized the vehicles. There were at least a half-dozen of them, maybe more. Army-issue security vehicles, moving at speed in his direction.

Something else caught his eye; a single person, dressed

in black, moving swiftly through the shadows on the far side of the fence.

Eden.

Whatever she was up to, it looked as though she'd done it. A silver aluminum case swung from one hand.

The muscles in Milo's arms and shoulders tensed, ready for action. He looked from Eden to the approaching vehicles. The howl of their engines thronged through the night air. Headlights cut through the air in strong, lancing beams. Blue lights strobed. Milo calculated their speed. He looked at Eden, her legs pumping as she ran toward the fence. She would never make it to the fence, let alone under it and on to the back of the bike.

Milo turned and looked down the gloomy perimeter road. He should just get out of here, that was the deal. He turned back toward Eden. But he couldn't do that. The twin flames of fear and excitement rose inside him. This was the sort of chase that Milo lived for.

Beneath the helmet, his lips twisted into a grin. His hand tightened around the throttle. His mind churned.

Eden had told him to go, but she was so close now. Milo steeled his gaze, narrowed his eyes, and yanked back on the throttle. He accelerated toward the hole which Eden had cut in the fence. The three-foot gap would be far too small to fit a bike through, usually.

Milo kicked the bike up a gear, accelerating wildly. Ten feet from the fence, he swung the bike to the right and powered into a skid. The tires tore up the ground, sending chunks of earth in all directions. The bike slid across the soil, ramming into the fence hard. A shock wave rippled down the chain-link for hundreds of feet in both directions. The impact split the wire almost in two. Milo tensed, trying to stay on the bike as it barreled through the fence.

Reaching the other side, Milo pulled the bike upright and hit the gas hard. The bike skipped forward as though nothing had happened.

The sound of the approaching vehicles was louder now. Milo glanced toward them. At least ten trucks, no doubt containing army personnel, screamed their way.

Milo hurried toward Eden. Ten feet before he reached her, Milo hit the brakes and squealed to a stop. Eden clambered on. Placing the case on the seat between Milo and herself, Eden grabbed hold. Milo passed Eden the helmet and she pushed it on.

"Cutting it a bit fine, aren't you?" Milo's voice immediately came through the headset.

"I was doing alright. I told you to go without me," Eden quipped in return.

Milo looked around, considering the best route of escape. He swung the bike around and powered back toward the broken chain link. The wire now sagged, a gaping hole in the center.

Three police cars, their blue lights strobing, squealed to a stop on the other side of the fence. The doors flew open, and several officers tumbled out.

Milo hit the brakes and swung the bike into a turn. He accelerated back toward the airport. From the left, a dozen military vehicles barreled their way. On the right, the landing lights of the vast and empty runway glinted almost as far as he could see.

"Hold on," Milo shouted, grinning beneath his helmet. "We're coming in to land."

7

Brighton, England. Present day.

THE SHRILL RINGING of Alexander Winslow's phone echoed
through his attic office. He glanced at the clock on the bookshelf opposite his desk. If the antique timepiece was correct,
then it was after 2am Winslow chided himself. The clock,
made by Galaliel Voyce in London, had been showing the
correct time for over two hundred years. It certainly wasn't
his place to doubt master clockmakers now.

Winslow removed the eye glass he was using to examine
a set of photographs from the 1912 dig on the Giza Plateau,
and picked up his phone.

"Richard Beaumont," he whispered to himself, reading
the name which scrolled across the screen. What could
Richard Beaumont possibly want at this hour?

Reluctantly, Winslow swept his finger across the screen
and answered the call.

"Have you heard?" Beaumont said, cutting straight to the
point.

"What?" Winslow asked, leaning back in his chair and

suppressing a tremor of frustration that moved through him.

"Paavak and Giulia. They've both been found dead. Giulia yesterday in Spain, and Paavak this morning in Sarajevo."

Beaumont's words hit Winslow like a bullet. He threw a hand to his chest and his mouth opened and closed several times, failing to construct a word.

Whilst he'd seen neither of the young and talented archeologists in several years, Winslow held them in incredibly high regard. They were both professional, skilled, and loyal to a fault.

Beaumont continued. Sounding flustered, his words came forth in a torrent. "Paavak fell in front of a tram. He just wasn't looking where he was going, apparently. And they're saying Giulia had some kind of undiagnosed heart condition."

"I don't understand. B-both on the same day?" Winslow stuttered.

Beaumont went silent for several seconds, letting his old friend absorb the news.

It just didn't make sense, as Paavak and Giulia were both so young and healthy. Paavak was also one of the most cautious people Winslow had ever met, there is no way he would cross the road without looking. A fear tightened around Winslow's heart. The room around him seemed to spin. He gripped on to the table with a shaking hand. "You don't think it's to do with the —"

"The Pushing Boundaries Summit," Beaumont said. Interrupting was one of the man's more irritating habits. On this occasion, Winslow welcomed not having to finish the sentence. "I couldn't say. You were planning something that was going to ruffle a few feathers, weren't you?"

Winslow tried to speak, but his thoughts ran faster than he could articulate. "Yes," he said, finally. Winslow knew that to be possibly the greatest understatement of modern times.

"But I don't see how. I just can't fathom how that involved Giulia and Paavak? Were they involved in the excavations?" Beaumont blustered on.

"They were involved in the original dig, back in 1998," Winslow said. He felt calm now, and knew what he needed to do. In many ways, he had spent two decades preparing for this. "We didn't find anything there, though. I've since learned the true location of the tablets."

Beaumont inhaled sharply.

"Yes, I'm the only person who knows the true location of the tablets." Winslow answered the un-asked question. "I had intended to retrieve them and move them to a secure location shortly before the summit."

"Was anyone else in Lebanon with you?" Beaumont asked.

A car accelerated up the street, three stories below. Winslow looked at the window, the sound reminding him that he was not alone.

"Yes, there was —"

A buzzing on the line cut Winslow off in mid-sentence. His own voice repeated the words back again a few seconds later. He suddenly felt very exposed.

"Thank you for letting me know." Winslow's hands were shaking, now uncontrollably. "I'll be in touch soon."

"Look after yourself," Beaumont said, but Winslow didn't hear a thing. He'd dropped the phone, shot to his feet, and was already halfway down the stairs.

8

Gatwick Airport Main Runway. Present Day.

EDEN GRIPPED ON TIGHT. The bike accelerated across the grass toward the runway.

Milo dragged the throttle to its maximum. The bike shook as they powered over rough ground.

Eden gripped on to the specially installed handholds behind her. She pressed the aluminum case hard between her stomach and Milo's back. She had no intention of losing what she'd come here for.

They shot onto the smooth tarmac of the main runway. The bike's rattling subsided into a quiet hum as it made quick progress down the uninterrupted asphalt.

"I've always wanted to do this," Milo's voice came through the earpiece. He pushed the modified Honda harder, moving up through the gears.

"Yeah, I bet," Eden replied, jolted back by their acceleration. She squeezed her thighs against the narrow seat. To the left, aircraft hangars shot past.

Confident she wouldn't fall off, Eden glanced over her shoulder. "They've stopped following us."

The vehicles which had been on their tail now sat in a line a few hundred feet behind.

Milo said something, but Eden couldn't hear what it was. An almighty roar filled her ears. The disorientating, powerful howl shook everything around them. Eden felt her bones shake against the cartilage. Even beneath the protective clothing, her skin tingled. She glanced around, her eyes bulging with panic, looking for the source of the noise. She tried to speak but couldn't even hear her own voice.

Eden looked up just in time to see the nose of an aircraft slide above them.

The high-pitched shriek of jet engines thronged through the air. The plane streaked across the sky less than a hundred feet above them. Eden looked up at the giant wheels, hanging, ready for touchdown.

Eden ducked her head, pulling in even closer to Milo. She felt his core muscles tense as he worked to keep the bike on a straight path.

The jet, a Boeing 747, roared on and thumped down to the runway some two hundred feet ahead. The ground shook beneath the wheels. The whining of the jet engines increased as the pilots reversed them to ease the beast to a crawl.

In a violent arc, Milo swung the bike onto the grass on the side of the runway. They bounced and skidded precariously. Milo skillfully feathered the brakes, his left hand simultaneously working the clutch. With the bike stabilized, Eden released a deep breath as they set off toward the terminal. Her ears buzzed, and she felt discombobulated by the movement.

"Which way?" Milo asked, his voice distant in Eden's headset.

"No use trying the normal exits, they'll be locked down for sure," Eden shouted over the buzzing in her ears. Recalling the plans of the airport which she'd studied in preparation for their escape, Eden searched for a solution.

They bumped up onto a taxiway. Eden glanced behind. The military vehicles had started in their direction again, further limiting their escape options.

Eden fished out her phone and scanned through schematics of the airport terminal.

"I've got an idea." Eden grinned. "It's so bonkers that it might just work."

"I'm game."

Eden pointed across the airport toward the terminal.

Milo accelerated the bike so hard it lifted on to the rear wheel.

They shot past countless aircraft, from four-engine behemoths to small private jets. Eden glanced up as they sped under the air-bridge — a pedestrian walkway which allowed passengers an aerial view of the planes.

After a few minutes, Eden saw what she was looking for.

"Baggage reclaim," she said, pointing toward an opening.

"Gotcha," Milo said, nodding. He rose to his feet and weaved them around a slow-moving baggage trolley. Eden turned and gave the astounded driver a wave.

They sped through the large plastic flaps which hung down over the airside entrance to baggage reclaim. Fortunately, at this time of day, the warehouse-sized space was largely empty. Two baggage operators at the far end of the hall, both dressed in pink high-viz jackets, ran for a door at the back of the room.

The space looked much like the reclaim hall on the opposite side, just with bare concrete and florescent lighting. Several large conveyor belts sat empty, ready to take luggage up into the terminal when the planes arrived.

"You sure you can do this?" Eden said, as they sped toward the first conveyer.

"Piece of cake. You just hold on tight."

Eden closed her fingers around the handholds again and tensed her core muscles. She pulled herself in as close to the machine as possible. The next couple of minutes was going to be bumpy.

Milo slowed and steered the bike toward the first conveyor. The noise of the bike's engine dropped. Suddenly an alarm shrieked through the building.

Eden muttered to herself. They were already running on borrowed time, and it wouldn't be long before the whole police force arrived.

Milo pumped the accelerator, as though toying with the bike. The bike skipped on to the conveyor belt. He played with the throttle, pushing them forward in bursts. They reached the ramp, which took the bags up into the baggage reclaim hall.

"Stay low," Milo hissed, crouching down over the handlebars.

Eden copied, holding her breath and tensing her entire body.

Milo yanked back the throttle. The bike shot forward, reared upwards, and then flew into the baggage hall above.

Eden gasped and looked around. Bright lights now flooded the room. The sound of the bike's powerful engine reverberated off the hard floors. Several groups of tired passengers scurried in different directions. Eden couldn't help but grin.

Milo swerved down from the carousel and onto the floor.

Alarms shrieked through the building. Several police officers ran around the corner, guns raised. Milo didn't give them the chance to take a shot. He pulled back on the throttle and bolted for the *Nothing to Declare* exit.

Less than thirty seconds later they pounded toward the airport exit. A group of policemen chased them on foot, but none had risked taking a shot with civilians nearby.

A pair of police cars slid to a stop at the door.

Eden swallowed. Her throat felt dry. Finally, it looked as though the game might be up. Still, adrenaline thronged through her veins. She didn't feel like giving up just yet.

Milo's body tensed again, and he stood up on the pegs of the bike. He wasn't giving up, either.

Another police car squealed to a stop, completely sealing their exit.

Milo's hand played with the throttle, pushing them on. The bike sneered and then shrieked.

Four officers piled out of the cars and raised MP5K submachine guns at the approaching bike. Eden pulled herself in closer to Milo. The seconds passed in slow motion. Eden's pulse slowed. It was now a dull, resonant thud, pounding deep within her chest.

"Hold on," Milo hissed through the headset. Eden nodded.

Milo jerked back the throttle and yanked up the handlebars. The Honda roared upward, the front wheel leaving the floor completely. Eden curled over the case, pulling herself into Milo's back. The pitch of the engine rose another octave.

The police officers leveled their weapons. Several pairs

of cold eyes bored into the approaching bike and its pair of riders.

Receiving the signal they needed, they opened fire. Two shots pinged from the bike's underside and three more thumped through the air nearby. They were shooting with exacting precision, Eden realized. Shooting to stop, not kill. She glanced down at the case wedged between Milo and herself.

Milo kicked the bike up a gear and accelerated again. Eden slid backward on the seat, almost falling off.

The acceleration continued. The bike was now balancing solely on its rear wheel.

Eden peered out at the assembled police officers. Two more shots ricocheted from the bike, neither doing any real damage. The Honda's engine roared. The noise of the thronging engine and the gentle hiss of radio static filled Eden's ears. She took a deep breath and held it. The next few seconds were make or break.

The color melted from the faces of the watching officers as the bike approached. The officers' eyes widened, flicking from the approaching bike to the cars beside them. Two officers lowered their weapons and shuffled back out of harm's way.

The Honda crunched hard against the front of a police car. For a moment, the bike's rear tire slipped against the asphalt. Then, with another twist of the throttle from Milo, the machine roared upward. The front of the car popped and thudded under the weight of the Honda. Now on top of the car, Milo steadied the bike and pushed on. The squad car's windscreen cracked like a spider's web beneath the weight. The Honda rolled on to the roof, crushing the strobing blue lights. With a final howl of the engine, they flew down onto the tarmac.

Eden inhaled a delicious lungful of the nighttime air. She couldn't quite believe what had happened.

Milo accelerated hard again, the needles bouncing into the red. Tires groaned against the asphalt as they made a series of short sharp turns to avoid giving the watching officers an easy target.

Eden glanced behind her, swallowing as the officers scrambled back into their waiting cars.

"Brilliant!" Eden said, gripping hard as they slammed around a roundabout. Excitement now buzzed through her veins. "But we haven't lost them yet." She glanced behind her. Blue lights flickered through the night sky.

"No bother," came Milo's reply. He sounded surprisingly calm.

They screamed toward the airport's perimeter road, the engine whining mercilessly. A large shadowy car park flashed past on the right.

Milo accelerated toward another roundabout. Eden gritted her teeth. As they approached the roundabout, another pair of police cars appeared at the third exit. A jolt shot through Eden's muscles. She pulled herself in toward Milo. She felt the tension in his back and arms.

Milo yanked back the throttle, forcing the bike into a high-octane bellow. They slammed around the roundabout moments before the police car, avoiding the front bumper by inches.

The bike barreled on, pulling ahead of the police cars. Sirens wailed. Somewhere above, Eden heard the heartbeat-like rattle of a chopper.

Eden glanced behind. The squad cars accelerated hard, pulling side by side to block the road. Eden frowned. In a flat-out flat race, the cars would probably beat them. That was if they played by the usual rules. Eden had no intention of doing that.

They screamed past a gas station, barely avoiding a blue Nissan pulling out into the road. The police cars dropped into single file just in time.

"Turn left," Eden screamed as they approached yet another roundabout. Milo complied without a break in the speed. The bike performed a miraculous lean beyond 45-degrees. They slid out on a four-lane road. They screeched past a fuel tanker, crawling in the outside lane. Woodland flashed past on either side of the road. Eden glanced behind them. The police cars shot from the entry ramp and increased their speed.

The deep hammering pulse of the helicopter rattled from somewhere nearby. Eden huffed out a breath. These guys were persistent tonight. The chopper loomed out from above the trees. The rotors thundered, whipping the branches into a frenzy. A bright spotlight danced across the surrounding asphalt.

"Up here, get ready to turn," Eden shouted, unperturbed.

Milo slowed the Honda. The chopper overshot and then doubled back. The road fell into darkness once again.

Eden glanced behind. The police cars were now less than a hundred feet behind. Forget the chopper; the cars were the real threat. Milo applied the brake again. The needles dipped below fifty. The police cars closed in further.

They approached a gap in the road's central barrier. Just three feet wide, there wasn't room for error. Milo slowed further. The gap loomed up ahead, impossibly small. The brakes locked and the Honda's tires squealed in protest.

The police cars were now less than fifty feet behind the bike.

Milo leaned forward and swung the wheel hard to the right. He pulled back on the throttle. The bike sprung forward, almost throwing Eden from her seat. They bumped up onto the central area and shot through the gap in the barrier. The police cars squealed to a stop, inches behind them.

Eden recovered her position in time for them to set off in the opposite direction at speed. The chopper's beam swept across the road, pinning them in its glare. More police cars wouldn't be far behind.

"Ready," Eden said, issuing Milo's next instructions.

Milo slowed again. The beam of the helicopter's search-light lanced forward. Then, slamming the wheel hard to left, they departed the road completely and bumped up into the woodland.

Eden studied the thick spring-time canopy of the trees high above them. A patch of light from the helicopter's beam swished across the branches before moving on.

Milo dipped the lights and cut their speed. They drove through the shadowy woodland for ten minutes, the shapes of trees and bushes swishing past on both sides.

Approaching the lights of a residential area up ahead, Milo cut their speed even further. Eden looked toward the sky. The tree cover was thinner here, and if the chopper came overhead, they would be in plain sight.

Eden listened closely. The thump of the chopper's engine echoed from somewhere nearby. Eden glanced at her watch. In a few minutes the whole county would be on lockdown. They didn't have time to waste.

"Go," she whispered.

Milo kicked the bike into gear. They pulled out into a quiet residential road, stopping beside a discolored van. Milo killed the Honda's engine.

Eden leapt off the bike and unlocked the van's back doors. She pulled out a ramp and together they heaved the bike inside. Eden climbed in behind the bike and threw the keys to Milo.

Milo caught the keys with one hand and slammed the van's back doors, plunging Eden into total darkness.

Eden glanced at her watch. The digital screen glowed. The whole operation had taken fourteen minutes and fifty-five seconds.

9

"JUST UP HERE," Eden said, pointing Milo in the direction of the forest track she knew so well. Milo had made short work of the journey, moving quickly through the anonymity of the motorway traffic in the decoy van. They'd ditched the van fifteen miles back and made the final leg back on the bike using only unmonitored lanes and walking trails. After nearly two years of living in this woodland, Eden navigated the tracks on autopilot

They bumped and revved up the rutted track. The bike's powerful headlight lanced through the trees, momentarily illuminating a bed of early bluebells. The flowers' cupped heads glowed ethereally for a moment before plunging back into darkness. Strange shadows moved behind the trees' twisted trunks.

To Eden, everything looked as it should. Her pulse crept back to normal. Apart from her and the deer and the foxes, no one came down here. That was the way Eden liked it. She glanced up at the sky, mostly hidden beneath a thick spring canopy of oak and beech leaves.

The bike sloshed through a puddle, sending a torrent of

dirty water spraying out behind them. Milo took the terrain slowly and carefully. There was no need to rush now.

"About half a mile up here," Eden said, as they lumbered up an incline. The deeply furrowed and uneven track made progress slow. That suited Eden perfectly. No one could sneak up on her here. Even on foot it could be hard work with thick mud and water lying in deep puddles.

A finger of pre-dawn mist snaked amid the trees, as though probing for something unseen.

A few minutes later, Eden saw her truck through the trees. Painted in matte green, and covered in parts by camouflage netting, the vehicle was only visible from very close by. Two large antennas extended up into the canopy.

"Stop just here," Eden instructed when they were fifty feet from the truck.

Milo slowed the engine and the thick tires slid to a stop. He kicked down the stand and indicated for Eden to get off the bike. Eden dismounted, her feet shaky from the ride. She slid off her helmet, and then tucked the aluminum case beneath her arm.

Milo hopped off the bike. He pulled off his helmet and arched his back, stretching out his muscles. "What is that?" Milo said, pointing toward the truck.

"That's a DAF T244. Military issue," Eden said, striding toward the vehicle.

"You live here?"

"Nearly two years now. Come in," she said, waving him over, "I have something for you."

"Nice," Milo said, striding after Eden.

Eden climbed the ladder and unlocked the door. She snapped on the light, bathing the inside of the truck in a warm orange glow. Milo climbed up and examined the place. Just twenty feet from end to end, it contained everything Eden needed. A bed, a kitchenette, and a small shower room took up one half of the space. Eden's workspace occupied the other half. Several large screens were mounted to the wall beside various sets of keyboards and computers.

Eden laid the case on the desk. A small electronic keypad sat on top. She tapped her phone a few times and then placed it next to the locking mechanism. The case whirred and then clicked as the lock disengaged. Eden removed her phone and pulled open the case. The metal groaned, now out of shape with the numerous bumps it had sustained during the journey. The contents would be fine. These cases were designed to withstand serious damage.

Eden removed a glass case and held it up to the light.

Milo examined the object and then recoiled in shock. The object inside the glass case looked like a human hand. The flaking skin was swollen and slightly orange in color. "Ewwww, what is that?"

"This is the right hand of Saint Francis Xavier."

Milo's eyes bulged, and his mouth gaped open. He pointed back toward the bike. "We did all of that for some dead guy's hand? I mean, it looks gross. How old is it?"

"Have some respect, please," Eden said, placing the glass case carefully back inside the box. "This is the hand of Saint Francis Xavier. He died four hundred and eighty years ago next month. If I work quickly, he should be back in his rightful place in time for the celebration."

Milo shook his head, clearly unable to understand.

Eden flipped open one of her laptops and scrolled through applications.

"Hold on, wait," Milo said finally. "We did all of that, you know, risking death or imprisonment, for the hand of a guy —"

"Saint Francis Xavier," Eden interrupted.

"Okay, fine, Saint Francis Xavier. We did all of that for his hand, because?"

Eden looked up at Milo. "Because it was stolen. The body of Saint Francis Xavier is displayed in the Church of Bom Jesus in Goa, India. Six months ago, when the body was delivered for its routine embalming process, someone broke into the facility and stole the hand."

"Why would someone do that?"

Eden shook her head. "The relics market is massive, especially for saints. Anyway, I did a little digging and found out that this particular relic was due to arrive in the UK today. Once it got here it would end up in a private collection and never be seen again."

Milo shrugged.

"This relic belongs to the people of Goa. It does not belong in the basement of some billionaire with a fetish for dead saints."

Milo exhaled slowly and shook his head. He walked up to the case and then closed the lid on the weird-looking hand. "Alright, fine," he said, sidling up beside Eden. "You got anything for breakfast?" He examined Eden's figure as she bent over the laptop.

"I don't eat breakfast," Eden replied, without looking up. She scrolled through various tabs on the laptop. Her fingers flashed over the keys. "Oh, that reminds me," she said, finally looking up.

Milo glanced guiltily away from her body.

"There's an envelope on the counter over there." Eden pointed in the direction of the kitchenette.

Milo strode over and picked up the envelope, which was about the size of a paperback book. He slid his thumb beneath the flap and flicked it open. The envelope was full of £20 notes.

"What's this for? You paid me already." Milo turned to face Eden.

Eden straightened up, grabbed her phone from the desk, strode to the door, and shimmied down the ladder.

"That's for the bike," Eden shouted up, tapping at her phone.

"What do you —" An explosion interrupted Milo's question. He rushed to the door. Fifty feet away, fire consumed the bike. Flames licked up toward the canopy of the trees.

"Oh man, I loved that bike. Why did you do that?" Milo shouted, leaping down to the ground.

"Sorry," Eden said as she shrugged half-heartedly, her face deadpan. "It was traceable, so it had to go."

Milo tried to protest, but Eden cut him short. "The nearest bus stop is four miles that way." She pointed off into the trees. "If you step on it, you'll be home in time for breakfast."

Eden scampered up the ladder and back into the truck.

Milo turned just in time to see the door slam and hear the lock click into place.

"Typical," he muttered to himself, tucking the envelope inside his jacket and dropping his arms to his sides. "I really did like that bike."

10

Hotel Bellevue. Kriens, Switzerland. Present Day.

THE MAN KNOWN as Helios stood at the terrace of the Hotel Bellevue and looked out at the scene beneath him. Built on the summit of Mount Pilatus, the hotel sat over two thousand feet above sea level. Helios gazed down on the shimmering waters of the bay of Lucerne. His eyes then moved across the rise and fall of the surrounding mountains. The cable car and the cog railway — the only two ways to reach the mountaintop structure — sat still and silent. The cable car's gondolas swung lazily in the breeze. No one left or arrived while The Council of the Selene was in session, that was the rule. Not a single guest had visited the Hotel Bellevue in the last six weeks in preparation for this meeting, and they would remain shut for four weeks after The Council had left. All staff had been replaced with those loyal to The Council and all electronic devices had been removed. When the assembly of The Council was finished, a team would work around the clock to return the hotel to its previous condition.

Despite the serene beauty of his surroundings, Helios scowled unhappily. Yet again, negotiations were moving very slowly indeed. Whilst he was the chairman of the organization, he needed the backing of The Council to make any real progress. His position and its limitations were written in the scriptures of The Council, a document which had been passed down through the generations of The Council's long and complex history. Although the chairman appeared to be in charge, really, he was just its guardian. His task, and one he took very seriously, was to ensure the success of The Council for the generations that followed.

The last twenty-four hours, though, had been frustrating. It seemed as though they were just arguing over the same issues time and time again. They all agreed that the world needed to move forward, and The Council of the Selene was central to that, but how they could go about making that change was a complex issue.

"The Council is ready for you," came a voice from the doorway behind him. Helios took another deep lungful of the cool mountain air and turned back toward the building.

"Thank you," he said, nodding to the secretary, then followed her inside.

Helios strode back into The Council chamber and took his customary seat at the head of the table. Buried deep within the hotel complex, The Council chamber was completely cut off from the outside world.

Seven men and women sat around a large table. The room was lit in such a way, that each member of The Council could only see the outline of the other members. The anonymity of The Council members was as important as the secrecy of The Council itself. No one, including Helios himself, knew the name, origins, or even gender of the people before him.

Recruited from all corners of the globe, the seven members of The Council were chosen to represent a cross-section of humankind. When sworn in, each councilor took the position for life. During their time within The Council, each member nominated seven eligible people for their replacement. Upon the death of a councilor, the remaining members chose a replacement from their nominations.

While serving The Council, members used the names of the original members.

"Back to the issue at hand," Helios said, glancing at the assembled men and women, and then down at the paper in front of him. "Azrael, before the recess you were sharing your report on the effects of this biotechnology on the plant life of Southeast Asia."

Azrael cleared his throat and continued. The Council were debating the release of a micro bot which could be used to enhance the yield of crops without the use of chemicals. Should the technology be used in the way it was designed, the repercussions for food production would be huge. Azrael and his team had been tasked with trying the system for a year-long period in a remote part of China. The results had proved to be nothing short of remarkable.

Helios listened in silence as Azrael completed his report.

"Thank you, Azrael, a very thorough and encouraging investigation," Helios said. "I will now open the floor to questions. Members, you know the protocol."

The screen in front of Helios lit up as various members indicated their desire to ask questions.

"Let's start with you, Uronion. You have a question regarding the safety of the technology?"

"That's right," Uronion began in her nasal British tone. "Thank you, Azrael, for such an interesting investigation, but how would we ensure the technology remains used in the way you've described? What's to prevent it being altered for personal gain by less scrupulous organizations?"

Helios suppressed a sigh. Although predicting and mitigating against possible issues was a part of The Council's remit, it seemed to have taken up most of their time in the last few meetings. There were no end of imaginary crisis situations the members could invent, which, in Helios's opinion, became increasingly unlikely the longer they talked.

Azrael considered the questions carefully, then spent several minutes explaining the safeguards that were built into the nanobots. Uronion listened closely, although Helios doubted it would make any difference.

Another three questions of a similar nature were asked by other members, which Azrael answered confidently.

"We will now recess to consider The Council's response to this," Helios said. "We will meet again to formalize our decision."

"Before we break, sir, I have a question for you." Helios looked around the room, scowling. It was against protocol to ask questions without prior authorization. Uriel, one of The Council's newest members, indicated his desire to speak.

Helios thought for a moment. He could refuse to answer an unplanned question, but that seemed pointless. During his tenure, Helios had endeavored to make The Council more transparent for its members. They were encouraged to ask questions — usually at the appropriate times, however.

"As you wish, Uriel. We have some minutes remaining, so I will answer your question."

"Last time we met you told us of a discovery which, if left to go public, could expose The Council and the work that we do. We were told that this was under control, and of course I have full faith in your ability, but do you have an update for us on this?"

All members turned from Uriel to Helios.

Helios cleared his throat. "Yes, of course. One of our interception teams learned some time ago that a collection of stone tablets was discovered, dating back to the time of The Council's establishment —"

"Sorry to interrupt sir, but just so that we're clear, if these tablets were found and decoded, it could expose the existence of The Council?"

Helios narrowed his eyes on the speaker. "It's very unlikely, but that is possible, yes."

The men and women around the table shared a harsh intake of breath.

"I must reassure you," Helios said, his hands outstretched, "that we are in the process of dealing with this. Two of the people who discovered the tablets have already been eliminated, one more will be dealt with shortly, then we will use the final one to lead us to the location of the tomb so we can seize the tablets for ourselves. During the recess I will communicate with my team on the ground."

11

The Godspeed Country Estate, England. Present Day.

ARCHIBALD GODSPEED CROUCHED on the lawn of the country manor which had been in his family for more generations than they could calculate. The house, as it stood now, had been built by his great-great-grandfather, Montgomery Godspeed, with the money he had accrued while owning several very successful plantations in the Caribbean. The fact that his family fortune was made on the back of slavery didn't matter to Archibald. In fact, it hadn't even occurred to him.

Godspeed slipped his Springfield hunting rifle from its case and lay it on the grass beside him. He gazed lovingly down at the machine, the matte-black twin barrels sparkling in the early morning light. The rifle represented everything Godspeed loved about human invention. It was stylish, effective, and very deadly indeed.

Godspeed shuffled down into a lying position with an ease that many people his age could only dream of. His expensive personal training routine with an ex-military captain, combined with a bespoke although boring diet, made sure he stayed in tip-top shape. Godspeed stretched out, ignoring the morning dew which soaked into his jacket and trousers.

Despite the dew, morning was the best time to find his prey. Plus, if there was a better way to start the day than killing a defenseless animal, he had yet to find it.

Godspeed swung the rifle out in front of him, rested it on its stand, and then gazed down the optical sight. Accurate to up to one thousand feet, the poor creature didn't stand a chance. They probably wouldn't even hear the rifle pop, or feel the bullet rip through its skull, if he had his aim right.

Godspeed made some adjustments to the rifle and scanned the woodland at the far side of the lawn. Thick and verdant leaves covered the trees, making his view inside the woodland impossible. In winter, when the forest's coverage was thinner, he could take down his prey amid the trees. During the summer months, though, he was forced to get creative. The tempting proposition of two feeding troughs nestled a few feet from the forest's edge worked well enough. Hunger was the ultimate motivator.

Godspeed swept the sight across the tree line, looking for movement amid the branches. He studied leaves, swaying gently in the light breeze. Having been hunting in all conditions, a light breeze wouldn't put him off his target.

Godspeed panned the sight from right to left again, looking for the telltale movement. A flash of white fur. A broken branch. Anything to show him that his prey was nearby. Nothing moved.

No matter, he would wait. Without removing his eye from the lens, Godspeed shuffled a cigarette from the pocket of his jacket, followed by a lighter. He plugged the cigarette in the corner of his mouth and lit up, puffing hard.

Enjoying the first nicotine rush of the day, he scanned the woodland again. They would come. They always came.

Suddenly, there it was. A flash of movement, a branch snapping back into place, right at the edge of his vision.

Exhaling hard, Godspeed adjusted the lens. He zoomed in and focused just on the area of the woodland where he thought he'd seen the creature.

Something deep in the undergrowth moved again. This time it was closer. A flicker of white fur followed the movement.

Godspeed's pulse increased as he focused hard. This looked like something big, something worth his deadly efforts. His jaw jutted forward in the tension of concentration. He made a minor adjustment to the rifle, then slipped his finger across the trigger. He was ready.

The animal moved to the edge of the forest now. He inhaled with excitement. A fallow deer slipped its slender head out through the low hanging branches. It was a young one too, he noticed. Perfect.

The deer looked this way and that, intelligent eyes searching the lawn for a threat. Noticing the food, the deer paused.

Two hundred feet away, the cigarette fell from Godspeed's lips and extinguished itself in the wet grass. He inhaled slowly, not wanting to make a noise.

The deer stepped forward, growing in confidence as no threat presented itself.

Godspeed tilted the rifle skyward just a fraction of an inch. The crosshairs now rested six inches in front of the animal. He would wait for the thing to step forward into the crosshairs. The last thing Godspeed wanted was the animal bolting at the final moment.

The deer made as though to move, then froze, scanning the lawn.

Then, a strange thing happened. The deer turned slowly, consciously, and looked in Godspeed's direction. The animal paused and stared directly down the barrel, as though locking eyes with its would-be killer.

"Sir. There's someone here to see you, sir. They say it's important and must see you immediately," came a voice, interrupting Godspeed's concentration.

Godspeed muttered and turned to see the man approaching.

"What is it Baxter? You know I'm not to be disturbed at this time."

"I know sir, but this is important," Baxter muttered in return.

Godspeed looked up at the man's imposing figure. Baxter had been working as his sole close protection operative for almost a year. The guy was intelligent, seemingly indestructible, and could operate almost any machine Godspeed threw at him.

"Who is it?" Godspeed scowled, struggling to his feet.

"The man wouldn't give his full name," Baxter said, almost nervously. "But he said you knew him as Helios."

Godspeed paled, his hands hanging limp at his sides.

Two hundred feet away, the fallow deer pounded back into the woodlands, its life spared, and a lesson learned.

"It's a nice place you've got here, Godspeed," the man known as Helios said, pacing across the worn carpet of the large drawing room. "I expect the upkeep is a burden, though. These places certainly weren't built to be economical."

Archibald Godspeed stepped forward, wringing his hands together. While he had heard of Helios, and the organization he overlooked, he had never met the man. Godspeed had to admit now, looking at him in flesh and blood, he just seemed normal. Helios wasn't imposing and didn't appear physically powerful, as Godspeed might have imagined. But then again, when your organization was as powerful as The Council of the Selene, physicality was almost obsolete. He was tall, though, towering over Godspeed by several inches.

Godspeed had been surprised to learn about The Council of the Selene as a young man. At the time he had been considering a future in politics, thinking, mistakenly as many do, that the men and women in the Houses of Parliament, Congress, Senate, or Assembly hold the power. They were all for show, he had soon learned. Little more than a troupe of actors, troubadours, or jesters, treading the boards and speaking in soundbites for public consumption. And how the public consumed such things, while failing to see the sheer obviousness of the truth.

Governments had no power. The real decisions were made in plain sight, all under the watchful eye of the man now standing in Godspeed's drawing room.

"I'm sorry to keep you waiting," Godspeed said, trying to calculate the man's age. Helios could have been anywhere between fifty and eighty. Although he moved with ease, a nest of gray hair encircled his crown, and lines bracketed his eyes.

"That's not a problem. I know you're a fan of some early morning gunplay."

Godspeed swallowed. He had not told Helios he had been shooting, and knew that Baxter wouldn't have either.

Helios spun around and fixed Godspeed with an icy gaze which seemed to communicate the fact he knew much more than he was letting on.

Helios broke the gaze and crossed to one of the large windows looking out over the gardens. He peered through the cracked glass, which could conceivably have last been replaced during the reign of Queen Victoria.

"I know you're a busy man, so I'll get to the point." Helios rubbed a finger down the glass, which came away stained. "I know a lot about you, Godspeed. I know about your family. You are the latest in a very long and distinguished line." Helios shook a handkerchief from his pocket and wiped the filth from his finger. "I'm particularly inspired by the work of your great grandfather."

"George," Godspeed interrupted and then instantly regretted it when Helios's icy gaze swung around to meet his.

"Yes. Exactly. I'm glad we're on the same page. Now, I know you've followed in your great-grandfather's footsteps with your interest in antiquities."

Godspeed nodded sagely.

"It's unfortunate, though, that you've done so with much less success."

Godspeed opened his mouth as though preparing to argue, then thought better of it.

"Fifty years ago, the Godspeed family was one of the wealthiest in the country. Your name was revered in the highest echelons of society." Helios shook his head like a cobra preparing to strike. "Now, however, I fear it's almost worthless."

"But, we, I still have —"

"Of course, I know about your secret vault beneath where we sit today —"

Godspeed paled. He had let only a handful of very trusted people see his private collection.

Helios held up a finger as though reading the other man's thoughts. "Don't you worry about how. I know a lot. This is, after all, my duty. It's an impressive collection, but its value is nothing in comparison to what it once was. Not after you factor in the repairs to this place, the cost of your staff, your vehicles, your aircraft. Let's be honest, old man, you'll be broke before the decade is out."

Godspeed clenched his fists and snarled at the other man.

"I'm just stating facts." Helios held out his hands in placation. "I'm here to offer you a way out. I need a job done, something important to my organization. In fact, it's something important to humankind."

Godspeed tilted his head and relaxed slightly. "Important, huh? What's in it for me?"

Helios smiled and pointed a long finger at the shorter man. "I thought you might ask that. I'm offering you a way out of the quicksand you've found yourself in. If you complete this small task, you'll get enough money to once again become one of the richest men in the country. You'll get to restore this place to its former glory." Helios examined one of the dust laden curtains. "Or you could just sell it and buy a private island somewhere. That's up to you."

"What's the job?" Godspeed barked, impatient now.

"Wait a second." Helios spun back around to face him. "When you do this, you'll also be publicly known as the man who made a discovery that changed the world. You'll be a public figure, who'll be written about for hundreds of years to come, rubbing shoulders with the likes of Bingham, Kane, and of course —"

"My great grandfather."

"Exactly!" Helios snapped his fingers, then walked across the room and settled into a faded leather armchair. "Now come, let me tell you what I need you to do."

Godspeed listened in silence for almost half an hour as Helios explained the job.

"It seems simple enough," he said, when the man had finished speaking.

"Yes." Helios leaned forward conspiratorially. "There are a couple of other details which you must know. I'm afraid this happens to be of a delicate nature. No one can know that your instructions came from me, do you understand?"

"Yes. No problem. When will I get —"

"Wait a minute. First, I need you to understand that under any circumstances, this must not be traced back to me or my organization. No one will know. But, I'm sure that won't be a problem for you, as you're more than capable of subtlety." Helios put his hands on the arms of the chair, preparing to lift himself up.

"Hold on." Godspeed held out a hand to stop the other man mid lift. "When will I get paid?"

A notification chimed from Godspeed's phone.

Helios grinned. "You just have."

Godspeed wrestled the phone from his jacket pocket. He read the figure and his eyes bulged.

Helios paced across the room and rapped his knuckles on the closed door. "Just to make sure you don't run into any problems, I've got two of my most trusted men to go with you."

"That won't be necessary. I have a very trustworthy —"

Godspeed stopped speaking as the door thumped open and two of the largest and meanest looking men Godspeed had ever seen walked in. Their heavy military-issue boots thundered over the old floorboards, no doubt shaking dust from the ceilings below. The men were so wide, they had to walk single file through the double doorway. The men were replicas of one another. Both wore black clothes which barely covered their rippling muscles, and their hair was long and tied back in ponytails. The only difference, Godspeed noticed before immediately looking away, was that one man had an ugly scar across one eye. The eye itself was pearly white and unseeing.

"My men will be with you every step of the way." Helios spoke as though the words were supposed to be reassuring. "Mr. Stone," — Helios indicated the man with one eye, then turned to the other — "and Mr. Croft, meet Mr. Godspeed. You will be under his command for the duration of the mission. Help him in any way you can."

The two brutish men nodded at Helios and then turned to face Godspeed.

"When do we start?" Godspeed said, turning to Helios.

"Oh, we already have," Helios replied, checking his watch. "In fact, the next event is just about to take place."

12

Heathrow Airport Terminal Three, near London.

DAWN BROKE SLOWLY over the patchwork towns and fields of southern England, painting the sky in swirls of mauve and purple. Mist hung thick in the air, churning through the fresh beams of sunlight. The springtime sun would soon burn the fog away, but for now it still clung heavy and thick in the shade.

In one of the terminal's many first-class lounges, Alexander Winslow checked his watch for the hundredth time. It seemed that, contrary to the rules of science, time actually had stopped, or at least, the last twenty minutes had stretched several times over.

He picked up and drained his fourth cup of coffee. He studied the coffee machine on the other side of the room, considering a refill. He knew that four was already too many. Caffeine surged through his veins, not helping with his growing sense of dread.

Winslow looked at the packet of chamomile cigarettes on the table. What he really wanted was one of those, but the smoking area was at least ten minutes walk away. He would have one on the plane. Fortunately, when flying private, normal rules did not have to be obeyed.

Winslow tapped his fingers on the table as the call from Beaumont spooled again through his mind. Giulia and Paavak were dead. Dead? How was that possible? At least fifteen years his junior, they deserved many more years.

Lowering his gaze, Alexander turned to examine the vast concrete expanse of the airport through the window. The flood lights had been extinguished in the soft, milky light of dawn.

What had they gotten involved in, to get themselves killed like that? Alexander wondered, before instantly rebuking himself. What had *he* gotten them involved in?

A suited man, the only other person in the lounge this early in the day, shuffled the salmon-pink pages of his newspaper.

Winslow had known for decades that what he was sitting on was huge. Bigger, really, than he could imagine. Maybe he had been too hasty, publicizing a lecture about the content of the files. Sure, he hadn't fully explored them yet, but he knew exactly where they were. They were in the same place they'd been for the last two hundred years. A clever bit of misdirection by a man named Horsam Rassam.

Winslow had always thought it essential that he didn't reveal the tablets too early. The most dangerous part of this whole process was the point at which he had revealed the location of the tablets before he told the world of their content. Once the world knew, the danger would have passed. That's why he had waited this long.

Winslow ran through the elements of his plan again. It was clever, but not perfect. It relied on several moving parts, which, under the balance of Winslow's analytical scrutiny, should stack up.

Winslow had secured the plan in the only way he knew how. It had never been committed to a single piece of paper, computer code, or even speech. It existed entirely within the confines of his brain. It was air-gapped, as the computer fraternity would say, with the rest of the world. That's the way it needed to be. Winslow thought that Horsam Rassam would probably agree.

His phone buzzed on the table before him, its shrill ringtone jarring through the lounge. Winslow grabbed up the smartphone. An unrecognized number scrolled across the screen.

"Hello," Winslow said, his eyes roaming the lounge suspiciously. The room's only other occupant flicked to the next page of his newspaper without concern.

"We're all ready, sir. Everything is set, just as you'd asked for," the man on the line said without introduction. Winslow knew exactly who it was.

"Excellent." Winslow slipped his fingers inside the collar of his shirt and pulled it away from his skin. It felt as though the temperature in the room had just increased dramatically.

"You and the team are in place?"

"Absolutely. Just as requested."

"Fine, good work," Winslow said, preparing to end the call.

"It's been a pleasure to work with you, sir." The voice sounded wistful now.

"Same to you," Winslow said, a flash of sadness entering his eyes. "I'll see you again, in this life or the next."

Winslow ended the call, gathered up his things, and tucked them inside the briefcase. He climbed to his feet as calmly as he could and strolled out of the lounge, turning in the direction of Gate 35.

Twenty minutes later, the first Pratt and Whitney turbofan of an aging Hawker 400xp private jet hummed to life, closely followed by the second. The Hawker, waiting at Gate 35, was enroute to Washington with one passenger and three highly trained crew on board.

With a clunk, the plane began the push back procedure, which would see it take to the sky for the last time in its long and arduous life.

13

A SMALL HERD of fallow deer trotted through the forest in the early morning light. Strafes and stripes of mist lay tangled with the trees, and dew sparkled from low-lying branches. Clouds of vapor streamed from the snouts of the calves, as they hurried to keep up with their elders. A doe, the largest in the group, raised her nostrils to the sky and inhaled the morning air. There was something different about the smell here this morning. There was something sharp about it, as though something had recently been burned. She examined the scene before them before moving on. All looked as it should. The small herd approached the trough and began to feed. They didn't concern themselves with how the food got there, or why it was replaced overnight. To them it was a free meal and a tasty treat.

Twenty feet away, inside the DAF T244, Eden typed furiously at the computer. She looked up as an alarm sounded, signaling movement nearby. On one of the screens above her, she saw the deer feeding, as they did every morning. That same herd of fallow deer had been visiting her for over a year. She'd watched their young grow from skipping calves into the young adults they now were.

She gazed out of the window to her right and saw them gathered around the food she left every day. A weak smile lit her face. In a world of struggle and complexity, there was something simple and beautiful about watching the comings and goings of woodland animals.

Eden turned back to her computer. A bar of thick morning sunlight lay across the screen. When Eden had brought the truck from a military surplus auction, via several shell companies, the only windows had been two square ventilation holes in the roof. She'd rectified that immediately by cutting a large window in each wall and one in the ceiling. This gave her a unique view of the forest, as though she were in the canopy herself. She'd also installed steel covers which slid down over the glass at the press of a button, giving her both privacy and security. She pressed one such button now, and the morning sunlight, along with her view of the feeding deer, disappeared.

Eden typed furiously on the laptop. Getting the artifact in her possession was only half of the challenge. The other half, sometimes the more difficult half, was getting it back to its rightful owner safely without anyone knowing she was involved.

The sort of people who stole these artifacts tended not to like the fact they'd gone missing and would often go to great expense in an attempt to get the item back.

A shrill buzz filled the truck, distracting Eden from her work. She looked instinctively up at the screens, which displayed security camera footage from the surrounding forest. The woodland was empty; the herd of deer had finished their food and wandered off amongst the trees. Eden looked at the clock. It was just after midday. She rubbed a hand across her face. She'd been working for several hours straight.

The noise came again. Eden looked around the desk. Her phone glowed in the gloom. An unknown number scrolled across the screen.

Strange, Eden thought, as she didn't give this number to anyone. It wasn't included on any public records, either. She grabbed the phone. Her hand hovered over the 'cancel' button.

There was only one person Eden had given this number to, and that wasn't him calling. Could he be using a different phone?

Maybe the call was about last night. She glanced at the case on the desk. Maybe they were on to her already. Was there a tracker on the relic that she'd failed to find? She'd checked carefully while they were in the van. But then, if they knew where the relic was, why would they be calling? She tried to speak but emitted only a croak. She cleared her throat and tried again.

Slowly, and for reasons Eden didn't understand, a dry but sickening feeling rose in her throat. She pressed the answer button and held the phone to her ear. For several long seconds, nothing happened. Eden was just about to remove the phone and check she hadn't become disconnected when a distant voice came down the line.

"Hello, I'm looking to speak with Eden Winslow."

Eden's tongue grew thick. No one called her by her father's name anymore. She had changed it several years ago. Not out of any dislike for her father or what he did, but since the archaeologist and his work were so well known, she found the constant 'how's your father?' very frustrating.

"Who's this?"

Silence again. Finally, a man spoke.

"My name's Daniel Grant. I'm with the British Transport Police. Am I speaking with Eden Winslow?"

Eden narrowed her eyes. If this wasn't about the relic, what did they want?

"Yes," she said, tentatively. "I'm Eden."

"Miss Winslow," the man continued, more quickly this time. It sounded to Eden as though he wanted to get the call over with too. "I've got some rather bad news. It's about your father."

14

Brighton Cemetery. Three weeks later.

EDEN PEERED up at the storm clouds which raced and churned overhead, threatening to spill gallons of rain across her, the cemetery, and the disparate group of mourners who gathered around the grave.

Encompassed by thick trees and overgrown bushes, the cemetery felt disconnected from the surrounding streets of the city. Eden studied the angular steeple of the chapel piercing the canopy a few hundred feet away.

The priest, dressed in a black cloak against the uncharacteristically cold spring day, stood at the head of the grave. His voice rose and fell in practiced repetition of the words.

Eden wasn't listening. She hadn't heard a word since she'd entered the church nearly an hour ago. Everything around her felt like it was underwater or behind glass. Tears prickled her eyes. She rubbed a hand across her face. She didn't feel like sharing her emotions today.

Eden looked down at her shoes, now splattered with wet

mud. They were new, as was the long sleeve black dress and jacket she wore.

She glanced across the cemetery through watery eyes. At the far side, beneath the shelter of a giant oak, a man in a high-visibility jacket smoked a cigarette beside a small excavator. Eden recalled such machines on the digs she'd attended with her father as a child. The excitement they'd shared uncovering secrets that had lain lost for thousands of years. Eden remembered how her father had the ability to weave each secret into a story. The object in question wasn't just a piece of pottery, it was a shard from the pot used to make stew for warriors, or the font used to baptize the king. Now only existing inside Eden's memory, those stories were lost to the world.

The priest's voice faded. In silence, four men standing around the grave lowered the coffin into the ground. Slowly, painstakingly, the casket sunk out of sight. The men were on hire from the undertaker. Alexander Winslow had no family members to lower him into the ground.

Nor did Eden, not anymore. Eden looked at the mourners gathered around the grave. Some she recognized from the archaeological digs she'd attended as a child, or from the university at which her father had been a professor. A few had greeted her with hugs and concerned smiles back at the church.

Many, she didn't know at all. Everyone seemed to know who she was, though, even if they didn't know her.

Scanning the assembled small crowd, Eden locked eyes with a man looking back at her. The man stood at the far side of the group. He wore a well-fitting black suit and overcoat. Probably in his early sixties, he was small, with fine features, and a closely shaved head.

Eden broke the stare as the coffin thudded gently into its

ultimate resting place. The four men stepped away from the graveside. Eden stepped forward and peered down at the casket. Her body felt cold and distant, as though the life had been stripped away from her as well.

She examined the casket's lid. In a way, it was the final image she would have of her father. Her eye caught on the brass plate mounted in the center. Eden hadn't noticed it before.

In a surprising twist of good fortune — if there was anything fortunate in this situation — her father had pre-planned his funeral arrangements. He'd engaged the funeral directors, chosen the casket, the prayers, picked his place in the cemetery, and written the wording for his tombstone and coffin. It was almost as if he knew it was going to happen.

As it turned out, all Eden had to do was turn up.

The words on the brass plate were big enough to read from where Eden stood. Alexander's name, dates of birth, and death were followed by a symbol. It was a symbol Eden recognized instantly: The Key to the Nile.

Eden reached for her neck and pulled out the chain she had worn every day for over half her life. She found the clasp and slipped the pendant from the chain. She closed her hand around the metal. The object felt warm, as though it retained some life itself. Eden opened her hand and looked down at the same symbol cast in silver.

The priest spoke again. Mourners stepped forward and dropped roses on top of the coffin.

Eden felt something close around her chest. She watched silently as the first shovels of earth thudded down onto the coffin. She stood trance-like until the coffin was covered. Then she blinked hard, turned away, and looked up at the sky.

The first drops of rain splashed down across Eden and the assembled mourners. Without looking at another person, Eden turned and walked away.

Eden passed through the gates of the cemetery and turned left. On one side of the road, ivy shrouded the high cemetery wall. On the other, a row of brightly painted Victorian terrace houses ran in both directions.

Water pounded in greedy droplets across the road, the parked cars, and Eden. Eden glanced behind her. A television flickered through the window of a pink-painted house. She thought momentarily about the residents, hunkered down against the sour weather. Eden wanted more than anything to be back in her truck, the small wood burning stove on, planning her next mission. This would all be over soon. Thrusting her hands deep in her pockets, she turned and wandered away from the cemetery.

In the distance, Eden heard the excavator's engine rumble to a start. She imagined the machine burying her father's coffin, sealing him from the outside world. It seemed fitting that a man who loved searching for things underground was being returned there. But where did that leave Eden? Fatherless, with a whole heap of problems to sort out.

She thought again of the symbol. She knew the symbol had a relevance between them, but why would her father have chosen it for the plaque on his coffin? Was it just a final show of affection toward his daughter, or was it something more? Thoughts spiraled like locusts through Eden's mind.

Something about it bothered Eden. It was almost as though he were trying to tell her something from beyond the grave. A message.

Eden dipped her head against the rain and quickened her pace up hill. Water ran through her hair and down the back of her neck, making her shiver. Once she was away from the cemetery, she would call a taxi. Right now, she just needed to move.

Somewhere behind her, a car engine purred to life. The gearbox clicked and the car started up the road.

The incline of the hill increased, and Eden's breathing intensified.

Eden wasn't paying any attention as a black Bentley slid past her, water hissing beneath the tires. The car pulled to the side of the road a few feet ahead. The tinted rear window slid down.

"Miss Black," came a voice.

At first Eden didn't notice it. Her thoughts turned and bubbled in her mind, sealing her off from the outside world. She walked past the car without turning.

"Miss Black, I'd like to speak with you if I may," the voice came again, more urgently.

Eden froze mid-stride, as though zapped by an electric shock. The name Black was Eden's preference since it gave her the freedom to operate without the association with her father, but how would someone at the funeral know that? They would all assume she was still Winslow, right?

Eden turned slowly on the spot. She locked eyes with the man in the back seat. He was about her father's age and had the air of aristocracy about him. Eden had met enough rich people to spot one from two hundred yards.

Eden stepped forward to get a better look at the man. She recognized him as one of the mourners at the cemetery. He'd locked eyes with her across the grave in a way that had made her uncomfortable.

The man pushed the car door open. "Get in, you'll catch your death out there."

Eden didn't reply. Her eyes narrowed on the man.

"Sorry, bad turn of phrase." He cleared his throat. "It is imperative that I speak with you. It's about your father. There's something I think you need to know."

Another car swished past, spraying water from the gutters, its wipers thumping across the screen in percussive streaks.

Eden took a step forward and then froze. A shudder of something more sinister than cold rattled her nerves.

The man held the door open, waiting for Eden to climb in. Rain spattered on the tan leather upholstery. Eden got the impression that he wasn't used to being kept waiting.

Eden looked from the man to his driver, who was probably a similar age to Eden herself. He wore a gray suit and sat stiffly, with gloved hands clutching the steering wheel, his eyes still fixed on the road ahead.

"We'll talk out here," Eden said, stepping away from the car.

The man scowled and waited a few seconds, as though Eden might change her mind.

Eden crossed her arms and shook out her hair.

"As you wish. Baxter, umbrella please."

The driver got out of the car, impervious to the rain, and took an umbrella from the passenger seat. Baxter was well over six feet tall, with a suit jacket that strained across his chest as he moved. Ex-military, Eden thought, focusing on his build.

Baxter opened the umbrella and held it out for his boss.

"He stays in the car," Eden said, pointing at Baxter. Her eyes held a challenge. She was wet and annoyed already and could just as easily do without whatever this guy had to say.

An expression of annoyance moved across the older man's face. He physically swallowed it down, a gesture which seemed to give him a great deal of discomfort. Finally, he climbed from the car and took the umbrella.

"Wait in the car Baxter. I'll be fine."

Baxter nodded and climbed back into the Bentley. The suspension sagged beneath his weight.

The man crossed to where Eden waited and extended his hand. "Archibald Godspeed," he said, waiting for Eden to take the proffered hand.

Eden ignored it. A few awkward seconds passed before Archibald continued. He stepped beside Eden and held the large umbrella over them both.

"My friends call me Archie, although there aren't many of them left," he said wistfully. He dug a packet of cigarettes from his coat, slid one out, and placed it in the corner of his mouth. "You don't mind, do you?" Godspeed said, the cigarette bobbing up and down.

"It's a free country," Eden said, and shrugged.

He lit up. "Over the years your father and I did a lot of work together. I'm part of the antiquities trade, you see. My family are one of the foremost collectors of antiques and artifacts in the country. We —"

"My father didn't deal in antiquities. He was an archaeologist," Eden interrupted

"Oh, my dear," — Godspeed exhaled a slow stream of smoke — "there is less difference than you might think. Archaeological digs are expensive. There are the workmen to pay for, the facilities, government officials to bribe."

"Get to the point," Eden snapped.

Godspeed took another drag on the cigarette.

A woman with a small dog straining at its leash shuffled past, both drenched by the rain but seemingly impervious to it. Godspeed waited until they were out of earshot before continuing.

Eden tapped her foot and gazed toward the end of the road. She resisted the growing temptation to walk away.

"Okay, well, I can see you're a very busy woman," Godspeed said finally. "I believe your father came across a set of tablets several years ago on one of his digs. 1998 it would have been, somewhere in Lebanon. Anyway, the tablets contain something of a diary, a journal if you will." He took another drag on the cigarette. "I have reason to believe that the contents of this diary are, well, very inconvenient for a lot of people. I'm not able to go into exactly what they contain here, out in public, but let's just say it would be life changing."

Eden turned to face Godspeed and suppressed a welling interest. He looked like a treasure hunter, but for all the wrong reasons.

"What I would hate is for these tablets to fall into the wrong hands. They could be used to solicit so much good in the world. They could also be suppressed or distorted and used for evil."

Eden scowled. The man talked like he had just walked out of a Dan Brown novel.

"I'm afraid this is rather more serious than I think you're taking it, Miss Black. This could be incredibly dangerous for you, and many other people." Godspeed finished his cigarette, dropped it, and crushed it beneath his shoe.

Eden's simmering frustration increased to a boil.

"Ahh, I see," Eden said, tipping her head back in a mock laugh. "Yes, of course. Why didn't you say? You're my knight in shining armor, right? I tell you what I'll do, I'll head over to my father's house, the father I've just buried, search through his things, and give you what you want. Does that work for you, Mr. Godspeed?" Eden spat the words.

"I think it would be best for us all if you did, yes. I have a secure facility at my home in which I can keep the tablets. Then, they'll be out of harm's way until we decide what to do with them." Godspeed grinned.

"Great idea," Eden said, suppressing a shiver.

"Excellent," Godspeed said, his grin widening further. "I can take you there now." He pointed toward the idling Bentley.

"But I have a better idea." Eden turned to the little man. "You get out of my business and leave me to grieve for my father." With that, she stomped away through the rain.

15

EDEN PAID the taxi and slipped back out into the rain. Despite the early hour, storm clouds had forced the sky into premature night.

She stared up at her father's house. The three-story Victorian monolith towered above her, as lifeless windows stared back down at her. Although the paperwork making the house officially hers had yet to come through, Eden had been given a key by one of the neighbors.

With no interest in living in the city, she planned to sell the place and its contents as quickly as possible.

Eden climbed the dozen tiled stairs which connected the house with the pavement, holding on to the iron railing to steady herself. Two panels of frosted glass gave a strange shadowy impression of the inside. She slipped the key into the lock and pushed open the heavy door. It swung back smoothly. She stepped inside and snapped on the light.

Glancing around at the large foyer, she looked fondly at the black and white floor tiles, the curving staircase, and the tapestries which hung across the walls. With a pang of regret, Eden tried to remember the last time she was here. It had been two years at least. Instinctively she dug the contents from the pockets of her coat and dropped them, along with the front door key, in a large glass bowl on the sideboard.

"What the..." Eden said out loud, picking up a business card which she'd just taken from her pocket.

Archibald Godspeed.

Antiquities.

"Sneaky man," Eden said, turning the card over. A note was scrawled on the back of the card in spidery handwriting.

You're right not to trust anyone. Strange things are happening. We need to speak.

Eden glimpsed herself in a wall-mounted mirror. She looked back down at the card, tapping it against her fingers. Maybe she would talk with him another time. Right now, she just wanted to be on her own.

Eden hung her coat on the stand and padded through to the kitchen, turning on lights as she went. She crossed the room and opened the glass doors of her father's drinks cabinet. She pushed aside several dusty bottles of whiskey and selected a cognac instead. She took out the oddly shaped bottle and examined it.

"Remy Martin Louis," she said, reading the label out loud. "That'll do."

She pulled out the cork, which made a satisfying pop as it came loose, then selected a glass and poured herself a large measure. Taking a greedy sip, Eden felt the smooth spirit warm her throat and stomach. It was a good feeling.

Glass in hand, Eden walked from room to room, considering the task ahead of her. It was fair to say that her father owned a lot of stuff. Shelves lined all available space, overflowing with books or other ancient curiosities. Pictures, tapestries, strange masks, spears, and things that Eden couldn't even determine the use for covered every available space. The problem was, without her father here, each of these objects was just that — an object. Wandering around the bedrooms on the second floor, Eden felt lonelier than ever. She finished her Cognac and returned to the kitchen for another glass. This time she poured herself an even larger measure. She took another sip, feeling the alcohol start to work its relaxing magic.

Then she climbed the winding staircase up to her father's office, careful not to knock any objects from the walls, and pushed open the door. Beneath the eaves in the roof of the Victorian house was the room in which Alexander Winslow had spent most of his time.

The pitched roof here was lower than those on the main floors. In the center of the room Eden could stand at her full height, but toward the slanted sides, she had to crouch.

She crossed to her father's large oak desk and slumped in his chair. Even the desk was a thing of beauty. Intricately carved and upholstered with green leather, it seemed far too big to have fit up the stairs. She took a sip from the glass and leaned back in the chair, examining the items on the desk in front of her.

Eden took a deep breath and suddenly felt overcome with grief. She gripped on to the tabletop, as though the room itself could melt away. She tried to push away the emotion. She didn't want to feel this now. Eden couldn't feel this now. She inhaled again, the smells of her father's chamomile cigarettes, combined with that of old books and aged leather, filled her senses. Eden glanced at the stubs of several cigarettes sat in an ashtray on the table. She picked one up and inhaled its strange, sweet aroma. Absorbing the smell, Eden felt strangely close to her father. It felt as though he had just popped downstairs and would return in a minute or two. Then he would light up another cigarette and continue with whatever story he had been telling.

Eden dropped the cigarette back into the ashtray. Tears sparkled at the corner of her eyes again, threatening to spill anew. She remembered all the times she'd moaned at her father for smoking — now she was glad he'd never stopped.

She cuffed away a tear, took a sip of the cognac, and tried to push away the emotions. She looked around the desk and locked eyes with a fossilized human skull made from black rock her father used as a paperweight. Eden remembered the thing but couldn't recall where her father had gotten it from.

She pulled a stack of paper from beneath the skull and flicked through it. She picked out one page and scanned the text. It looked like a report from a dig in Cyprus the year before. She put the papers back in the pile. Two framed photographs sat on the opposite side of the desk. In one of them, Eden and her father grinned at the camera. Eden recognized it, taken maybe fifteen years ago at a dig in Lebanon. She held the photograph to her chest and exhaled. Grief swelling inside, Eden closed her eyes for a moment and imagined her father's voice intoning of ancient civilizations, merciless kings, or fearless warriors.

She exhaled hard and forced the grief away. Mourning didn't suit her. She didn't want it to suit her. Alexander Winslow had been a man of work and passion, and while he clearly loved and provided for his daughter, the only way she ever got to see him was to go to work with him.

Eden noticed another picture on the desk. It too had been taken some years ago and showed her father standing with several other men. Again, it looked as though it had been taken on a dig site. Behind the assembled men, several trenches stretched out in the sand.

Eden examined the men in the photograph one by one. Recognition dropped like a stone. She snatched up the picture. There was no mistaking it; the man to her father's right was Archibald Godspeed.

Eden looked at the picture for long seconds. Maybe Godspeed had been telling the truth — he had worked with her father. Eden's fingers tightened around the frame.

Had she really known her father that little? Or maybe he had told her about this man, but she hadn't listened. Grief flowed through her anew, now riding on a river of guilt.

Eden stood the picture of her father and Archibald back on the desk and picked up the one in which she was a child. She wished that she could speak to her father again, just to ask him what to do. What would he want her to do with all this stuff? Who could she trust to help her?

She gazed at the picture and longed for the simple days of childhood again. Eden looked up and stared absently at the bookshelf across the room. Built into the far wall of the attic office, it contained several rows of red and gold books, what looked like an animal skull, and two small terracotta pots. Eden smiled as a memory flashed into her mind. The bookshelf also contained a tiny crawl space behind. Eden remembered many afternoons as a child crawling into the hidden space in the pretense that she too was on an archae-ological dig — rediscovering treasures lost to the world for thousands of years. Strangely, she'd never felt closer to her father than she did in those days, peering out from behind the shelf at him working at his desk.

Eden emptied the glass of cognac into her mouth, swallowed and crossed the room. She pushed a trunk aside, exposing the gap behind the shelf. Then, using the light on her phone, she peered into the void. The space ran for about ten feet, getting thinner and thinner as the eves of the roof met the floor. Eden crawled slowly into the space. It wasn't as easy as it used to be. She wiggled herself inside and then pulled the trunk back over the gap. She peered out from between the books. Everything was just as she remembered. The only thing missing was him.

Suddenly grief welled up inside her again. Hot tears sprung forth, streaking down her face. She curled up on the floor. Eden buried her head in her hands, clamped her eyes shut, and let the emotion flow forth.

A crash echoed through the house, waking Eden with a start. She looked up, wide-eyed, trying to understand her surroundings. She remembered crying some hours ago but must have fallen asleep. She peered out into her father's office. Everything was as she'd left it, except now the windows mounted into the ceiling showed only black squares of night sky. She checked her phone. It was just before 2am. She had been asleep for several hours.

Another thump reverberated through the floor beneath her.

Eden rubbed her eyes. She remembered her father's house always making noises in the night. The floorboards readjusting to temperature shifts or the heating system cooling — the place ticked and thumped as though it were alive.

What was that? Eden held her breath and listened, closing her eyes as though it might enhance her hearing. A soft methodical thud echoed through the floor. Eden's eyes shot open. There was someone else inside the house.

Eden heard the footsteps clearly now, moving from room to room on the floor below her. It sounded like two pairs. One would move, and then go quiet. Then the other would move, then pause too.

Whoever they were, they were looking for something. And they were coming her way.

Silently, Eden shimmied further into the void behind the bookcase. She had shifted the trunk to the side to ensure it blocked the gap through which she'd come. The only way someone could see her would be to look directly into the void — with a light.

A whisper carried up the stairs, followed quickly by a reply. From her hiding place, Eden couldn't make out the words.

Then, slowly at first but increasing in speed, the footsteps padded up the stairs toward her.

16

THE FOOTSTEPS DREW CLOSER, tapping up the tightly wound staircase toward the attic room.

Deep within the confines of her childhood hiding hole, Eden froze. Her fingers bent into the dusty floorboards, as though scrabbling for a way out she knew wasn't there. Her heart beat impossibly loud in the enclosed space. Loud enough to give her location away for sure, she thought. She reduced her breathing until it was nothing more than a shallow, repetitive gulp of air.

The footsteps reached the top of the stairs and stopped. The door mechanism clicked open. The door swung back on its hinges.

Eden's curiosity rose, and she peered around the bookshelf. The only light in the room came from the green-shaded lamp on the desk. Eden cursed herself for leaving it on.

A beam of light swept through the room like a probing finger. Footsteps thudded through the doorway, vibrating the floorboards against Eden's ribs only feet away.

A pair of boots clobbered into Eden's view. Even in her

frightened state, she was intent on noting everything she could about them. They were made from some kind of tough synthetic fabric and looked like military-issue.

The boots did a full circle of the room, then a deep voice hissed. When the reply came, it was tinny. The men were talking using a comms system. The fact that they weren't using in-ear headsets meant they'd assumed the building was empty.

Eden's fear suddenly increased. She knew a thing or two about professional military types — and that's exactly what this man was. And, possibly more alarming, they were searching for something, and wouldn't quit until they found it.

The man stepped close to one of the bookshelves on the far side of the room, giving Eden a better view of him. He was tall and muscular, with long hair pulled back in a pony-tail. Eden scrutinized his black tactical clothing and the weapon holstered at his hip. For some reason, seeing the weapon at the man's side sent a bolt of shock through Eden's body. Then she realized that of course he would be armed. This man, along with his colleagues in the house below, was on a mission.

The man swept his light across the bookcase, systemati-cally checking each book and artifact in turn.

Eden widened her gaze, willing more light into her struggling eyes.

The man paused and slid a book from the shelf with his gloved hand. The gold embossed leather hardback shim-mered. He checked something and then slid it back onto the shelf.

Eden had often asked her father the value of his collec-tion of books and artifacts.

"Monetary value is not the only measure of an item's

worth," he would reply. Eden had always suspected he had a very valuable collection.

These men were not interested in its perceived value or lack thereof, though; they were after something specific. An indication about the location of the tablets Godspeed had mentioned, perhaps? Eden blinked hard at the realization. Hadn't Godspeed mentioned something about powerful forces at work here? Was this it?

Eden steeled herself, swallowed down her fear, and shuffled slowly to the left, giving herself a better view of the man as he moved methodically along the bookcase. Her fear merged into curiosity and then ballooned into anger. How dare this man, these men, rifle through her father's possessions?

Her body stiffened as she resisted the temptation to leap from her hiding place. He was armed and she had no idea how many others there might be down below. One at least, she suspected, maybe more.

Eden slipped out her phone while the man's back was turned. She turned the screen to its dimmest setting so as not to give away her location. Then, making sure the flash and sound were disabled, she took several photos of the man. She made sure to get one of his boots, the make of his weapon, and any other identifying marks she could find. She would analyze them later, although she expected him to be a ghost.

The man did a full rotation of the room, checking each of the shelves in turn. Then he turned to the large wooden desk and slid open each of the drawers. He rifled through each one but found nothing that interested him.

"Clear. There's nothing. It's not here," he barked into the radio. Eden made out his crisp British accent this time. An unintelligible reply squawked from the receiver.

The man stomped back across the room and down the stairs, the old wood creaking beneath his considerable weight.

Eden took a deep breath and let relief wash over her. Whoever he was — whoever they were — they hadn't found what they were looking for. Maybe the information wasn't here at all.

Eden listened in closely as the footsteps reached the floor below. The movement stopped and the sound of whispered voices drifted upward. Eden strained her ears, longing to hear what they'd said. She pushed herself slowly toward the opening in a bid to hear better, but still couldn't make out a single word.

Then the footsteps turned and thumped their way back toward the staircase. Eden pushed herself silently backward again, into the safety of the shadows.

The man reached the top of the staircase and walked into the attic room. Although dressed identically, there was something slightly different about this man. He was larger and moved with a more cumbersome stride. He made no efforts to silence his movements, clearly confident that no one was around to hear him.

The brute dropped a heavy object to the antique Persian carpet.

Eden peered out, trying to notice as much as she could. The lamp on the desk cast the man in shadow. Eden focused on the object. The thing was large, square in shape, and from the way the man had lugged it into the room, heavy.

The man picked up the object again and moved to the back of the room. In the dull lamplight, Eden saw that it was a metal fuel can. Fear welled in her. Her muscles froze in shock. It felt as though the scene was taking place in a dream. She blinked, trying to wake up, but came straight back to the harsh reality.

The man bent down and unscrewed the cap from the top of the can. He stood, picked up the can, and poured the contents around the room. Liquid splashed over the floor, up on to the bookshelves, across the desk, covering the priceless artifacts of her father's life and work.

Now on the other side of the lamp, Eden got a look at the man's face. For a moment, she couldn't look away. A deep and jagged scar ran across his right eye, permanently closing the colorless orb to nothing more than a slit.

It was the smell that snapped Eden from her trance. The thick and noxious stench of fuel filled the attic.

Eden watched in silence as the man continued to cover her father's office in fuel. He apparently took sick pride in systematically splashing the liquid across all parts of the room, concentrating specifically on the books and artifacts. When he was satisfied, the man tilted the can and walked back to the stairwell. A thin stream of fuel splashed out behind him.

Eden's heart thudded against the floorboards. The chemical-laden air filled her nose and throat. She felt sick, tired, and cold all at once.

She listened closely as the man retraced his steps, slowly descending the staircase. The man reached the floor below and Eden scurried out of her hiding place.

Walking on the balls of her feet, she crossed to the door. The floorboards felt slippery beneath her shoes. Whatever accelerant they'd used, it was thick and viscous. The deadly smell of the fuel rose further in her throat, making her feel light-headed. She held on to the door frame to prevent herself from fainting. She willed the feeling to pass.

Eden forced herself into action. She grabbed a satchel

which hung on the back of the door and tiptoed around the room, stuffing things inside. First, she took the photo of her and her father from its frame and stuffed it in the bag, then slipped the one of Archibald Godspeed in beside it. She folded the papers she'd glanced through and slipped them inside the bag, too.

Eden froze in her tracks. A wall of heat moved up the stairwell, pushing her clothes tight against her skin. Eden turned to the door. The accelerant was slow-burning but powerful — no doubt designed to mirror the behavior of a real house fire. Eden wondered for a moment how many times the men had done this.

She turned to face the only window in the attic room. The dormer window was set into the roof behind the desk. Brighton's night sky glowed slightly orange through the glass.

Eden paced across the room, the heat growing beyond bearable levels. She unlocked and shoved open the window. The pane moved about six inches and then stopped. A wisp of cool night air streamed through the gap. Eden shoved the window again, her sweat-drenched hands slipped across the glass. Again, the pane of glass shuddered to a stop, making her escape impossible. The window had a safety measure which prevented her from getting outside.

Eden glanced behind her. The dull orange glow from the hallway now flickered with approaching flames. Something on the floor below her crashed. Her breathing became labored as smoke filled the air.

Eden looked around for something with which to break the glass. Panic drove her heart beat into double-time. The stone skull looked back at her from the desk with its long-dead eyes. The flickering flames gave the skull a devilish appearance.

Eden picked up the single piece of rock. It felt heavy and cold against her burning skin. She crossed back to the window and raised the stone skull high. With all her strength, she slammed it down against the windowpane. A large crack spread across the glass, but it didn't shatter.

Something crashed from the stairs behind her. Another wave of heat wafted into the room. Eden could feel the heat rising through the floor beneath her. It wouldn't be long before the timbers of the old Victorian building lost their strength and collapsed into the flames.

Eden steeled herself against the rising heat, and her rising fear. She raised the skull again. Sliding her fingers into the eye sockets, she swung the it with all her strength. The skull crashed through the glass, shattering the pane it into tiny pieces. Eden smashed out the remaining shards and scrambled out on to the roof. She took a deep, beautiful breath of the night air and spat out the taste of the fire.

The fire engulfed the attic room with the new influx of oxygen. Eden glanced behind her. Fire completely consumed the attic room.

Keeping low and careful to keep her footing, she scurried across the roof slates. Fifty feet below, enough for a fatal fall, she saw her father's small yard lit by violent hues of red and yellow.

Eden moved on to the roof of the neighboring house. She peered over the edge and down into the neighbor's yard. There was nothing here to help her descend to ground level. She turned and scurried up and across the roof slates, sliding down the other side. The road stretched out fifty feet below her, heading in the direction of the city center. In the distance, the celebratory lights of the Palace Pier glittered incongruously.

Eden looked down at the cars in the street beneath her.

On the opposite side of the road a black van stood at the curb, it's engine idling. As though responding to her presence, the van's lights clicked on, and the vehicle pulled out on to the empty road.

"Waiting to check the job was finished?" Eden muttered, pulling out her phone and snapping several shots of the van as it drove away. "You'll wish you hadn't."

Then, all at once, Eden's energy left her body. She struggled to keep upright on the slates as her breathing became light and her head spun. She looked out at the city around her but couldn't focus on anything. She used one of the chimney stacks to support her as she crouched down.

Somewhere far beneath her she saw the strobing lights of a fire engine power around the corner. Then, the remaining strength left her body and she sunk into darkness.

17

EDEN DIDN'T KNOW what she expected to see when she opened her eyes, but it wasn't this. She blinked several times, but the view didn't change.

She was lying in a brightly lit room. Blue curtains hung around her, billowing softly in one direction and then the other. There was movement behind the curtains, but at first, she couldn't make it out.

Then her hearing drifted back into service, too. Shoes squeaked across the floor. One voice spoke and another answered.

Eden looked around frantically, panic rising in her throat.

She was lying in a bed, half covered by blankets. She noticed that she wasn't wearing her own clothes anymore. A jug of water sat on a cabinet to her left, and to her right lay a couple of other things she didn't recognize.

Footsteps squeaked from somewhere beyond the curtains again. A head appeared between one curtain and the other, followed quickly by a body and two legs.

"Hello," said a woman, stepping toward the bed. "You're awake. That's fantastic."

Eden tried to speak. Her voice was croaky and hoarse. "What? Where am I? What happened?"

"You're in Hospital," the woman said, in a tuneful Irish accent. "You've only been here a few hours." She pulled a clipboard from the end of the bed and examined it carefully. "You were involved in a housefire. They were surprised to find you alive. Apparently, you'd managed to pull yourself out on to the roof to safety. If you'd stayed inside, there was no way you'd be here now."

The nurse slid the clipboard back on to the foot of the bed.

"What's wrong with me? Am I —"

"Smoke inhalation, mostly. Some scrapes and bruises too, but nothing serious. It's a miracle, really. From what I heard, that's better than can be said for the house. It took them ages to get the blaze under control. Is there anyone you'd like me to call? People must be worried about you."

Eden blinked again, trying to make sense of things. She remembered the van pulling away, and then everything going black.

"No. You don't need to call anyone," Eden said. "Where's my phone?"

"Your bag is on the side up there." The nurse pointed at the cabinet to Eden's left. "Anything from your pockets I put in there too. There's a buzzer on the top there. Press it if you need anything and I'll be right along." The nurse disappeared back through the curtain and into the hubbub of the hospital.

Eden turned to the cabinet. Her muscles ached, although nothing felt like it was specifically injured. She heaved the small satchel down onto her lap with a lot more effort than would have usually been necessary. Eden flipped open the lid and flicked past the photographs, the pair of books, and the stack of papers. She dug out her phone and thumbed the unlock button. The phone glowed for a second, then the empty battery sign flashed before fading to black.

Eden dropped the phone to the bed. Maybe they would have a charger that she could use, although she didn't intend to stay that long.

She opened the bag again and noticed a business card sitting at the bottom. She dug it out. Archibald's name glittered under the hospital's anemic light. She put the card to one side and dug out the photograph of Godspeed and her father. Eden examined the background of the photograph, trying to work out where it might have been taken. Although her father had been an expert in Middle Eastern archaeology, he had travelled all over the world at one point or another.

She lay the photo on the bed cover and looked at the loosely billowing curtains. If her father had trusted Archibald Godspeed, then maybe she should too.

She leaned back on the pillow and ran the events of the last few days through her mind. She missed her home in the woods and longed to get back there as soon as possible. She closed her eyes and imagined the bluebells covered in the morning's dew, the animals whose lives intermingled with hers, and the silence of the still night air.

A noise which sounded like a slamming door brought Eden back to the present. She opened her eyes and looked around. The blue curtain which had billowed slightly, now lay still. An air conditioner rattled somewhere out of sight. Other than that, all was silent. Unsettlingly silent. Dead silent. Although Eden hadn't spent long in the hospital, the silence felt unnatural. She expected there to always be the tapping of footsteps or the rumble of a passing trolley.

She listened closely to the silence and then heard a sound which caused her to physically shudder. Her blood ran cold, and her muscles tensed.

The sound was only faint at first, but it made the hairs on the back of her neck stand on end. The deep thud of heavy boots on a linoleum floor.

An image spooled through Eden's mind. She was back behind the bookcase in her father's house, watching the boots stomp into the room. A bookcase that no longer existed, in a house that was now burned to the ground.

Eden's hands clenched into fists on top of the cover. Her heart beat aggressively in her chest. She sat up straight, ready to fight or run.

Another step echoed through the room. A door thumped closed.

Eden turned her ear toward the curtain. One set of footsteps were slightly heavier than the last. Two people headed her way. They were coming to finish the job they'd started; Eden was sure of it. She focused on the sound, trying to work out where the men were. It sounded as though they were still a fair way off. They had only taken three steps since coming through the main door.

Slowly and silently, Eden pulled off the cover. Careful not to let it fall, she arranged the pillows and folded the cover back over the top. To the casual observer it might look as though someone was still asleep in the bed. She turned off the light. The gloom hung thick across the bed. Seconds of confusion could be the lifeline she needed.

Adrenaline coursing through her veins now, elevating her into a sense of hyper awareness, Eden ducked behind the bed and tightened the satchel over her shoulder. The bag wasn't ideal to run with, and nor was the hospital gown. She would have to find some proper clothes as soon as possible.

A few feet beyond the curtain, the footsteps paused. Eden imagined the men looking for her bed. Keeping low, she ducked through the rear curtain and into the next bay. The bed was empty. A heart rate monitor on a trolley sat beside the bed, its screen glowing dully.

The footsteps moved forward again. Gloved hands tore the curtains aside. Two faint pops echoed through the ward.

Eden suppressed a gasp. A silenced weapon. An urgent voice whispered, another answered.

The men had fired into the bed without realizing it was empty. In moments, they would pull aside the thin curtain she hid behind and see Eden there. Her eyes darted from side to side, looking for a way out.

Eden knelt down and unclipped the brake on the wheels of the heavy heart rate monitor. She shoved the machine as hard as she could through the curtain, then turned and ran. Eden screamed inside as her bare feet slapped the linoleum. Her pulse clicked into overdrive and the sound of her panicked breathing filled her ears.

Behind her, the heart rate monitor smashed to the floor. Glass shattered. One of the men shouted.

Eden pounded on without looking back. Her head whipped right and left, searching for an escape. Cold air streamed past the bare skin of her legs. She felt exposed and vulnerable. Without pausing, she ran past empty beds and the nurse's station.

Two more distant pops sounded. Eden took a deep breath and held it, waiting for the tearing heat of a bullet. None came. She powered on.

"Whooah, my dear, you shouldn't be running. You

shouldn't even be out of bed," came the nurse's calm, lilting tones as she bustled out of a side room.

Eden tried to shout a warning but couldn't do it in time. Two slugs smashed through the air, thumping the woman in the chest. The nurse gasped; a scream caught in her throat. Crimson bloomed across her uniform, and she fell to the floor. A wheezing, gurgling noise escaped her lips.

Eden stared down at the woman, now writhing on the floor. She then turned and looked behind her. The men charged her way. In a flash she saw the greasy ponytails and the scarred face. There was no doubt about it — these men had come to finish what they'd started.

Eden ran on, a fist of guilt twisting in her stomach. She swerved toward a set of double doors. Her bare feet easily finding traction on the linoleum, she crashed through and found herself in a concrete stairwell. One set of stairs rose and the other fell. On instinct, Eden climbed. It was logical to assume that she would head down. Down usually meant out. And escape.

18

Reaching the next floor landing, Eden froze. The door below her thundered open. Heavy boots pounded out into the stairwell. The sound of a whispered voice rose toward her.

She stood silently, her muscles tightened, ready to run or fight.

"Clear, I'm heading down," the man said. Eden didn't recognize his voice, although he had a British accent. The response came over a radio, meaning the men had split up. Eden didn't dare move, or even breathe. Eventually, the footsteps faded as her pursuer descended to the floor below.

Eden dragged a breath and shook herself back into action. She turned, silently pulled open the door, and slipped inside. A long corridor ran in both directions, doors lining both sides. Strip lights mounted in the ceiling washed everything in an eerie glow.

Eden turned right, slipping into a slow jog. Running on her toes, her bare feet barely made a sound against the cool linoleum floor. She passed two wards on the right and another on the left. Eden paused and peered through the door's glass panel. The space lay in gloom. Patients tucked in beds lined both sides of the ward, their sleeping figures silhouetted against the glow of various machines.

She glanced behind her. No one had come through the door, yet. A machine hummed somewhere nearby, but other than that, the place was silent. No footsteps came her way.

Eden turned and jogged on. Her breathing and pulse slowed, as her muscles tingled from the exertion and adrenaline. The next room was a set of toilets, and then one marked *Staff Only*. She pushed inside. A light clicked on automatically. A small kitchenette took up one side of the room with some comfortable chairs in the center. Various colorful pieces of paper pinned to a notice board fluttered in the draft from an air vent. A bank of lockers occupied one wall, above which a clock read a quarter past four. No wonder everyone was asleep; it was still the middle of the night.

Eden looked down at her hospital gown. Finding clothes and shoes was a top priority.

She grabbed a knife from a drawer in the kitchen and jimmied open a locker. She rifled through the clothes but found nothing of use. This one was obviously owned by a person much larger than her. She ripped open two more lockers and found a pair of trainers, some jeans, a black t-shirt and a jacket, all of which fit well enough. She also took a rucksack from one locker and switched it for her father's satchel. Then, she cut the hospital's ID tag from her wrist and shoved it and the hospital gown into a bin.

Eden pushed open the door and peered out. The corridor was empty. She stepped through. The door whispered closed behind her. Reaching the end of the corridor, Eden slipped through another set of double doors. A bank of three large lifts took up one wall, and a window looked out over the hospital grounds from the other. Eden crossed to the window and peered out. She was on the fifth or sixth floor of the building. She looked down on various smaller buildings and a snaking access road which led back out toward the city.

Eden turned back toward the stairs. She guessed a building of this size must have several stairwells and exits. Hopefully, she would lose her pursuers in the labyrinth of corridors.

Tightening the rucksack across her shoulders, Eden headed for the stairs. She made her way down slowly, stopping at each landing to make sure no one was waiting for her. Reaching the ground floor, she ignored signs for the main exit and headed for the nearest fire escape. A door with a push bar sat at the end of a corridor. Eden glanced behind her. An eerie silence hung across the building. She examined the door. Electrical sensors mounted in the center suggested that opening the door would trigger an alarm. Eden figured she'd be long gone by the time that mattered.

She shoved the door. The lock clunked, and the door swung open. Eden stepped out into the cool night air. Before she could take a full breath, though, heavy footsteps pounded the floor behind her. Eden spun around. She slipped into a fighting stance, her muscles taut and ready. Two men rounded the corner and charged her way, their boots thundering in the enclosed space. It took Eden a nanosecond to recognize their imposing figures. She glanced up at a small camera on the ceiling above her head. The men must have radio contact with someone monitoring the hospital's security system.

Eden turned and ran. Running was clearly better than

fighting two armed men. They hadn't caught her yet, and she certainly wasn't giving up.

She charged down the length of the building, skipping over flower beds and benches. The beat of her heart quickened to match her pounding legs. The ill-fitting trainers flopped around on her feet, but Eden pushed on.

She darted to the left and shot past a row of cars parked in the gloom. She risked a glance over her shoulder. She had created some distance between her and the men. At least half their size, she was quicker on her feet.

She reached an access road and paused. Ahead of her, a brick wall loomed upward. It was well over twelve feet high, with nothing nearby to help Eden over it. Eden's breath came out in enormous clouds. She looked left and then right. The access road curved out of sight in both directions. The glow from overhead streetlights pooled every hundred feet, leaving the rest of the road in gloom. Various hospital buildings hung cloaked in the shadows, their windows barred.

She looked back at the men, maybe sixty feet away now. One pulled out his weapon and raised it high.

Eden's heart thundered in her chest, again. Her lungs ached from the fire, and now strained from running. She looked left and then right, trying to decide. Nether direction offered her safety.

A noise surged above the distant murmur of the hospital. The growling of a car's powerful engine. It rose and fell as the car moved through the gears.

Eden looked back at the men, closing in on her now.

Bright headlights swung around the corner of the access road as the car squealed toward them. Eden raised her hand to her eyes against the blinding light. The car revved forward and then screeched to a stop between Eden and the men. The men stopped running and raised their weapons, their mouths set in snarls of anger.

The passenger door nearest to Eden swung open and the cabin light snapped on. Eden's eyes sprung wide, and her hand covered her mouth in recognition of the man inside.

19

"How did you know where I was?" Eden shouted over the roaring of the engine. She was in the back seat of a black Bentley now, pulling out of the hospital grounds and onto the main road.

Archibald Godspeed considered Eden, the passing streetlights patterning across his face.

"I heard about your father's house on the news, and when I couldn't get through to you, Baxter and I did some research."

Baxter, who was clearly more than just a driver, nodded from the front of the Bentley. They turned a corner and accelerated.

"There's much you don't know, Eden. As I tried to warn you before, there is a lot at stake here. Powerful people want what you have."

Eden looked from Godspeed to the city flashing past the windows. Everything felt alien, and unsettling, as though she didn't even know where she was any longer. It felt as though the life she knew was slipping away and there was nothing she could do about it. Then her disquietude turned to anger, and then, grief. Her hands closed into fists.

"Wait, no, stop!" Eden shouted, trying to regain control. "Let me out. This is madness!"

Baxter's eyes focused on Godspeed in the rearview mirror. Godspeed nodded once and Baxter pulled to the side of the road.

Eden burst out of the car and leapt onto the pavement. She leaned on the front of a closed-up shop and pulled several deep and nourishing breaths. After a minute, she stood up and looked out in the city's direction. After the rain of the day before, the night was cool and calm, unlike Eden's turbulent emotions.

Godspeed lifted himself out of the car, too. He still looked smart, wearing a pale blue shirt and black trousers.

Eden crossed back to the car and leveled a finger at the older man. "First you told me you needed something my dad had, then his house burns down. Then, I'm almost killed when two men turn up at the hospital. I'm not getting back in that car until you tell me what's going on."

Movement in the shop doorway behind her caused Eden to glance over her shoulder. A man, seeking refuge in the recessed doorway, turned in his sleep. Finding the unlikely comfort he required, he settled down again.

Godspeed took Eden by the elbow and moved them away from the sleeping figure.

The Bentley idled at the curb. Baxter sat in the driver's seat, his eyes locked on the road ahead.

"I don't intend to keep anything from you," Godspeed whispered. "But we can't talk here, it's not safe. I will tell you everything. You deserve to know what your family's involved in. But we must do it somewhere safe."

"I'm not getting back in —"

"Listen," Godspeed hissed, more forcefully now. "You have two choices. You come with me and find out what's really going on here, or you try your luck out there alone." He pointed down the road toward the city center. In the distance, a pair of shapeless figures lumbered toward them.

Godspeed walked around the Bentley and climbed back inside. The door thumped closed. The engine continued to idle softly.

Eden looked one way and then the other. Not one vehicle had passed since Eden had climbed from the car. She thought about calling a taxi, but her phone was dead and useless. Then she thought about the picture she had found of Godspeed and her father. Beneath the grief and fear, a hint of curiosity gnawed. If her father had really been up to something dangerous, she wanted to know what it was.

"Fine," Eden said, sliding back into the car. "But you're talking as soon as we get there. No more time wasting."

With no expression of frustration at the delay, Baxter clicked the Bentley into gear and accelerated away.

Eden stared morosely out of the window as the Bentley cut quickly through Brighton's traffic-free roads and out into the countryside. Before a word had even been spoken between the car's three occupants, they were speeding past fields and blink-and-you'll-miss-them villages.

"Do you mind?" Godspeed said, digging his silver cigarette case from a pocket. Eden shook her head. Godspeed wound down his window and lit the cigarette. Catching a scent of the tobacco, Eden remembered the chamomile cigarettes her father smoked. She had encouraged him to give up. Now, as a memory, it felt sort of nostalgic.

After another few minutes of silence, they turned off the

main road and onto a gravel driveway. The Bentley paused for a pair of vast iron gates to swing open. Baxter sat silently, staring through the windscreen. Godspeed, his cigarette now finished, drummed a pattern on his knees.

The Bentley rolled on, crunching over the gravel, and passing landscaped gardens on both sides of the driveway.

"Put the lights on for our guest, will you?" Godspeed said, leaning forward and tapping Baxter on the shoulder. Baxter pressed a button on the Bentley's central console. Lights flared, illuminating a grand manor house set on the crest of a hill.

The Bentley purred to a stop at the front of the house. Eden got out and looked up at the expansive building. A wide stone staircase led between regency columns up to a vast vine-covered façade.

Eden snapped her mouth shut and turned to Godspeed. "I hope it's not cold," she said, swinging her bag over her shoulder and wandering toward the front of the house. Two stone dolphins with unseeing eyes seemed to consider her from the top of a column.

"You won't be cold. This way." Godspeed pointed her in the opposite direction.

Eden followed him around the side of the house and into a smaller, much less grand entrance. Godspeed snapped on the light to reveal a large kitchen with an old-fashioned stove, oak counters, and several large, red leather armchairs.

"Take a seat," he said, pointing toward the chairs. "Tea, or coffee?" He filled the kettle. "Or something stronger?"

Eden liked the room. It had a cozy warmth that made her feel at home. She dropped her bag and flopped into the first comfy chair she saw.

"Hold the drink, it's time to talk," Eden snapped.

"Well, I'm having one," Godspeed replied, bustling around the kitchen. "It's been a hell of a night, and I fear this is only just getting started."

Eden glanced at the dying embers of a fire in the grate.

"I'll get another log on the fire in a moment," Godspeed said, noticing Eden's scowl. "It'll be toasty hot before you know it."

Eden feared it wasn't the temperature that caused her discomfort. Her stomach clenched in fear and expectation at what Godspeed was about to reveal.

Godspeed placed a Baileys, a strong coffee, and a glass of water on the small table beside Eden's chair. Glancing at the drinks, Eden realized how thirsty she was. With a nod of thanks, she snatched up the water and drained almost the entire glass.

Godspeed re-stoked the fire and then settled himself in the chair opposite Eden.

"When my grandfather lived here, this would have been the servants' quarters. He would have hardly ever come down here. Now, it's my favorite room. I rarely use any of the other rooms." He signaled upward.

Eden took a deep sip of her drink and made a show of looking around. "Yes, I like it. Start talking."

Godspeed nodded and his expression hardened. He placed his glass on the table beside Eden's. "There's no easy way to say this, Eden."

Eden shifted in her chair and nodded. She leaned in. "Go on, tell me."

"I know, beyond doubt, that your father's death wasn't an accident."

20

_____

EIGHT MEN, all dressed in black, moved toward the perimeter wall of Archibald Godspeed's manor house. The men were on high alert, their Heckler & Koch MP5-SF Parabellum machine pistols scanning the grounds for movement.

The leading man, only recognizable by his single working eye, which darted left and right in a well-practiced pattern of survival, gestured silently to his men. The men scurried easily across the ten-foot wall.

The leader listened, watching the hillside for movement, as eight pairs of heavy-duty boots thumped quietly to the soft earth on the other side. The hillside was quiet tonight. No backup waited nearby. No air support was available. There was no extraction point. They had to get in, get the job done, and get out.

On the other side of the wall, the men scurried behind the cover of a nearby bush. Now in the area of conflict, the next few minutes of their mission would either yield success or failure. In their line of work, those few minutes felt like a lifetime.

The leader heaved himself up onto the wall, the old bricks crumbling beneath his gloved hands. He swung himself over easily. Dropping to the ground on the other side, he turned and studied the wall. He rearranged a strand of ivy which had been displaced as the men climbed over. Professionals. Leave no trace.

The leader stepped behind the undergrowth and peered out at the manor house. Floodlights washed the building in a warm glow. Three hundred yards of well-trimmed lawn stretched between the men and the house. The leader had no doubt they would be seen crossing the lawn, but that didn't matter. Their instructions were to wait undercover. For now.

GODSPEED'S WORDS hit Eden like a fist to the stomach. The room spun and wobbled around her. She bolted upright and looked deep into the eyes of the man sitting opposite her.

"You mean... you mean, he was murdered?"

"Yes. Murdered. Let me explain. In 1998 your father uncovered a tomb in the mountains of Lebanon dating from around 4000 BC. He had hoped to discover something that would send shockwaves through the archaeological community. Oddly, however, they reported to have discovered nothing." Godspeed's wiry brows knitted together. "Here's the strange part," he continued, biting his lip, "in the last few weeks, everyone that took part on that dig has died."

Eden sat motionless for a few seconds, considering the implications of the events Godspeed had unfolded before her. When she spoke, a single word came out softly and slowly. "Nothing?"

He pointed at Eden and smiled wryly. "Nothing." His

hands made the shape of an explosion. "The tomb had already been opened and the contents stolen, apparently."

"You think my father was lying about what he found in that tomb?" Eden's gaze held a challenge.

Godspeed straightened up, surprised by the assertion. He cleared his throat. "Yes, actually I do. Your father was a brilliant man. It was rumored that he expected to find something explosive in the tomb. The sort of thing that would send shockwaves, not just through the archeological community, but through society. Your father knew this. It's my belief that he's been keeping what was really in that tomb under wraps for twenty years, waiting for the right time to come clean."

"But why wait this long?"

"Your father knew that if this information was released at the wrong time, it would be swept undercover by the establishment. Powerful people would discredit him and his work. He was waiting until the world was ready for such a change."

"Okay, but what was supposed to be in the tomb in the first place, if it's so important?"

"Those aren't the questions you really want to ask," Godspeed said, his eyes glittering in the firelight, "are they?"

Eden narrowed her gaze. Frustrated, for a moment she considered standing up and smacking the man in the face. The effects of delayed grief, a short night of sleep, and being hunted by two heavy-booted men had caught up with her. And now, the annoying request to answer an unsolvable question. "Don't patronize me," she spat, her fingers closing so tightly around the glass of Baileys that it began to shake. The ice cubes tinkled. Eden pointed at Godspeed, her eyes burning into him. "Don't patronize me, and don't play games with me. I'm not here to talk in riddles or solve

your problems. Tell me what you know about my father, or
—"

"What I mean is," Godspeed cut in, "we need to start this in the right place." Godspeed extended his hands in a gesture of placation. "What's important first of all, what I need to tell you —"

"Whose tomb was it?" Eden shouted, her voice echoing around the kitchen.

"That is the key to this whole sorry mess," Godspeed said, pointing at Eden. The tone of his voice took on that of a master storyteller. "The tomb belonged to a young lady called Aloma who lived approximately five thousand years ago. Now, Aloma came from a very notable family. In fact, her father-in-law is still spoken of today in certain circles." He paused for effect. "He went by the name of Noah —"

"You mean... No way. The guy with the ark?" Eden shook her head.

"Correct. Aloma kept a diary, a sort of journal, which detailed her life *before* the great flood." His voice lowered, as though he were about to reveal a great secret. Eden shuffled forward on her chair. "To summarize, this diary is proof that the history of the world is nothing like we believe it to be. Imagine a world where people lived for up to a thousand years, where angels and demons walked side-by-side, where human memory was so great that they could remember everything they were told. A world in which they could construct great wonders without the benefits of modern technology and machinery —"

"Like the pyramids," Eden interrupted, wide-eyed.

"Oh, there are more, so many more." Godspeed had warmed up now and spoke with confidence. "In the modern world we seem to think that we are so successful, but we are really just a shadow of what came before. What's in that diary is a living witness's testimony of our true past." Godspeed became more animated, his voice increasing in pitch. "It completely turns on its head the ideas peddled by modern-day scientists, religious leaders, even governments. This is the sort of thing scientific outcasts like von Daniken have been writing about for decades, now suddenly they'll be proved right. Forget Ancient Aliens on TV, the contents of this journal make Darwin seem like the class clown."

Eden scowled, watching the man explain. "Right, let's say for a second that I believe you, and that you haven't just made this up for your own delusional entertainment."

Godspeed drew a sharp breath, as though he were about to argue with Eden. Eden suspected he lived in a world where people did what he demanded of them at every turn. She held up a finger to silence the older man.

"Why would the rest of the world believe this? What you're talking about here is getting billions of people to change their belief structures. It's not just letting the air out of a balloon. This is complicated. You'll need real proof."

"If the diary is found in its original form, written on stone tablets in cuneiform, it could be dated. We would know, without doubt, when it was written." Godspeed sat back and steepled his fingers. "If this comes out, many people will have to face some pretty embarrassing facts. The whole world dynamic would change."

"But in 1998 they didn't find the diary?"

"That's what your father said. He wrote that it was clear the diary had already been taken. In fact, he also knew when it had been taken, and by whom."

Eden raised a disbelieving eyebrow. She tried to think logically and impartially about what Godspeed was saying, but it was becoming increasingly difficult. "How would he have figured that out?"

"Some clues left in the tomb, apparently."

"Who did he think took the tablets?"

Godspeed took a long sip of his drink and let the question hang. Then he grinned. "Your father believed that the tablets were taken in 1876, by two men." Godspeed puffed out his chest a little. "George Godspeed and Horsam Rassam."

Eden pointed at Godspeed. "Your great-grandfather?"

A smile spread across Godspeed's face.

"Then you know where these tablets are —"

"I'm afraid it's not that simple," Godspeed said, his eyes focusing on the fire. "Shortly after discovering the tomb, George Godspeed died in Baalbek. However, I suspect that's not true... I'll explain why shortly. Rassam, the man who, alongside George, had discovered the tablets, would have been able to facilitate his fake death. Rassam's father was high up in the Lebanese government at the time. Same as today, these men knew that the content of these tablets was life-threatening. Coincidently, Rassam is actually buried in the same cemetery as your father." Godspeed paused, lost in his thoughts.

"Right, and?"

Godspeed snapped out of his reverie and shot to his feet. "It's better if I show you. For this part of the story, we need to go for a walk."

Eden finished her drink in one large gulp and climbed to her aching feet.

Godspeed pulled open the door at the back of the kitchen and set off at a sprightly pace down a long corridor. Their footsteps clacked over the uneven stone floor tiles.

The stuffed heads of a dozen furry creatures nailed to the walls looked down on Eden and Godspeed as they moved along the corridor. Eden recoiled at the sparkling glass eyes.

"Shot these myself," Godspeed said, chin up, pointing up at the dead animal heads. "I'm something of an enthusiast. I haven't got anything more than a deer in recent years, though."

Eden thought about the beautiful, peaceful animals that flourished in her patch of woodland, their eyes so alive. She tried and failed to suppress a wave of revulsion that someone should be entertained by shooting them.

At the end of the corridor, Godspeed pulled open a door to reveal a narrow staircase. He snapped on a light. The staircase curved out of sight twenty feet beneath them.

"Watch your step," Godspeed said over his shoulder, as though he weren't at least thirty years Eden's senior.

Eden gripped the handrail and took the stairs slowly. At least two stories below, the staircase opened into a space roughly hewn out of the rock. To the right, another passage led into the gloom.

"Feel that?" Godspeed said, turning to face Eden and holding a finger in the air. He took an extra breath. "It's exactly twelve degrees centigrade down here, year-round. Over the years it's been used as cold storage, for brewing beer, even as an air raid shelter during the Second World War. Now I use it for a very different purpose."

Godspeed turned toward a steel door set into the far wall of the space. "I had this installed about thirty years ago."

Godspeed punched a number into a small digital keypad.

Eden instinctively counted the digits. Ten.

"Over ten billion combinations of the access code," he said, as though reading Eden's thoughts. "Get it wrong three times and the vault locks for twenty-four hours and my off-site security team are here in ten minutes."

"You must have a lot of very valuable stuff," Eden said.

Godspeed pushed open the door. A waft of dry air streamed out.

Eden followed the man inside and looked around. Her eyes bulged as she took in the immense collection.

Although not large, the room was filled — wall to wall and floor to ceiling — with all sorts of antiquities. In one corner, the dead eyes of a figure carved into a sarcophagus stared malevolently across the room. Ancient books lined the shelves. Chunks of stone, carved into all manner of hieroglyphs and symbols, lined the walls.

"Quite a collection, yes?" Godspeed said, turning to Eden.

Eden nodded slowly. "Where, how, did you get all of this?" she said.

"This is just part of it, really. I have several pieces which I loan to museums and galleries across the globe. It would be a shame to hide these items from the public. Every so often, I let another of these beauties go out for a while, as long as they come back. But this," — Godspeed stepped toward a stainless-steel chest on the far side of the room — "I'd never let this go."

Flicking his hand in the way a magician would reveal a trick, Godspeed pointed at a stack of yellowed papers behind a protective pane of glass.

Eden read the text on the front page. Her eyes grew wide.

The Diary of Aloma.

21

ALEXANDER WINSLOW HAD BEEN unable to answer when first asked by his daughter why he had dedicated his life to archaeology and antiquities. Was it merely the unconscious obsession of a passion that had led him there, along with dogged persistence, study, and the ability to do whatever it took and suffer any hardships in pursuit of the dream?

Years later, though, he realized the explanation was actually something quite different.

"It's very hard to explain, but there's a feeling I get when I'm with something of importance."

Eden looked up at him.

"I know what you're thinking. That sounds like mumbo-jumbo. I'm not saying I have any special powers or anything like that. Although, maybe it is like that. I don't know. I don't think I really understand it myself. But what I mean is, when I touch an object that has some historical significance, it's as though I can feel it. I can smell and taste and touch those bygone times. In my imagination, at least. It's as if that object had some umbilical connection with my past, with our past as inhabitants of this planet. I feel that through me — as though I'm some kind of medium, or conduit — the past gets to live again."

EDEN SHOOK HER HEAD. In the chilly cave beneath the manor house in rural England, for the first time, Eden understood the words her father had spoken all those years ago. It was, quite literally, as though she could feel the importance of this document.

She shook her head slowly, her brow knitted. "I don't understand. I thought you said it was never recovered?"

Godspeed extended a long index finger. "You're right. My great-grandfather supposedly died, and the tablets were never recovered. Then two years later, his widow received this anonymous document telling the story of Aloma and her diary."

Godspeed flipped to the first page of the document. "He's even included an account of them finding the tablets." He read from the text: "The white blossom of the trees was thick and the sun strong as we sat for a rest on our long journey."

Eden listened for a couple of minutes. The account told of two men riding on horseback through the hills of a mountainous country. One of the men grabbed hold of a tree bough to save himself from falling. He inadvertently pulled the tree away from a cliff face, revealing the entrance to a tomb, and inside they found the tablets.

"Why can't you just share this, and then the world will know?"

"Because this is not proof." He tapped the glass cabinet. "It's written anonymously, two hundred years ago. There is no reason for anyone to believe it. If — no, when — we find the tablets, they'll be certified as from that period. They are proof that the incredible story of this document is true."

Ideas swirled in Eden's mind as she searched for understanding. She stepped back from the document and turned to face the man. "Okay, okay, back up. Let me get this straight. How do we know this was even from your great-grandfather? Maybe he did actually die in Baalbek. Maybe this was sent by a colleague, or someone else."

"Good question. The tablets were written in cuneiform. In 1876 there were only two people in the world that could have translated them. One was my great-grandfather. The other was on a dig in the deserts of northern Africa for the entire year, totally cut off from the outside world."

"Okay. So, you think that your great-grandfather faked his death and ran off to America with the tablets."

"Not exactly, no. The tablets would each have been about five inches by three inches, made from stone, and there would have been over one-hundred thousand of them. They would have been heavy, and cumbersome. Impossible to move without a team and transport arranged."

"Then how did he do this?" Eden pointed at the diary.

"The tablets are essentially letters scratched into stone." Godspeed snatched a piece of stone from the shelf. Eden winced with the carelessness with which he handled the object. "I suspect George had a team of people place a piece of paper over the writing and —"

"Brass rubbings, like we did at school," Eden interrupted.

"Exactly! Just like that, and that would mean that the —"

"Tablets never left the tomb to begin with," Eden interjected again.

"That's what I believe. And further to that, I believe your father did find the tablets in 1998. But, knowing how important they are, I believe he left them in position, hiding in plain sight, waiting for the right time to share them with the world. And now, eventually, that time was approaching."

"The Pushing Boundaries Summit at Cambridge," Eden stated, a realization forming. "He told me it was the most important presentation of his life. But why wait all this time?"

"To move them back in 1998 would have been such a massive undertaking. You couldn't keep that secret. It's my belief that your father took one or two tablets from the tomb, for research and carbon dating, and left the others. He may even have gone back to Lebanon several times to collect more samples." Godspeed beckoned Eden over to a table in the center of the room. He pulled out and unfurled a map, clipping the ends down flat.

"That means that the tablets are somewhere in this area," Godspeed said, drawing a circle on the map with his finger. "It's taken me years to even get that close. All the research your father did on this was off the books, you see. The problem is, everyone who's ever seen the tomb is now dead, so there's no way to know exactly."

"Not quite." It was Eden's turn to act smug. She pulled off her backpack and slid out the photograph of herself and her father. "There's one person alive who may be able to help you."

Godspeed's eyes bulged and his expression melted into one of amazement.

A high-pitched alarm sounded through the vault.

22

Archibald Godspeed stared toward the sound of the alarm and then back at Eden.

"Blast," he shouted, his fist crashing onto the table. He slid out his phone, tapped a few buttons, and then held it to his ear. "Baxter, what's going on?"

Eden listened closely but couldn't hear the response.

"Intruders," Godspeed said, hanging up the phone and sliding it back into his pocket. "Somehow they've found their way here. They must have tracked us from the hospital. I don't know how." He turned and stared at Eden. "That makes sense now. It's you they want. You're the last living person who knows where the tomb is. You are the key to this."

Godspeed grasped Eden by both shoulders. His forceful grip caused Eden to step back. Her hands suddenly felt clammy.

"You are in great danger, Eden. These people will not stop until you are dead, or until they have the tablets. And if they get the tablets, they will never be shared with the world. Their employers are heavily invested in keeping things as they are. They fear change and losing control."

A bolt of fear shuddered through Eden's body. "To find the tablets, we need to get out of here. How?"

"Luckily my ancestors thought of that too. Follow me." Godspeed turned and hustled out of the vault. He pushed the door shut with a resounding clunk. The locking mechanism buzzed as it re-engaged.

"This way," he said, beckoning Eden to follow him down a different passage, away from the stairs. "Baxter says there are three tactical units are approaching the house now. Four men in each. They look like a professional lot too. Night vision, all the gear."

The passage was thinner here. Eden fell in behind Godspeed. Bare bulbs hung from the ceiling at twenty-foot intervals. After two minutes, the passage curved to the right and rose upward. Eden glanced at the thick walls, constructed in slabs of discolored stone.

They climbed in silence for another minute. A set of stone stairs materialized at the end of the passage. Godspeed climbed the stairs at speed until they reached a hatch blocking their progress.

Godspeed pulled out his phone again. "Baxter, we're in position. Okay. Yes." He turned and beckoned to Eden. "Come here. I need your help. We need to shift this hatch to the side and then run to the car, on my count. Got it?"

Eden shuffled up the stairs beside Godspeed and wedged her shoulder against the hatch. Moisture seeped into her clothes.

"He's coming now," Godspeed said, the phone still clamped to his ear.

Eden felt the ground around them vibrate. At first it was just a gentle rumble, growing in ferocity and volume until the hatch thumped hard against her shoulder. Eden gritted her teeth and prepared to push.

"Ready. On my count!" Godspeed shouted from behind her. "Three."

Eden tensed her muscles. Her toes curled, pushing into the stone steps.

"Two," Godspeed shouted.

The rumbling sounded as though it were coming from right above them now. It coursed through the ground, shaking dust from the tunnel's walls and roof.

"Push now,"

The noise moved above their heads, just inches beyond the flimsy hatchway.

Eden heaved upward. Pain shot through her shoulder. Her muscles strained with the pressure. One of her feet slipped, sending her crashing against the wall. She got up and pushed on.

The hatch moved. First an inch. Then two. Then it was wide open, the damp night air flooding in. They heaved the hatch up vertically and shoved it down against the ground beside the opening.

Eden peered out. As her eyes adjusted, she saw that they were in a wooded area. Ten feet away, a Land Rover Defender idled. With its lights off, it was barely distinguishable against the night.

"Go now," he hissed.

Eden leapt out of the tunnel and charged for the Land Rover. Wet earth slipped beneath her feet.

Baxter sat poised and ready in the driver's seat. He leaned behind him and shoved open the rear door.

Eden leapt in, scrambling across the seat. She straightened up, panting, her heart thumping against her ribs. Then she heard the first howl of automatic gunfire. Bullets zipped through the trees. Hot metal thumped into the door through which Eden had just passed, shattering glass, and tearing the vehicle's interior to shreds. Another strafe of bullets thudded into a nearby tree, showering them in bark and leaves.

A grunt of pain filled the woodland, followed by the deep thud of something hitting the earth. At first, Eden didn't know what it was. She turned and peered back toward the tunnel's opening. The hole, twenty feet away across the woodland floor, lay empty. Godspeed wasn't there.

Eden shimmed back along the rear seat of the Land Rover and peered out into the woodland.

Godspeed lay amid shards of glass and chunks of wood, splayed out on the ground.

"Godspeed," Eden shouted, scrambling out of the Land Rover. Another volley of gunfire whizzed past, barely missing her. She leapt back up into the safety of the vehicle. Two more bullets thwacked into the earth, just inches from his prone figure.

Eden gazed into the darkness. Godspeed rolled slightly, his body moving toward the vehicle in tiny increments. He wiggled around, clutching a hand to his stomach. Blood covered his pale skin. Archibald Godspeed looked up at Eden, his eyes wild and pained.

"You must go," he said, straining. He peered off into the woodland behind them. Somewhere out of sight, footsteps pounded the wet earth. The men were approaching. "It's you they want. They've got no business with me. You are the only person alive who knows where this tomb is." He gasped for air. "You can blow this thing wide open."

Eden nodded, her eyes wide, her heart beating heavily.

Godspeed turned with some effort to face Baxter. "Your work is now with Eden. You must go with her. Go to the airfield and take the jet. You will provide everything Eden needs to find the tablets. Do you understand?"

Baxter nodded and revved the engine.

Anther volley of gunfire hammered through the air. Two bullets thrashed into the open door. Boots pounded through dry leaves.

"Go now. You must go now!" He strained against the pain and rolled over once more.

Baxter obeyed without a second thought. The Land Rover's engine growled and the tires tore into the earth. Eden sunk back into the seat as they accelerated away. Baxter snapped on the headlights as they smashed through a wooden gate. Chunks of wood flew in all directions. Tires screeched as they hit the tarmac of a tiny lane. Baxter swung the wheel and accelerated hard.

Eden peered over the broken glass, listening to the woodland behind them. Somewhere, carrying on the wind, she heard another bout of gunfire.

23

EDEN, finally coming to her senses, slipped off the rucksack and pulled the door closed. The noise of the engine muted, although wind still howled through the shattered window.

Eden glanced at Baxter, his face glowing eerily in the light from the dials. She had yet to exchange a single word with the man, but right now she had nothing to say. The image of Godspeed, lying there bleeding on the forest floor, spooled again through her mind. Whatever this was she was involved in here, it had already claimed too many lives.

Baxter accelerated into a corner, and the Land Rover skidded sideways for a few seconds before the tires gripped the wet earth. An old wooden gate came into view between two hedgerows.

"Hold on," Baxter barked, gripping the wheel with both hands.

Acceleration pushed Eden back into the seat. She gripped hold of the door handle.

The Land Rover barreled toward the gate, branches whipping the windows. The old gate shattered across the grill. Chunks of rotten wood smashed up across the windscreen.

Baxter swung the wheel to the left as they flew out onto a narrow country lane. The vehicle bounced several times before picking up speed again. Baxter drove more smoothly now. He obviously knew the corners and undulations of this road by heart. The Land Rover's strong lights swept through the night, warning anyone nearby of their approach.

"Where exactly are we going?" Eden asked, raising her voice above the growling engine and the wind hammering through the window. She scrambled through to the front and strapped herself into the passenger seat.

"Godspeed keeps a plane, several planes actually, at the airport at Shoreham. We'll be there in just under an hour."

"Then what, we just fly to Lebanon and stumble across these ancient relics?"

"That's as much of a plan as we've got so far." Baxter glanced at Eden, a glimmer in his eye.

"I'm more of a plan-it-all-out-before sort of person," Eden said. "Flying by the seat of my pants makes me nervous."

"You mean you planned to drive through Gatwick's South Terminal on a motorbike?" Baxter quipped, glancing at Eden again.

"How do you know about that?" Eden glowered.

Baxter shrugged and almost smiled, although not quite. He didn't reply.

"I didn't exactly plan that, no," Eden conceded. "Let's just call it a stroke of lucky genius."

"I hope you've got some more lucky genius ready to go now," Baxter said, eyes fixed on the rearview mirror. "Because it looks as if we've got company."

Eden swung around in the seat. Two headlights pierced

the night behind them. She glanced at their dashboard — Baxter was currently doing fifty, and the lights behind were gaining fast.

Baxter shifted gears and pushed the Land Rover harder. The engine increased from a compliant purr to an all-out bellow. The lights behind them continued to gain.

Then the rat-tat-tat of gunfire resounded through the night. Eden ducked down just in time. Several bullets whizzed through the vehicle, shattering the windscreen and one of the mirrors.

Baxter slipped down as low as he could in the seat, his expression paling.

"I don't suppose you've got anything useful in here?" Eden said, cracking open the glove box. "You know, like a gun?"

"One of Mr. Godspeed's shotguns is in the back, I think," Baxter said. He feathered the brakes and swung the Land Rover around a tight corner. Branches and leaves whipped at the sides. The tires screeched across loose gravel. "How's your shooting?"

"Better than your driving," Eden quipped. She scrambled into the back of the vehicle and pulled down the rear seats. She unzipped the bag and examined the shotgun.

"Nice piece of kit, this," Eden said. She snagged a box of cartridges too and pushed the rear seats back into position.

For several seconds, their pursuers were hidden around a corner. As the road straightened out, the lights appeared behind them again. The two pursuing vehicles accelerated hard.

"They're on quad bikes," Eden said. "It looks like there're two men on each. One driving and one —"

Another volley of hot metal thudded into the back of the Land Rover, cutting Eden off in mid-sentence. Eden stayed well out of range beneath the rear seats. Another barrage of bullets further obliterated the rear windscreen, showering shattered glass across Eden and the vehicle's interior.

Baxter accelerated again, pulling away from the quads. On the open road, the Land Rover would have the advantage, but quads handled the corners of these twisting lanes with ease.

Still ducked below the rear seat, Eden slid two cartridges into the shot gun. The pellets from this gun were unlikely to kill someone wearing protective gear and a helmet, but a good shot could force them off the road.

"On my signal, hit the brakes," Eden commanded, swinging the shotgun across the rear shelf and through the shattered windscreen. She flattened herself as another barrage of bullets flew their way, hitting nothing but the hedgerow to their right. She took aim at the front of the leading quad.

"Now!" Eden shouted.

Baxter hit the brakes hard.

Eden fired both shots into the front of the lead quad, one after the other. The headlight went out, plunging the scene into darkness.

Eden flung herself back around behind the seat. With a growl, and a thunderous crack, the leading quad bike collided with the back of the Land Rover. She looked up to see the driver had been flung from the bike and through the Land Rover's rear window. He lay across the rear shelf, his legs dangling out the back of the vehicle.

"Go!" Eden shouted. Baxter didn't have to be told twice. He accelerated hard. Eden grabbed the quad driver beneath the shoulders, ensuring he stayed inside the Land Rover as they pulled away. The stricken quad remained in the middle of the road, it's front-end smashed in.

The quad rider came to a few seconds later. He turned and looked up at Eden. His legs continued to dangle out the back of the Land Rover. Eden grinned at the man, then forced her elbow into his spine to stop him from struggling.

The second quad picked its way around the wreckage and accelerated after them. As Eden had suspected, no bullets came their way. They didn't want to risk hitting one of their own, hanging from the back of the vehicle.

Watching their pursuers, an idea occurred to Eden. She explained it to Baxter.

"Is this a stoke of lucky genius?" he asked.

"It is if it works," Eden replied.

24

THE RIDER of the second quad bike watched as the Land Rover accelerated hard on a straight section of road. His colleague's legs hung limp from the rear of the vehicle.

They hadn't seen the attack coming. One moment they were chasing the Land Rover down, peppering it with gun fire, and then next the lead quad lay on its side, the rider incapacitated.

The second rider accelerated cautiously. He was afraid to let the Land Rover get too far ahead, but they weren't going to fall for the same trick a second time.

The Land Rover disappeared around a bend two hundred feet up ahead. That was fine, he thought, he knew this road. A stretch of country lane between farms and villages, there wasn't a crossroads for the next two miles. Fields flashed past on either side of the road. To the right, the hillside rose steeply, and to the left it fell away toward a river at the bottom of the valley.

"It's alright, we've got them," yelled the man on the back of the quad, holding his gun ready. "It's all bends from here. We'll catch them up easily."

The driver nodded and accelerated smoothly toward the corner up ahead. The powerful quad bike thronged beneath them, begging for speed. Reaching the corner, the rider cut their speed. He wasn't getting tricked like last time.

Another stretch of road came into view, winding for a mile or so upward toward the summit of the hill. Hedges lined both sides. No sign of the Land Rover.

Both riders looked ahead, searching for a flash of tail-lights, or any other indication that the Land Rover was nearby. Nothing. The scene lay in darkness.

"Wait, slow down. What's that?" The passenger pointed at something on the road a few hundred feet ahead. The driver squeezed the brakes, bringing the quad to a crawl. They pulled to a stop just before the body of the lead quad driver. He lay across the asphalt, almost blocking the entire lane. The two men examined their colleague for a moment. His chest rose and fell gently, indicating that he wasn't dead.

"We can't get past, you're going to have to move him," the driver said.

"Why me? You move him. I'll cover you in case —"

At that moment, bright lights flooded the scene and the Land Rover roared out from the entrance to a field on the right-hand side of the lane. The driver and passenger scrambled in panic away from the quad. The passenger stumbled, dropping his gun.

The Land Rover collided with the quad and pushed it with ease across the narrow lane. The quad screeched across the asphalt, leaving thick rubber marks beneath the tires.

Baxter hit the gas harder, pushing the quad up the verge on the other side of the lane and then through a gate. With one final stamp on the gas, he nudged the quad towards the slope. The quad teetered on two wheels and then rolled, shedding parts as it tumbled toward the river some two-hundred feet below.

Baxter threw the Land Rover into reverse and pulled back out into the lane.

"Get him out of the way," Eden said, appearing at the window of the Land Rover with the shotgun.

The two riders, now unarmed and without their vehicle, held up their hands in surrender. They hurried across to their fallen colleague and pulled him out of the lane.

Baxter gunned the engine, and the Land Rover tore off up the lane in a cloud of dust.

Half an hour later, Eden peered through the cracked windows of the Land Rover as they approached Brighton City Airport. The sky was beginning to lighten with the purples, pinks, and blues that Eden knew so well. She glanced in the direction of Brighton, lurking unseen across the horizon. Although it was only yesterday that Eden had been in Brighton to bury her father, it seemed like an age ago. It was a day, she knew, that she wouldn't forget in a long time. Deep in her stomach, Eden feared that things were a long way from getting better.

Fortunately, traffic around the airport was light. Their now battered-up Land Rover would certainly turn heads in the daylight.

Baxter slowed the vehicle to a crawl as they passed the airport's tiny terminal building. The place looked as though it was built in the era when air travel was a thing of intrigue and glamor.

Baxter slowed behind one of the private hangars. He climbed out and tapped a code into a keypad on the wall. A rusting metal shutter creaked upward. He climbed back into the Land Rover and pulled them inside the hangar, parking in close to the rear wall of the building and then killing the engine.

Eden shuffled across the backseat and climbed out, hanging her bag over one shoulder. She left the shotgun in the rear footwell.

The aircraft hangar was unlike those Eden had seen before. A discolored steel roof arched overhead. Birds clattered about between the structure's broken metal ribs. Dawn light seeped in through the cracked windows and crumbling holes, coloring the entire space in an ethereal glow. In the middle of the hangar, in contrast to the building itself, sat three glinting aircraft.

"Mr. Godspeed was something of a plane enthusiast," Baxter said, moving toward the aircraft. "He came here frequently. He loved the Tiger Moth the best." Baxter pointed at an aircraft with double wings. "He took the Piper Warrior up sometimes, too." Baxter touched the wingtip of another propeller-driven aircraft.

"What's that one?" Eden pointed at the aircraft on the far side of the hangar. It was the smallest jet powered machine she'd ever seen.

"That's what we're using today," Baxter said. "A Cirrus SF50. It's the smallest jet on the market, and with a range of two thousand miles and a speed of nearly six hundred per hour, it should get us to Lebanon well before lunchtime." Baxter removed a small remote control from his pocket and unlocked the aircraft. The door opened outward, lowering a ladder down to the concrete.

"Climb inside and make yourself comfortable. We'll be airborne in twenty minutes."

"Are we waiting for the pilot?" Eden asked, stepping toward the plane.

"You're looking at him," Baxter said, the hint of a smile curving his lips.

Eden scaled the ladder and into the plane. The inside was no larger than a car, with two seats in the front and three in the back. Eden took one of the back seats and placed her bag down beside her.

Sure enough, twenty minutes later, they powered down the runway and up into the clear morning sky.

25
_____

ARCHIBALD GODSPEED LAY in the mud, clutching his stomach and listening to the sound of heavy boots pounding toward him. The growl of the Land Rover's engine faded into the night.

There was a strange taste in his mouth — something chemical or metallic. The smell of the forest floor tickled his nose.

He shook as the sound of several more gunshots rang through the forest, but he didn't feel a thing. He continued to lie unmoving on the ground. The footsteps thundered in from all directions. It sounded as if the men now surrounded him on all sides. He didn't dare speak. Not yet. He didn't even say a word as a last pair of boots walked slowly up to his side.

He lay silent and still, waiting, just in case. No one spoke for several seconds. Godspeed listened to his breathing.

When the voice came, it meant business.

"We're clear, sir, they've gone."

Godspeed removed the hand from his stomach and sat up. He looked up at the men surrounding him. Helios's men,

Croft and Stone, stood at the front, surrounded by the additional hired support. "And?" he barked.

"Everything went just as you said it would, sir. Baxter is with her now, and they are on their way to the airport. Our men have set off in pursuit. They'll keep them running for a while, but won't get in the way."

"It looked very convincing," another man said.

"Excellent." Godspeed looked down at the mess of fake blood and dirt on his hands and clothes. He spat the blood pellet out onto the ground and wiped the red smear from the corner of his mouth.

"Somebody, help me up." He reached out his hand. Stone hoisted him back to his feet. Godspeed peered into the woodland. Two thick tire tracks ran off toward the road.

"Good work," he said, looking around the group of men. They stood upright, submachine guns pointed down at the ground.

"She's got some fight," Croft said. "We didn't expect such a show at the hospital."

"We got the job done," Godspeed replied, brushing the mud from his clothes. He spat again. The strange taste of the blood pellet, which he had slipped between his teeth as they pushed the hatch open, lingered on his tongue. "But now we have to keep the pressure on. She's already running scared. Let's keep it that way. She needs to be left no choice but to lead us to that tomb. Get me back to the house. I need to get this mess off me."

Stone barked into a radio, and the lights of an all-terrain quad bike cut through the forest. The vehicle pulled up beside the men, its engine now idling. Godspeed clambered on behind the driver.

"We don't let up the pressure until we have those tablets,

you hear me? We keep them running all way to the tomb. Roll out in twenty minutes."

EDEN WOKE up and gazed through the windows of the Cirrus. Several thousand feet beneath the tiny plane, the Mediterranean shimmered like a bed of diamonds.

She rubbed her eyes, yawned, and stretched. She unclipped her seatbelt and scrambled into the front seat beside Baxter.

"Where are we?" she asked, looking out through the windscreen.

"We've just passed Cyprus," Baxter said, glancing down at the controls. "If you look out of the left window, you'll see it."

Eden saw the island spread hazily beneath them. She lay back into the seat and watched Baxter adjust one of the controls.

"You're a pretty clever guy, aren't you?" she said, observing the confidence with which he handled the plane.

Baxter grunted in reply.

"Not much of a talker, though," Eden said, turning back to the window.

"We have a job to do. We'll be landing in forty minutes. Get some rest."

A few minutes later, land crept into view over the horizon. Eden peered down as rows of concrete buildings, clinging to the coast like the dirty teeth of a shark, came into view. The Cirrus slid across the land, and the buildings dissolved into desert. Baxter pushed forward on the controls and the aircraft drifted groundward. Eden looked out as a country of deserts, mountains, and mysteries scrolled beneath them.

"Put your seatbelt on," Baxter barked, as a dusty runway came into view.

"Yes, captain." Eden smiled, buckling herself in.

As they circled the airport, Eden thought about the last time she was here, over twenty years ago. In 1998, she had been barely more than a child. A cloud of doubts passed through her mind. Was she foolish even attempting to remember the location of somewhere she'd visited so long ago?

Baxter brought the plane down gently and taxied to the end of the runway. They cruised past a hulking cargo jet waiting for take-off.

Eden looked out at the discolored airport building as they slid past. This place really was in the middle of nowhere.

"Where are we?" Eden asked.

"Just outside Baalbek," Baxter mumbled.

They finally rolled to a stop outside a sand-colored hangar at the far end of the airport building. Baxter tapped at the controls and the engine noise dropped to a whisper, and then ceased completely.

A dirty Jeep Wrangler charged across the tarmac toward them.

Baxter climbed to his feet and moved across to the door. He turned to Eden. "Stay here and don't say anything." He disappeared down the stairs.

The noise of whining jet engines and the tang of fuel filled the air. Heat streamed into the cabin. Eden's skin prickled.

Baxter paced across to the Jeep, dug a wad of notes from his pocket, and passed them through the driver's window. The driver slipped the notes out of sight and the two men exchanged some words.

"Let's go!" Baxter shouted up into the Cirrus.

Eden's muscles tensed. She huffed out a deep breath and slung her bag over her shoulder.

Eden stepped out of the Cirrus and paced across to the Jeep. The air felt like a wall of heat as sweat instantly dabbled her skin. Eden clambered into the back of the Jeep and Baxter got into the passenger seat. The driver, wearing a soiled khaki shirt and shorts, leered at her in the rearview mirror. Eden scowled in return.

The Jeep's engine growled, and they set off, bumping across the airstrip at high speed. They reached a security checkpoint. The driver raised his hand and the guards, dressed in military fatigues, waved them straight through.

A wad of notes has that effect, Eden thought.

For half an hour they climbed through the rugged landscape. Eden examined everything, searching for something that looked familiar. Farms spread out on the hills below, crops shimmering in uniform lines. Here on the higher land, less grew. They passed the occasional flock of sheep, bells clanging around their necks. A sign welcoming them to Baalbek, in both Arabic and English, flew past. Nothing looked familiar to Eden yet.

The Jeep slowed as they neared the center of the town. Buildings constructed in ancient stone jostled for space next to modern concrete monoliths. People, bikes, and animals filled the roads. They slowed behind a lumbering truck, coughing great clouds of blue smoke from its engine. The air was different here — hot, thin, and riddled with the fumes of cars so old that they should have been condemned years ago.

Eden noticed several ancient structures looming over the city on a nearby hillside. They looked Roman, she thought, suddenly missing her father. He would know what they were, who built them, and why. Eden steeled her expression and looked even harder for something she recognized.

The Jeep crunched to a stop outside a large stone building. Built in the Arabic style, it had several lattice-fronted balconies, arched windows, and an ornate domed roof. Eden gazed up at the intricate architecture. Stylized lettering high above their heads claimed that this was the 'Saint George Hotel.'

Eden turned and examined a market on the opposite side of the street. With excitement and nostalgia, she noticed the rows of vegetables, fruits, spices, and fabrics which stretched out in colorful layers as far as she could see. She had spent many afternoons with her father roaming around such markets. They may have even visited this particular one.

The smell of sweet spices drifted into the Jeep. After dropping her bag in the hotel, she would look around. Maybe something there would jog her memory. At the very least she would get some more appropriate clothes for the trip.

Baxter climbed out of the Jeep, motioning for Eden to follow.

The pair pushed through a brass revolving door and into the hotel lobby. In contrast to the bright afternoon sunlight, the inside was gloomy. A vast domed ceiling loomed above them. Lights in crystal shades hung on long chains, swaying gently in the breeze. A vast curving staircase swept up one side of the lobby.

A man wearing a red waistcoat swept the floor. Another stood behind the reception desk. Other than the distant murmur of the traffic and the creaking of the revolving door, the building was deathly silent.

Baxter strode across to the reception desk and spoke to the concierge in hushed whispers. He swapped another few notes for a pair of keys. Then, beckoning Eden to follow, he trotted up the stairs to the third floor.

Baxter unlocked a door, revealing a large room leading out to a balcony. Long white curtains, framing a view of the market, swept in on the breeze. He beckoned Eden inside.

"This is your room," he said. "You want anything, call reception and they will bring it to you. Get some rest. We head out first thing tomorrow."

Baxter swept past Eden and shut the door behind him. Eden was about to follow when she heard the key crunching in the lock.

26

ARCHIBALD GODSPEED SAT BACK in the wide leather seat as the Gulfstream G650 thumped to the tarmac of Baalbek airport and began its taxi toward the private hangar. Godspeed suppressed a small flash of frustration that he'd let Baxter take the Cirrus, and as such had been forced to hire the more cumbersome Gulfstream.

Godspeed glanced at his Rolex. They were already running several hours behind schedule. They should have been here just a few minutes after Baxter and Eden had landed and been able to follow them from the airport. But the fact that Godspeed had been forced to travel to Heathrow to board the Gulfstream had taken almost two hours longer than planned.

It didn't matter, ultimately, Godspeed thought, glancing out of the window.

The Gulfstream crawled to the far side of the airport. Several large jets waited on the tarmac a few hundred feet away.

It wouldn't matter, because although Eden Black's record might look good on paper — she knew a thing or two about stolen relics — she wasn't used to being alone and this far from home. She wasn't a soldier. She wasn't an espionage operative. She was a spoilt brat with an authority complex.

Godspeed slid his phone from his jacket pocket. It was time to add a little more pressure, he thought. He dialed the number of a sergeant in the Baalbek police force. A man that, he'd been informed through a contact, could deal with all manner of nefarious tasks. The phone rang several times and then clicked. Finally, a whispered voice strained through the speaker.

"I need you to kill a man," Godspeed said, getting straight to the point. "He's staying at the Saint George Hotel, in Baalbek. Checked in today. Make it look like a robbery gone wrong."

"Of course, sir," replied the sergeant, as though the request was commonplace. "What's the gentleman's name."

"Baxter."

It was a shame Baxter had to die. He was a good soldier. He could run, fight, and fly planes with the best of them — but the cause was always bigger than a single soldier. Baxter would understand that, Godspeed thought.

The police sergeant asked a few questions about Baxter's appearance, and how Godspeed planned to pay for such a service, then ended the call.

It was all too easy, Godspeed thought as the Gulfstream finally juddered to a stop and the door dropped open. The balmy smell of dust and heat streamed into the cabin.

Within thirty minutes Eden would be alone in a strange land. Apply some pressure in the right place and she would be running scared. She would lead him right to where Helios wanted them to go.

No sooner had Godspeed slid his phone into the pocket of his jacket, it rang again. The unusual ringing tone sent a cold chill through his nervous system. It was a noise that, despite the settings on his phone, Godspeed couldn't turn off. Helios was calling.

Godspeed fumbled the phone from his pocket, his hands numb. He swiped to answer.

"Mr. Godspeed, Helios would like to speak with you." The sterile voice of the secretary streamed from the handset. Godspeed sat bolted to his seat, the mention of the man's name caused a sickening feeling to bubble in his stomach. He sat in silence, the phone pinned to his ear. After several seconds another voice boomed down the line. Godspeed knew it instantly: Helios.

"Godspeed, you better have a good reason as to why this is taking so long."

Godspeed tried to answer, but it felt as though his tongue had been tied in knots.

"Are you there?" Helios barked.

"Yes sir, absolutely. I can assure you I have full control of this. I know where they're going. I have a man on the ground, right now."

"Do you know, Godspeed, what has allowed this organization to retain its powerful position for the last five thousand years?" Helios said, his tone deep and malevolent. He continued before Godspeed could speak. "We are always ahead. We prepare for every eventually. We hold all the aces. As far as I can see it right now, you are blindly chasing one young woman in the hope that she might remember where these tablets are. It doesn't seem to me that you are holding all the aces. In fact, right now you're sitting in the Gulfstream while they are almost thirty miles away."

Godspeed looked around guiltily, as though expecting to see the man nearby. Helios knew everything.

"I have it all under —"

"It hardly seems that way," Helios interrupted. "I asked you to do this because I thought you were the right man for the job. Do not let me down. We need to recover those tablets, and then myself and The Council will decide their fate. It is not up to you, and it is certainly not up to Eden Black. I'll remind you this once, Godspeed, and once only." Helios spat the words. "If you fail to bring The Council the outcome we desire, we will have no choice but to dis-communicate you."

The line went dead. Godspeed removed the phone from his ear and stared down at it in his shaking hand. All the color had blanched from his face.

Godspeed had always known The Council demanded the best from their people, but the personal threat of dis-communication from Helios himself struck like a hammer to an anvil. Godspeed had heard many rumors about what being 'dis-communicated' actually meant. Some people thought they made you disappear, even erasing your existence from public records. Others suggested that The Council brought some public shame against you, enough to discredit you for life. Godspeed had read enough accounts of the rich and famous falling from grace to see the effect of such claims. Whatever it was Helios had in mind, Godspeed didn't intend to find out.

JUST FIFTY MILES AWAY, the man known as Helios crossed the deck of the Balonia, the two-hundred-foot yacht from where his operations were run and controlled. He gazed due east, toward the distant shores of Lebanon. He leaned on the railing, narrowed his eyes against the bright afternoon sun, and tried to make out the shadowy smudge of land several miles from their current anchorage.

He thought about the call he'd just shared with Archibald Godspeed.

The man was a fool, that Helios knew for sure. But a fool had a certain amount of reliability to him. You could trust a fool to do what came naturally to him, and behave in a foolish way. Helios had no doubt that Godspeed would behave now with the same nonchalant persistence in which he'd been acting for the whole of his life.

It would serve The Council to have a backup though, just in case.

Helios tapped his phone and then held it to his ear. After a moment the voice of his secretary came cut through the speaker.

"Get me Athena,"

Although the secretary was trained not to show any emotion on the events of The Council, her momentary silence spoke volumes. "Yes of course sir. I will send her up to you now."

"Good. Thank you." Helios hung up the phone. He gazed down at the device for a moment, tapping it against his hand. His desires to keep the situation discreet and draw it to a speedy conclusion conflicted in his mind. If he was going to send in just one more person, Athena was the woman for the job.

Helios nodded, his decision made. This was the right thing to do.

He turned and looked up at the sleek architecture of the huge craft. Behind the tinted windows and beneath the wooden decks, a team of the world's most impressive technical minds worked tirelessly to make sure the aims of Helios's organization were met. During his stewardship, The Council of the Selene had seen much change. He had worked tirelessly during his ten year reign to streamline and modernize the organization. Of course, The Council of the Selene had always been the very pinnacle of modernity. In their various labs around the world, always cloaked under the names of multiple companies, scientists worked on the technology that may shape the future. Ultimately, the impact a certain technology had on the world would come down to Helios and his council. The seven members of The Council would assemble every ninety days to discuss new developments and decide the fate of new developments.

Helios thought again of that last frustrating meeting. He had always led with a progressive stance. He believed that where possible, the development of technology should be as transparent as possible. If the world's population could have a use for something, then it should be allowed through their system.

Certain members of The Council, however, were not as free willed. They believed in strict control and were rarely swayed to see the other side. This had been a thorn in Helios's side since he had been elected as The Council's chairman all those years ago. But, it was something he would have to work with, as all the holders of his position for the last several thousand years had done.

A set of doors slid open, and Athena walked out on to the deck. One of the council's most reliable fixers, Athena was a force to be reckoned with. Despite her young appearance, Helios had seen her infiltrate some of the most well protected organizations on the planet.

"You asked to see me sir," she said, leaning on the railing beside Helios. Her voice was soft, and her accent had a subtle Eastern European texture. Helios knew she could sound like almost anyone at a moment's notice. The setting sun sparkled in her large almond-colored eyes.

"Yes." Helios cleared his throat. "I have a job for you."

27

EDEN LOOKED AT THE DOOR, her mouth open in disbelief. She couldn't understand why Baxter would want to lock her in the room, as though she were some kind of criminal.

Snapping her mouth shut, Eden paced across the room and yanked the doorknob. Locked solid. She pulled at the handle again. Constructed in heavy wood, the door didn't even shudder.

Eden grunted and turned toward the bed. She dropped her bag and then stalked out onto the balcony. She was here of her own accord, helping to discover whatever was at the bottom of this mess, and now, like a petulant teenager, she'd been locked in her room. Eden scowled and forced one fist into the palm of her other hand. This is exactly why she didn't like working with other people — they were unpredictable. At least working alone, Eden knew whom she could rely on.

Eden tried to shake out the anger and leaned across the railing, looking at the market below. She should have told Godspeed to screw it and gone back to her truck in the woods. No one had treated her like this, not ever. She thought about the time her father had attempted to send her to a boarding school. That hadn't worked. On the first evening, they'd found her wandering around the nearest town. The headteacher had quickly suggested that, for the benefit of Eden and the other students, she should continue her education elsewhere. The memory brought a grin to Eden's face as she pictured her father trying to act cross with her. She knew he hated schools like that as much as she did, and would have done exactly the same thing.

A powerful gust of wind rushed up from the street, bringing with it the scents of the market below and dragging Eden from her memories. Eden inhaled slowly, trying to recognize the smell. There was something familiar about it. She thought about it for a while, trying to place the aroma, but couldn't. The breeze brought with it a snatch of conversation, too. Eden couldn't understand the words but looked around for the speakers. The nearest person she could see was at least sixty feet away, yet this voice sounded as though it were coming from just a few feet away.

Eden peered further over the balcony, looking for the voice owners. Two hotel workers, recognizable by their red waistcoats, smoked on the balcony below hers. Eden's face melted into a smile, as an idea took root.

She strode back into the room and seized one of the long, flowing curtains. She unhooked the curtain from the rail and tied it to the stone balustrade. Now, with a sense of excitement flowing through her, she pulled the curtain to test the strength of the knot. No one could keep Eden Black locked up, not for long anyway.

Eden shuffled her bag onto her back, and then tightened the straps. She looped the curtain around her wrist, swung her legs over the railing and shimmed down to the balcony below.

The men watched with open mouths, cigarettes burning away, as Eden slid down the makeshift rope and stepped onto the balcony.

"Sorry," Eden said, smiling. "Forgot my keys." She shrugged and walked from the room, down the stairs, and out into the muggy afternoon air.

Eden wandered through the markets, stalls, and shops, losing track of time. Only the sun dipping behind the surrounding buildings, combined with the rumbling of her stomach, reminded her that the day was drawing to a close. The noise of the market was muting now as traders packed away their wares.

Eden looked back in the vague direction of the hotel. She thought about Baxter returning to her room and finding her gone. Eden grinned. That would show him she couldn't be pushed around.

Eden selected several shawls from a fabric stall and handed them to the wizened merchant. The man folded them with a dexterity that belied his age. Without negotiation, Eden slid several notes into the man's palm. It was far more than the shawls were worth, but she didn't care. The man nodded in thanks as Eden stuffed the purchases in her bag.

Eden turned and, following her nose, she headed further into the warren of narrow streets in search of something to eat.

She stopped outside a small restaurant and sniffed the air. A fragrant scent of spices intertwined with meat cooking over charcoal. This was exactly the sort of place she loved visiting while she was traveling. The sort of place where you could get a good local meal without any fuss.

Eden peered into the restaurant. Smoke hung thick in the air. A group of men paused their conversation and turned to look at her. Having travelled across the world many times, Eden didn't mind. She had learned long ago that the attention she got was more out of curiosity than anything malevolent. Eden smiled at the men, generating a room full of smiles in return, then stepped inside. Eden took the table nearest the window and let her eyes lose focus. What she really needed now was some time to think. Everything in the last few weeks had seemed to happen so quickly, and now she was in a foreign land on a mission that she didn't really understand.

Eden gazed through the window out at the street. She questioned again whether it would be possible for her to remember a place which she'd visited all those years ago. She would have to try, she supposed. Otherwise, she may never understand the circumstances behind her father's death.

Suddenly Eden sat bolt upright in her seat. A figure crossed the street outside the restaurant. Eden recognized him instantly. Baxter.

Eden watched Baxter for several seconds as he paced down the street. Fortunately, his eyes remained forward, never straying her way.

Curiosity rose inside her. She wondered who Baxter really was, and why he had ended up working for someone like Archibald Godspeed. It seemed like a strange position for a young and seemingly very capable man like Baxter.

Then, two more figures moved down the street. It took Eden a few moments to work out what was happening in the dying daylight.

Two men picked their way down the street behind Baxter. From the speed of their steps, it looked as though they were in a hurry. From her position in the restaurant,

Eden saw no more than their broad backs. Both wore linen shirts, one white, one grey.

Eden looked from the men to Baxter, now several hundred feet ahead. Baxter turned left and disappeared down a side street. The men quickened their pace again. Eden leaned forwards in her seat, her rickety chair creaking. Unless she was seeing things, those men were following Baxter.

Thoughts of confusion swarmed her mind again. There were things going on here that she didn't understand. Dangerous things.

Without another thought, Eden rose from her seat, rummaged in her bag, and draped a shawl around her head and shoulders. She glanced at herself in the window's reflection. It wasn't exactly a disguise, but if Baxter or the men happened to look her way for just a moment, she wouldn't draw attention.

She paused at the door to give the men another few seconds to pull ahead and then exited the restaurant, much to the confusion of the smoking men huddled around their tables. Hunching over slightly, to give herself the posture of someone three-times her age, Eden hurried down the street.

The men reached the side street down which Baxter had disappeared. They looked around, suspicion filling in every movement.

Eden ducked in behind a slow-moving truck and quickened her pace. She closed the gap in time to see the men disappear down the side street. She sprinted up to the junction. The street was little more than a narrow alleyway. Eden stopped just short of the corner and peered into the passage, her senses on high alert.

Discolored cement walls rose high on both sides. Water

dripped from somewhere, thumping to the stained concrete floor with the regularity of a heartbeat.

Eden felt a sense of disquietude rise within her. There was something going on here, and Eden didn't like it.

She stepped into the passage and peered into the darkness. Twenty feet ahead, the men stalked forwards. Now in the shadows, they had a predatory swing to their gait.

Now fifty feet ahead, Baxter strolled on. He moved through a shadow, almost obscuring him from her sight.

The smell of rotten food drifted from several overflowing bins. Something squealed and scuttled beneath a pile of boxes.

Baxter slowed. His head moved from left to right as though he was looking for something.

Then, in unison, the men unsheathed knives, flashing menacingly in the gloom.

28

THE NEXT FEW moments passed as though time had slowed. The noise of the city shrunk to nothing more than a distant murmur. The thump of Eden's heartbeat rose in her ears.

Baxter turned to face the men. At first, his expression was one of confusion, before realization distorted it into fear. He backed away. His arms rose into a fighter's stance. His hands balled into fists.

The man in the white shirt struck first, swinging his knife in a wide, downward arc. Baxter avoided the knife easily and sent a right jab in to follow, striking the man in the neck. White Shirt took a step back, almost falling on the uneven stones.

Grey Shirt lunged forward, thrusting the knife outward in a stabbing motion. Baxter side-stepped and elbowed the man in the ribs. The knife wobbled in the would-be assassin's grip, but he kept hold. Grey Shirt stepped backward, clearing the way for White Shirt's next attack.

White Shirt lunged forward, swinging the knife toward Baxter's neck. Again, Baxter twisted out of the way. Now

Grey Shirt took his chance, leaping forward with the knife outstretched.

To Eden, tucked out of sight just a few feet away, the intention of the men was clear. They were here to kill Baxter.

Baxter tried to twist out of the way of Grey Shirt's attack. His foot struck something on the ground, and he stumbled. The knife slashed across the side of his ribs. Baxter cried out and his hand shot to the side of his abdomen. He pulled it away, now slick with blood.

Fury knotted in Baxter's expression now. He crouched backward for a moment before exploding toward the two men. Baxter punched White Shirt in the stomach and then the nose. White Shirt's knife clattered to the ground.

Baxter swung around and smashed an elbow into Grey Shirt's face. Grey Shirt staggered to the left, almost colliding with the wall, but stayed upright. Grey Shirt lurched forward again, keeping the knife low, aiming for Baxter's stomach. Baxter retorted with another strike aimed for Grey Shirt's face, but missed. Grey Shirt struck out, but Baxter knocked his knife away at the last moment.

Baxter took another step backward.

White Shirt picked up his knife again. The attackers stepped forward; weapons raised. They were relentless. Now it was kill or be killed.

Watching from the doorway, Eden felt a knot of horror twist in her stomach. Sure, she and Baxter had hardly got on like a house on fire, but they were here for the same reason. They were — supposedly, at least — fighting for the same thing. Him being stabbed to death in a filthy alleyway wasn't good for anyone.

Eden looked around, assessing the scene for weapons.

White Shirt and Grey Shirt stepped forward — predators stalking their prey. Grey Shirt's nose was bleeding, and probably broken.

Baxter took another step backward. His foot connected with the rear wall of the passageway. He'd reached a dead end.

Eden watched Baxter, his chances of victory ebbing away. She forced her lips together in a sneer and scanned the surrounding rubbish for a weapon. She saw nothing that would help her battle against two knife-wielding maniacs.

She gazed up at the walls towering above them. Wires and pipes crisscrossed the filthy concrete, all of them out of reach. All, except one. One of the pipes had fallen from its bracket and dangled by a single screw just two feet above Eden's head. Eden scuttled across the alleyway, leapt up, and grabbed hold of the pipe. The rusted fixing came away easily, screeching as it separated from the concrete. Eden whipped around to face the assassins. No one had noticed the sound.

Eden weighed the pipe in her hands. It was a solid weapon. She locked her gaze on the men and made her way stealthily toward the action.

White Shirt lunged forward, but Baxter shoved him away just in time. Then Grey Shirt tried to bury his knife in Baxter's stomach. Baxter kicked him hard, sending the man reeling back. White Shirt found his footing and pushed forward again. The assassins' relentless attempts were wearing Baxter down and his movements became more labored.

Eden saw that the man in the grey shirt was about to lunge again. Dismissing her furtive approach, she charged forward, the pipe raised high. Without saying a word, she brought the heavy metal tube down across Grey Shirt's head. A deep clunk echoed throughout the passage and the man crumpled to the ground.

Baxter spun around and froze, meeting Eden's gaze. Surprise and then relief flashed in his eyes for a moment. He turned his attention to the second assassin.

White Shirt looked from Eden to Baxter and back again. Facing two assailants, he seemed to diminish in stature. He glanced at the mouth of the passage behind Eden.

Baxter moved in. He punched White Shirt in the guts. White Shirt swung the knife in Eden's direction.

Eden shuffled backward, and then sprang in with the pipe. The metal cracked against the thug's wrist. Bones cracked, vibrating through the metal. The man howled, dropping the knife. His hand drooped at a distorted angle.

Baxter pushed the man up against the wall. He drew his fist back, ready to pulverize the man's nose. The thug's eyes bulged.

"Who sent you here?" Baxter growled.

The man's lips quivered. He didn't say a word.

Baxter thumped the man in the mouth. White Shirt yelped. His lip split and a trickle of blood ran down over his chin.

Eden noticed then how young the men were. White Shirt was probably only in his late teens, and was already killing people for money. Attempting to, at least.

Baxter drew his fist back again. "That was just a warm up. This time I'll break your jaw. Who sent —"

A gunshot rang out in the passageway. An electric shock rang down Eden's spine, tensing all her muscles. Her ears whined.

White Shirt slipped to the ground, the left side of his face a bloody mess.

Eden leapt to the concrete and rolled over to face the shooter.

Baxter threw himself against the wall and turned.

Grey Shirt, his face a broken mess of blood and bone, lay on the ground looking up at them. His smashed-up lips contorted into something of a smile. In his shaking hand, he raised a gun at Eden and Baxter.

Eden rolled toward him, swinging the pipe at his quivering hand.

Another shot rang out. A white-hot pain jarred through Eden's body. The pipe, which was already in motion, connected with Grey Shirt's shoulder. The gun flew from his hand, clattering against the far wall. Grey Shirt's shoulder cracked. He shrieked and uttered a string of obscenities.

Ignoring the pain, adrenaline coursing through her body, Eden repositioned the metal bar and drove it down hard across the man's skull. The crack vibrated through the steel and the man fell silent.

Eden exhaled, pain engulfing her from somewhere near the base of her neck. She rubbed a hand down the side of her face and across her neck. Thick blood slewed out across her shirt. Suddenly she felt cold and dizzy. Eden pushed her hand hard against the wound. From what she could tell, a lot of blood was escaping, but the fact she hadn't lost consciousness was a good sign.

Baxter hurdled White Shirt's prone figure and took her arm. They locked eyes. Baxter pulled the shawl from around Eden's neck, balled it, and pressed it hard against the wound.

He slid two fingers beneath the shawl and felt the pressure of the blood flow.

"You're lucky," he said, removing his fingers and pushing

the shawl firmly against the wound. "It's just a skin abrasion."

Eden gripped on to his shoulder for support. "I don't feel very lucky," she said, looking up at him. "Anyway, what are you, a doctor now too?"

"Part of my Royal Air Force training, yes. Just battlefield injuries, bullet, knife wounds, that sort of thing."

"Maybe that is lucky," Eden muttered.

Baxter looked down at the two men. "We need to get out of here. They'll probably send more once they realize these guys failed."

"Wait a minute, d'you know why these guys came for you?" Pushing the shawl against her neck, Eden felt the blood slowing already.

"No," Baxter said, a beat too slowly. "But they clearly meant business."

"They were just kids," Eden said, glancing back at the crumpled figures.

"A gun in the hand of a child is just as deadly," Baxter said. "We need to get back to the hotel, and then get out of town, fast."

29

"TELL ME IT'S DONE," Archibald Godspeed said, pacing the length of his hotel suite like a caged tiger. The man on the other end of the line, a sergeant with the local police force, was being less than helpful.

No reply came down the line.

"With the amount you're getting paid, you should be able to give me a description of the dead man." Godspeed strode to the window and peered out between the curtains. Night had fallen across Baalbek some time ago, although traffic still wrestled through the narrow streets.

Godspeed heard the man bark instructions into a radio. Godspeed just needed confirmation that Baxter was dead. That would leave Eden on her own. They needed to keep her isolated and keep the pressure on. The line buzzed and clanged, and the police sergeant came through again.

"We have one man dead, and one with a serious concussion. Both are known troublemakers in the town," the sergeant said.

Godspeed dropped the curtain and paced back into the room. His jaw tensed and his knuckles blanched around the phone. He only just resisted throwing the phone against the wall.

"No Englishman is dead?" Godspeed barked.

The sergeant spoke into the radio again. Several long seconds of silence and strange banging noises came down the line. Then the sergeant's voice came again.

"No sir, I'm afraid not. Just the two local boys. One shot in the eye and the other, we suspect, has a cracked skull."

Godspeed fumed. This was supposed to be a simple job. Kill a man in an alleyway, then make it look like a robbery gone wrong. He knew deep down that he should have sent someone more experienced.

"You said these guys were the best," Godspeed bellowed. "How have they got this so wrong?"

"I don't know, sir. Seeing the injuries the men sustained, I think there may have been more than one person there. When I know more I'll —"

"I'll tell you exactly what you'll do," Godspeed bellowed, frustration boiling over into pure rage. "You'll find the man and tell me where he is. You've messed this up once. You need to get it right this time."

"No problem," the sergeant said. "I do that for you this very instant."

Now we're getting somewhere, Godspeed thought. The sound of rustling papers filled the silence. The sergeant cleared his throat.

"The dead man has been taken to morgue, and the man with the cracked skull to the hospital. I give you address now. You have pen?"

"No, you idiot!" Godspeed screamed, all semblance of calm evaporating. A vein stood out, pulsing from his forehead. "Not those men. I don't care about them. I need you to find and eliminate the man called Baxter."

. . .

EDEN PULLED another shawl from her bag and looped it around her shoulders to cover the blood. The movement aggravated the wound and a stinging pain shot through her body.

Baxter peered out into the street. It was quiet and gloomy now.

A car groaned up the road, dazzling Eden with its single working headlight. Eden turned away as the car passed.

The call to prayer echoed across the city. The ghostly words, which once had made Eden feel the excitement of travel and an intrigue for distant lands, now sounded like a warning.

They picked their way up the road, sticking to the shadows where possible.

"In here," Eden hissed, pulling Baxter into a doorway as a pair of police cars screeched around the corner.

"They got on to that quickly," Baxter said.

"Maybe someone heard the gunshots."

"I doubt it," Baxter replied. "They'll be looking for two tourists with blood on their hands." Baxter looked down at his hands, caked in blood. "Literally."

"How? You think someone told them about us?" Eden pictured the grizzly scene they were due to find in the alleyway.

"They knew I would be there, didn't they? Someone doesn't want us to find these tablets."

The sound of the sirens faded. Baxter assessed the scene. When he was satisfied that the street was deserted, they pressed on back toward the hotel. They crossed the empty marketplace, sticking to the darkness where possible. Compared to the bustle of the daytime, the place was now eerily quiet. Somewhere nearby, a pack of stray animals clattered between the bins — cats, probably. Eden whipped around all the same, searching for movement.

They paused opposite the hotel. The extensive building loomed above them, most of its windows unlit. In the darkness, the ornate architecture looked strangely sinister now.

"We should find another way in," Eden said, remembering the attentive receptionist watching her leave. Bright light radiated through the hotel's revolving door, in stark contrast to the gloom of the city. The curtain which Eden had used to escape her room still hung from the third-floor balcony, swaying gently.

Baxter nodded. He noticed the curtain, but said nothing.

They walked further down the street, sticking to the shadows, and then crossed the road. A narrow alleyway ran down the back of the hotel, not unlike the one they'd just been in. A pair of overflowing bins sat next to a service door.

Baxter took out the knife he'd relieved one of the assassins of and pried open the hotel's back door. Eden and Baxter snuck inside. Baxter pulled the door shut silently. They hurried down a sparse corridor, passing a brightly lit kitchen and a small staff room. The sound of idle conversation drifted from a room nearby.

Reaching the end of the corridor, Eden peered into the reception area. As she had expected, a man watched the main door from behind the reception desk. They climbed the stairs silently, resisting the temptation to rush in case anyone came the other way.

Reaching the third floor, Baxter fished two keys from his pocket.

"I'm sorry about... you know." He unlocked the door to Eden's room.

Eden glanced at him, daggers in her eyes. "You ever do that again, and I'll let the killers have their way with you."

Baxter nodded, glancing at the floor.

"Five minutes," Eden said, stepping inside her room. "Then we're out of here."

Baxter stepped toward his own room.

A couple of minutes later, Eden pushed through Baxter's door, her bag slung over her shoulder.

Baxter packed some items into his bag. His eyes lingered on Eden's neck. "We need to get that wound cleaned up before we go. There's clean water here. You really don't want it getting infected."

Eden touched her neck. The blood was still damp, although it had stopped flowing. "Does it really look that bad?"

"A bit of a mess, yes." Baxter pulled out a chair and beckoned Eden to sit.

"Charming," Eden muttered, dropping her bag and sitting in the chair.

"Do you mind if I...?" Baxter pointed at the strap of Eden's top. Eden slid the strap from her shoulder.

Baxter tenderly cleaned her neck and shoulder with one of the hotel's towels and water from the kettle.

"You might get charged for that," Eden said, glancing at the bloodstained towel.

"I think we should leave without checking out," Baxter said, his face expressionless. "It's probably better we don't alert them too —"

"It was a joke," Eden said, her eyes rolling.

Baxter nodded, his face serious.

"It's not as bad as it looked," Baxter said, now that the blood was cleared up. He poured antiseptic onto a ball of cotton wool. "You won't need stitches. It should heal nicely on its own. You are very lucky. An inch to the left and —"

"And an inch to right and maybe it would have hit you instead," Eden said between gritted teeth. Baxter dabbed the wound gently.

"What kind of name is Baxter, anyway?" Eden asked, looking at the man in the mirror across the room.

"Baxter's my surname," he said flatly.

"Yes, I figured out that much," Eden said.

"Another joke?"

"Sort of." Eden forced herself to stop laughing. "Do you have another name, then?"

"Gavin," Baxter said without looking up.

Maybe it was the released tension of the last few hours, or the draining of adrenaline, but Eden couldn't help but laugh out loud. "Now you're joking?"

"No, I'm not." Baxter pulled a dressing from the first aid kit. He caught Eden's eye in the mirror.

"Seriously? No one born since 1960 has been named Gavin."

This time Baxter grinned too.

"Hence why I go with Baxter most of time. I think only my mum still calls me Gavin."

"Yeah, it would be weird if she called you Baxter."

The pair looked at each other in the mirror.

Baxter broke off the stare and continued applying antiseptic. "You're pretty good in a fight, for a —"

"For a woman?" Eden cut in, bristling at the comment. "Just because I'm a woman, you don't think I should be able to fight? If it wasn't for me, Mr. Action Man, you'd be sitting on a cloud and playing a harp right about now."

"For a civilian," Baxter said flatly, ignoring the outburst.

"Some of the best people I've ever fought beside were women. Have you had a lot of practice?"

Eden relaxed slightly. "Yeah, I train every now and then." She pictured the hours spent, both with her personal instructor, and perfecting her moves alone in the woodland. The short scuffle with the assassins had barely demonstrated her skills. "How long were you in the Air Force."

The sound of revving engines drifted through the window. Brakes squealed and then the engines died. Baxter glanced toward the window, applied the dressing quickly, and hurried across the room.

"Three police cars outside," he stated, rushing to the bed and stuffing the first aid kit inside his bag. "By the way, keep that clean and dry for at least forty-eight hours."

"Yes, doc." Eden's fingers instinctively explored the place where Baxter's hands had been. "Let's get out of here."

30

EDEN CLIMBED to her feet and crossed to the door. The wound felt better already. Although she had teased him, Baxter had done a good job.

Eden peered out into the hallway. The sound of running footsteps echoed up the stairs. Eden shut and locked the door, then she and Baxter shoved a chunky dressing table in front of it. That wouldn't hold the police for long, but would at least delay them.

"We're going to need another way out," Eden said, crossing to the window. She peeked out. Baxter's window was on the side of the hotel, overlooking the flat roof of the neighboring building. "That's a ten-foot drop," Eden said. "I think we can make that."

Baxter examined the drop and nodded.

The sound of footsteps stopped, and whispered voices came through the door. Eden imagined the man in the red waistcoat hunting for the correct key. Sure enough, a few seconds later, a key grated in the lock.

Eden carefully slid her bag over her shoulders and ran to the window.

The locking mechanism clicked, and the door swung open a fraction, thumping against the dresser. Raised voices streamed through the gap. Eden glanced back at the door but saw only shadows.

She swung the bag out of the window and dropped it to the roof below. It thudded hard against the concrete.

A shoulder crashed against the door, moving the heavy dresser by an inch.

Eden swung herself up on to the windowsill. Gripping on to the ledge, she lowered her body flat against the outside wall, then dropped.

Baxter followed.

Eden snatched up her bag and charged across the roof. She dove behind an air conditioner. Baxter leapt in beside her. They sat shoulder to shoulder for several seconds, trying to pick out noises from the open window behind them.

After a minute, she turned and glanced back up at the window. A shadow moved around in the room. She waited for several seconds, frozen to the spot. With each pulse of her heart, she expected to hear the snap of gunfire or the heavy thump of boots on the roof. None came.

She counted out another minute and then peered back at the room again. Several shadowy figures moved about inside now. Eden imagined them thoroughly searching the space. The towel, still wet with blood, would show they hadn't left long ago. Right now, they might be setting up a search perimeter on the city streets below, sealing their way out.

Two minutes later the figures disappeared.

"They've gone, I think," Eden hissed, breathing a sigh of relief.

The pair waited silently in their hiding place for a further five minutes.

"Let's get out of here," she said, climbing to her feet and pacing to the far end of the rooftop. She glanced over the edge. A police car remained at the hotel entrance, a pair of officers watching the door.

"This way," Baxter hissed, beckoning Eden to the other side of the rooftop. They looked down the thin alleyway at the rear of the hotel. Another pair of officers stood at the hotel's back door. Each held a light, swaying it this way and then that through the gloom.

"That's easy." Baxter tightened the straps of his backpack and then paced away from the roof's edge. "Tell me when they're facing the other way."

Eden assessed the jump. It was at least six feet from one building to the other. Certainly possible, although she'd rather not think about what could go wrong. She watched the officers below. One of them wandered further into the gloom and then called for his colleague.

"Now," Eden stated, when both officers were facing the other way.

Baxter sprinted across the rooftop and leapt across the gap. He landed with a thump, and with several inches to spare, on the opposite roof.

Eden peered back across the edge. The officers were still examining something at the far end of the alleyway.

"Easy," Baxter hissed from across the roofs.

"If you say so," Eden quipped. She tightened the straps of her bag and paced back from the edge, just as Baxter had done.

Baxter crawled to the roof's edge and peered down at the officers.

Eden rubbed her hands together and considered the

jump. Although she wasn't afraid of heights, the drop was certainly a distraction. She huffed out her breath and then pictured herself landing perfectly on the other side.

Baxter gave her a thumbs up to indicate the officers were still facing the other way.

Eden dropped into the position of a sprinter on the blocks, and then, counting down from three in her head, she charged. Her feet thumped heavily across the roof as she approached the precipice. Six feet remaining. Four feet to go. Two feet. Eden glanced down at Baxter and then at the opposite rooftop. She jumped. The air rushed past her ears. She drew her legs up in midair.

On the other rooftop, Baxter paled. He looked up at Eden, knowing it was too late to shout now.

Moving through the air, Eden heard a raised voice and then the distant report of a gun. She drew her legs up further and landed hard on the rooftop. She rolled forward away from the edge. The sound of two more gunshots pounded from the alleyway. Bullets ricocheted from the roof's edge, scattering concrete fragments.

"You told me they were facing the other way," Eden hissed. She took a deep breath, relieved that she'd made it across the gap.

"They turned at the very last moment. Seeing you in midair must have given them a fright."

Eden gazed down into the alleyway. One of the officers remained below, barking instructions into a radio. The other sprinted off in the direction of the building's entrance. "We better get moving. How do we get down from here?"

"Stairs over there." Baxter pointed to the far side of the building.

"Lucky," Eden said, setting off at a sprint.

They reached the staircase and hustled down to street

level. Somewhere nearby the whining of a siren carried through the still air. Eden and Baxter scurried away, using the network of thin interconnecting passages between the buildings. They reached a junction with the main street and peered out. The road was empty in both directions.

"This way," Eden said, indicating left, away from the hotel. She wanted to put as much distance between herself, the hotel, and the dead assassins as possible.

Closed signs hung from the shops which lined both sides of the street, their shutters drawn down tight against the night. Boxy concrete buildings jutted up into the sky. The windows of apartments on the upper floors glowed invitingly.

Eden and Baxter walked for ten minutes, keeping out of sight as much as possible. Two or three times, hearing a vehicle heading their way, they slunk into the doorway of a shop or hussled into a shadow.

They passed a junction with an unlit backstreet. Something clattered. Eden froze in mid-stride. She glanced toward the noise. Something scurried through the gloom.

"It's just a cat or something," Eden muttered to herself. *Get a grip.*

Then, almost totally obscured by the darkness, she saw a row of parked vehicles. They needed to get out of the city as quickly as possible without leaving a trail. Taking a car was their only option.

"This way," she hissed to Baxter, stepping into the gloom.

Eden examined the vehicles and was instantly drawn to one. A dust-covered Volvo 114. She approached the car. The age of the vehicle suggested it wouldn't have an immobilizer or an alarm, and the thick layer of dust told her it hadn't been used for a long time. She had also seen several similar vehicles grunting and groaning around the city in the last few hours, which would allow them to blend in.

Eden asked Baxter for the knife and, within a few seconds, she had pried open the door. She slipped into the driver's seat and dumped her bag in the back. She unlocked the passenger door and Baxter slid in beside her. Eden examined the ignition block. She would have no problem getting this started.

Just in case, though, before tearing the cover off and messing about with the wires, she pulled down the sun visor. A set of keys fell into her lap.

"Your guardian angel's nearby tonight," Baxter said, smiling for what Eden believed was the first time.

"It looks that way." Eden started the engine. The Volvo growled to life. She pulled out of the bay and accelerated away.

As the Volvo's taillights merged into the mayhem of the city, a cigarette flared. The light was followed by a cloud of chamomile smoke.

31

GODSPEED PULLED ASIDE the curtain and looked out at the surrounding rooftops. Hillsides loomed around the edge of the city. The town wasn't that big. It really shouldn't take this long for a competent police force to locate and remove one man.

Godspeed's phone chirped from the table beside him. He snatched it up and answered.

"You've got him?" Godspeed barked.

"Not exactly, sir. Although we know where he is."

Godspeed threw the curtain back into position and stalked into the room. He sucked a lungful of air through gritted teeth. "Well go and get him, put a bullet between his eyes, and dump his body somewhere it'll never be found."

"Of course, of course," the sergeant chimed in reply. "But it's not that simple."

Godspeed's fists clenched. He knew exactly how simple it was, or at least how simple it should be.

"They have been seen leaving the town to the north. Our officers were in pursuit, but then it was the end of their shift, so we had to let them go. We can't have officers not making it home in time for their families, I'm sure you understand."

Godspeed felt as though all the air had been sucked out of the room. He tried to breathe, but his jaw was clenched so tightly he barely got a gulp of oxygen.

"The two officers that followed them actually did a very good job, I think you'll agree. They were seen running across —"

"Shut up. Just shut up!" Godspeed roared.

Croft and Stone, who had been standing at ease by the door, bristled upright at the sound.

Godspeed held the phone at arm's length for several seconds. A vein in the side of his head bulged as though it was ready to explode. He placed the phone back against his ear and his voice faded to little more than a whisper.

"I'll do this myself from here on. Tell me what you know."

"I can assure you, sir, that is not necessary. We totally have this one-hundred percent under control."

"Just tell me what you know."

"Okay. They're in a blue Volvo. We think the car is probably stolen but are running checks now. They're heading north out of the city."

"Fine," Godspeed hissed.

"How would you like to make the payment?"

Godspeed didn't hear the sergeant's question as he had already hung up the phone. He strode back to the window and studied the landscape. He tapped a finger against his chin. After several seconds he turned back toward Croft and Stone.

"Gentlemen," he said, barely above a whisper. "It's time we went to work."

. . .

THE VOLVO CLANGED and wallowed through the night. Driving on pure instinct, Eden took them north. The highway was almost deserted at this time of night, just the occasional long-distance truck rumbling in the opposite direction.

Baxter sat silently in the passenger seat, watching the occasional light of a farm or a tiny village stream past.

Eventually, after what seemed like several hours, they arrived in the town of Maalqa. Little more than a collection of buildings along the highway, Eden hoped the town was big enough to provide them with a bed for the night.

Sure enough, midway through the town, they approached a building which advertised itself in both Arabic and English as a hotel and restaurant.

Not wanting their borrowed car to attract any attention, Eden drove beyond the hotel and pulled into a side street. With something like a sigh of thanks, the Volvo hissed into silence. They grabbed their bags and walked back around to the hotel.

"I'll go inside," Baxter said as they neared the entrance. "You've still got a bit of blood on you."

Eden looked down at her strap top. Whilst the blood on her neck had been cleaned away, it still covered her top.

Baxter jogged up the stairs and knocked on the glass doors at the front of the building. A sleepy-looking man appeared and let him inside.

Several minutes later, Baxter returned with keys to a pair of rooms on the first floor. He gave one key to Eden and together they climbed the stairs in silence.

Eden let herself into the room, stripped off her bloodied clothes, and collapsed onto the bed.

She awoke the following morning with the sun streaming through the curtains. A knock pummeled the door. Eden blinked hard and then rubbed at her eyes. She looked around, disorientated. It felt like just moments ago that she'd climbed into the bed.

The knock sounded from the door again, more aggressive this time. With no idea why someone would knock so hard, a fission of fear moved through her body.

She sprung to her feet and slipped on the hotel robe. She looked around for something she could use as a weapon if necessary. A large glass vase sat empty on a side table. Eden picked it up, hefting it to feel the weight. It probably wouldn't kill anyone but would afford her the time to get away.

She moved to the door, slowly. Another knock shook the flimsy door against its fixings. She held the vase high in her right hand and twisted the handle with her left. She edged backward into a crouch, ready to run or fight at a moment's notice.

"Hello madam," came a voice in sing-song tones through the gap in the door. "I have your breakfast. Last night sir ordered it for 10am. I am sorry it is," — the man looked at his watch — "twelve minutes late. I will have cross words with the chef."

Eden stepped backward, adrenaline still coursing through her veins. She considered the man again. Almost as wide as he was tall, with a nest of greying hair, he didn't seem to pose a threat. Eden glanced down at the tray. Several small bowls containing yoghurt, chopped fruits, fried eggs, grilled haloumi, and several slices of bread made her realize how hungry she was. Her stomach replied with a growl.

"Thank you," Eden said, her voice croaky. She accepted the tray and padded back to the bed, hunger now replacing her tiredness.

. . .

THIRTY MINUTES LATER, having demolished the food, showered, and changed, Eden and Baxter unfolded the map of Lebanon across her bed and set to making a list of the tomb's potential locations.

A fresh pot of coffee sat on the bedside table.

"I have to be honest, I don't remember that much," Eden said, scrutinizing the map. "Wherever we look, it's going to be a real long shot."

"That's okay," Baxter said, looking at her from across the bed. "I know it was a long time ago and you were very young. We've got more to go on than anyone else, though."

Eden caught Baxter's eye and forced a smile. She knew the search was comparable to finding a needle in a haystack. She guessed Baxter knew that too but was just going through the motions out of loyalty to his boss.

Eden slipped the photograph of her and her father out of the bag at her feet. "This picture was taken on the morning we went to the tomb. I can't remember how we got from the place this picture was taken to the tomb site. We might have gone in a car, we might have walked, I can't remember."

Baxter accepted the photograph. He studied it carefully, then turned it over and checked the back.

"As you can see, it's taken from a hillside overlooking a town with the sea in the background."

"Any idea what town that might be?"

"No. I told you, I can't remember," Eden snapped, more aggressively than she'd intended.

Baxter nodded.

"Sorry, I didn't —"

"It's fine, honestly." Baxter forced a smile and turned to

the map spread out on the bed. "Okay. Let's assume that Godspeed's calculations here are correct." Baxter indicated the markings which Godspeed had made on the map.

"How did he calculate this?"

"He looked at some old logs from the various digs that took place around that time."

"I thought this one was totally off the books?" Eden said.

"It was, yes, but things still leave a trace. They would have needed men and transport, and such things leave a record. It was his theory that his great grandfather and Rassam had effectively embezzled resources from other sites and moved them here."

"That would make them close by, right?"

"Exactly. So, he's highlighted these areas on the map in which he thinks it's more likely the tomb could be positioned."

"More likely sounds good to me," Eden agreed. "I also remember that the tomb was built into a hillside. It was rocky, and quite steep. My dad made me sit to one side on a large rock and not move for fear I might fall down the mountain." Eden felt her eyes moisten at the memory. She turned and looked out the window for a few moments.

"That's useful, actually." Baxter's finger traced a line on the map now. "Do you remember if there were any plants or trees growing there?"

Eden narrowed her eyes. "Yes, actually. There were several trees growing around the entrance to the tomb."

"That rules out this part of the country then." Baxter swept his hand over the eastern part of the map.

"That would also have taken us a long time to get to if this picture was taken on the morning of the visit." Eden pointed at the photograph. "Although I don't know exactly where it was taken, I suspect it wasn't too far away."

"Yes, I agree. I didn't know your father, but I imagine he was a practical man, and wouldn't have wanted to drive halfway across the country for no reason."

"Absolutely," Eden said, nodding. "He did everything for a reason."

"Kadisha Valley," Baxter said, circling an area with his finger. "Godspeed's research suggests that they could have carried out an off-the-books dig there pretty easily."

Eden slid out her phone and brought up a few pictures of the area. She scrolled through various images of tree-covered hills, waterfalls, and cliffs. "That looks about right to me," she said.

"It's also about forty minutes' drive from the sea."

"It's a good place to start," Eden said.

Baxter folded the map and slipped it into his bag.

Despite Eden's efforts to think positively, the search felt insurmountable. Even with her strands of memory and Godspeed's research, there remained any number of places the tomb could be. Eden slung her bag across her shoulders and forced a smile. Her father always said that he reveled in the unlikely. Now it was Eden's turn to do the same.

32

For the first hour of the journey, they drove south back toward Baalbek. Baxter insisted he should drive, to give Eden the chance to look out at the landscape just in case anything should occur to her. Initially, Eden had disagreed, preferring to be in control, but in the end, she conceded that Baxter's plan was logical.

Eden found some reassurance, because the landscape they passed didn't look at all familiar. Sand-colored hills reared up on either side of the road, already baking under the cloudless sky. They passed through several small towns, which consisted of a few hundred concrete buildings, all clustered around a mosque. All the structures in the towns seemed to be the same color as the surrounding hills, as though the dust that passed through the town stained everything in its wake.

Just beyond the village of Rasm AL Hadath, they turned off the highway and headed west. The road wound through a changing landscape, becoming lusher and more tree-covered with every downward turn.

Eden shuffled forward in her seat and scrutinized every passing mountain crag or clump of foliage.

Thirty minutes later, they turned from the asphalt and onto a narrow dusty track, cutting in a zigzag through a patchwork of lush undergrowth. The road wound up a hillside, the plants giving way to overhanging cliffs.

"We're close," Baxter said, navigating the Volvo slowly around a steep bend. The Volvo's tires, inappropriate for use on the steep roads, juddered and slipped. The nose of the heavy car swung from one side to the other. Baxter shifted into a lower gear and slowed the engine. Finally, the tires caught some purchase, and they growled onward. "There's a monastery just up ahead," he said, wiping a hand across his forehead. "I suggest we look there. We might even find someone who can help us."

"Sounds good," Eden said, gazing out the window. She'd relaxed over the course of the journey, but now they were approaching their destination she felt the pressure rise again. They hadn't seen another car since they'd left the main road, which was the way she liked it.

"They'll see us coming two miles away," Baxter said, pointing a thumb at the great cloud of dust kicked twenty feet in the air behind them.

"It means we can see anyone coming too," Eden said, glancing behind them at the downward snaking road. So far it was empty as far as she could see.

"How far?" Eden said, turning back to face Baxter as he slowly navigated another corner.

"A mile, maybe two," he said, gripping the wheel tightly.

"Next time we see a place to stop out of sight, use it," Eden said. "We'll approach on foot."

"You can't seriously be worried about —"

"Right now, I'm worried about everything," Eden

snapped. "And if I wasn't, you'd be lying dead in an alleyway."

Baxter nodded.

"Up here," Eden said, pointing at a collection of tin-roofed building slightly off the road to the left.

Baxter swung the wheel and the Volvo skidded down a narrow, rutted access road. He pulled around the back of the structure, which contained a pick-up truck and a decrepit tractor with half its innards missing.

Eden scrambled out of the Volvo and slipped two bottles of water into her bag. She glanced up at the sky. Whilst the heat of the day had yet to reach its peak, the temperature had already climbed far beyond comfortable. A pair of large birds wheeled and swung overhead, their calls echoing down across the landscape. Eden narrowed her eyes against the bright sky. Birds of prey, probably, waiting for an easy meal. Maybe they'd sensed the disquietude which had been rising in Eden's guts all morning.

Eden watched the birds for another few seconds, slicing in great arcs across the thermal currents. Then her eyes picked out something else. A tiny flicker in the sky, several hundred feet above them. She looked down at the ground. Her feeling of uneasiness rose into a bubbling fear.

"Don't look up," Eden said, locking Baxter with a stare. "I'm pretty sure we've got company." Eden motioned upward with her head.

"A drone," Baxter stated, doing a much better job of appearing calm than Eden was.

Eden nodded. "We better start walking, don't want to give them any sense that they've been spotted."

Baxter swung on his bag and the pair walked up to the road, climbing the final few hundred feet toward the monastery.

As they walked, Eden shuffled her phone out of her pocket and, while carefully looking as though she was checking something, took several pictures of the sky. She then used the photo editing function to zoom in and scan the sky above them.

"There," Eden said, showing Baxter the zoomed-in picture. Sure enough, at least a hundred feet above them, the device hovered, beaming its pictures back to someone nearby.

"I wonder how long they've been following."

"I expect they were following in another vehicle back on the main road. Then put the drone up when we headed down here." Eden strode up the hill. A cliff reared above them on the left, creepers and vines obscuring much of the surface.

"They're not a danger to us unless they think we've found something," Baxter said, striding onward.

"Let's check this place out," Eden said, nodding forward. "Then what do you say we give them something to get excited about?"

Baxter nodded and the pair quickened their pace up the incline.

Eden and Baxter climbed slowly, both aware of the eye in the sky floating above their heads. Eden risked another glance over her shoulder. The road, snaking downward to the valley floor, was empty. Still, no cars had passed them since they'd left the main road. No clouds of dust gave away the existence of approaching vehicles, either.

The pair pushed on up the hill, Eden digging deep to keep up with Baxter's long strides. By the time they reached the next corner, Eden's heart was thumping like a jack hammer and each breath felt as though it was coming up short.

"It's the heat, it makes this sort of exercise so much more difficult," Baxter said, as though reading her thoughts. "Back in basic training they used to make us run up mountains with full packs. I think I would prefer that, to walking in anything above thirty."

"Absolutely," Eden said. "I'm sure it'll be easier on the way down."

"That depends on what company we've got," Baxter said morosely. "Do you recognize anything yet?"

Eden stopped and looked up at the hills surrounding them. With the distraction of their pursuers, she hadn't thought about the fact that she may have been here before, since they'd left the car.

"It certainly looks more familiar than the dry landscape we came through this morning, but nothing stands out to me just yet."

"That means we could be nearby."

"Maybe," Eden huffed between breaths. "Or we could be hundreds of miles away in a place that just looks a bit similar."

Baxter shot her a look and noticed a wry smile flash across Eden's expression.

"Let's hope that's not the case."

The pair trudged around a bend in the road ahead and then froze in their tracks. Appearing to defy gravity, the monastery hung from the cliff face just a few hundred yards away. The building itself was constructed in tan colored stone. Beautiful carved arches and balustrades adorned windows and balconies. Statues of saints perched on the rooftops, regally surveying the valley beneath them. The whole effect, especially when juxtaposed to the rugged and isolated valley, was dreamlike and almost otherworldly.

"That's quite a place," Baxter said, leaning back on his heels to take the structure in.

"A clifftop monastery, deep within a remote valley. It's definitely the sort of place I would hide a set of ancient tablets." Eden scrutinized the structure, looking for something that she remembered.

"What, you remember something?" Baxter flashed her a look of excitement.

"No, nothing I'm afraid." Eden nodded upward. "But they don't know that. Let the wild goose chase begin."

33

Two miles away, a black Toyota Land Cruiser sat at the side of the road. The vehicle stood out to any passing local drivers because of its sleek black exterior. The engine purred gently. Beyond the tinted glass of the rear windows, a shadow moved.

Sitting in the back, Archibald Godspeed watched the drone footage on a tablet. The man sitting beside him had a similar screen attached to the drone's control unit.

"Keep right on top of them," Godspeed barked, as Eden and Baxter set off at a run toward the monastery. "We're not losing them now. I want to be there within minutes of them making the discovery."

Stone, or was it Croft? — Godspeed hadn't made the effort of remembering — made an adjustment, and the camera drifted forward, staying directly above their quarry.

"And you're sure they couldn't have seen this?" Godspeed pointed at the screen.

"It's possible, but unlikely. They won't hear it either, not at that distance."

Godspeed nodded. Although this case had seemed fun

to start with, his patience was now wearing thin. Initially he had loved the chance to follow in his old great grandfather's footsteps and impress a man as important as Helios. But Godspeed hadn't realized then just how much hard work would be involved.

Sure, Godspeed needed the money, what with the upkeep of the stately home, and his flamboyant lifestyle to pay for, but he hadn't intended to actually *work* for it. This job was starting to look a whole lot like work.

He turned away from the screen and looked out at the landscape. He had hoped not to actually have to see things through "on the ground." Was it too much to ask to have someone else do all the work, and just call him in at the last minute to make the collection? He wouldn't mind hanging out in one of Lebanon's five-star beachside resorts while these men did the dirty work.

Godspeed glanced at the two men sitting with him in the Land Cruiser. Despite the long hours they had spent together, he hadn't heard the men say a single unnecessary word. They just seemed to bark instructions at each other all day in some strange military language.

The sooner he got back to England, the better.

"Any sign?" Godspeed asked, scrutinizing the screen.

Eden and Baxter had stopped fifty yards from the front of the monastery. They looked up at the buildings as though deciding where to go.

"Negative," the drone controller barked.

Negative, Godspeed thought to himself. What was the point in that? *"Negative"* is actually longer than just saying *"no."*

"Three minutes flight time remaining," the man grunted.

"I think we go in," Godspeed said. At least that would

break the boredom of just sitting in the car. "They're obviously on to something. They've come here for a reason."

The men looked at each other.

"Affirmative. We move in."

Godspeed rolled his eyes.

The drone controller pressed a few buttons. The machine shot back toward them at an impressive speed.

"But until we get a visual confirmation of the tablets, you should stay in the vehicle."

Archibald Godspeed swallowed a fission of frustration. Who was this man to speak to him like that? At least now things were going to get a little more interesting.

EDEN AND BAXTER walked up to the front of the monastery. Up close, the place was even more impressive. It seemed to hover, either attached to the cliff face by some magical force, or placed there by nature herself. The effigies of countless religious figures looked down over Eden and Baxter, as though judging them from on-high.

Eden turned and looked out over the valley floor some two hundred feet below. It appeared that the only way to get to and from the monastery was via the path they'd used.

"Hello, welcome!"

Eden physically leapt at the sound of the voice. She and Baxter spun around to face the speaker.

A small man, with a head that seemed too large for his slender body, strode toward them. He wore a simple black cloak with the hood pulled up. His long grey beard swung with the movement.

"I am Simeon," he said, stopping before Eden and Baxter and sounding slightly out of breath. His English was disjointed and accented, but perfectly understandable. "You have come to see my home?"

"Yes," Eden said, surprised by the little man. "You live here alone?"

"That is the case, yes. This monastery was built in the thirteenth century but was abandoned one hundred years ago. I look after it the best I can."

"You do a great job," Baxter said, looking about the walls of the building. "It looks to be very well kept."

"I try." The monk shrugged.

"Do you have many visitors here?" Eden asked.

"Sometimes yes, sometimes no. People know I am here and often hike past to see me. I do not know how they know that I am here. Someone must be telling them." He tilted his head from side to side.

"We're actually here looking for something," Eden said. She watched the man closely for any indication of dishonesty. She saw none.

"Everyone is looking for something," the monk replied, cryptically.

"We're looking for a tomb —"

"The Lord works in funny ways," Simeon interrupted Eden, turning to look out across the valley. "No one visits me for over a week, and then two people come at once. Look!" He pointed at a cloud of dust rising over the access road a few hundred feet away.

Eden and Baxter glanced at each other.

"We need to go." Baxter touched Eden on the shoulder and pointed the other way down the valley. "Is there another way out of here?"

Simeon tilted his head and considered Baxter. "I do not think these people have good intentions." He pointed at the access road. A large black vehicle was visible now, speeding in their direction. It was making quicker work of the dusty road than the Volvo had.

"You're right," Eden said. "They're looking for the tomb too, but they want it for bad reasons. We need to get there first to make sure they don't get it."

"There are many tombs in this sacred valley," Simeon said. "I can show you some if you like."

"I don't think the tomb we need to find is here," Eden said, looking around. Nothing had seemed familiar since they'd arrived. "But if you could show us another way out of here, that would be fantastic."

Simeon looked up at the sky for a moment, his lips pursed together in thought. He ran a hand through his beard. "I know just the place," he said, a finger raised. "They will never know where you have gone."

Simeon set off at a quick step toward the building from which he'd appeared.

"Are you coming or not?" Simeon said, turning around as he reached the door.

Eden glanced at Baxter. Baxter shrugged and a grin almost broke through his rugged countenance. They jogged up to the door and stepped inside.

From inside, Eden understood how the building seemed to defy gravity. While the front half of the structure was made by human hands from blocks of stone, the back half consisted of caves either hewn, or naturally occurring in the rock. Sunlight streamed through high windows in thick beams.

"These caves have been home to monks like me for thousands of years," Simeon said, closing the heavy wooden door. Just before the door swung shut, Eden saw that the approaching vehicle was now less than a hundred feet from the front of the monastery. The growl of the engine hung in the air for a moment before the door thumped into position.

Simeon pushed a heavy bolt across, securing the door in place.

"Over the years these caves have been sanctuary for many people. This way." Simeon wandered across to a gas lamp, hanging from the wall. "No electricity in here, you see. We live in the way people have in past times." He slid a box of matches from beneath his habit, struck one, and offered it up to the wick.

The sound of the vehicle's engine grumbled through the door. Tires crunched to a stop on the gravel outside.

Eden tapped her foot impatiently.

"Come on," Simeon muttered, willing the lamp into life. The match fizzled and then went out. Simeon muttered again and stuck another match.

Heavy footsteps thudded across the ground outside the door.

The tempo of Eden's pulse increased. She looked from the door to Simeon and back again. "I really think we should —"

"There we are," Simeon crowed as the oil lamp glowed reluctantly to life. "This way then." He pointed further into the cave.

A thump echoed through the door, shaking the wood against its fixings. A muffled voice followed. Another voice answered.

Eden listened carefully. There were at least two men, maybe more. She wondered whether they were the men who had tried to kill her at the hospital. Either way, she knew they weren't pilgrims visiting the old monk.

Simeon shuffled further into the darkness.

Eden and Baxter followed.

It looked as though most of the caves were naturally occurring, with interconnecting tunnels cut between them. Light streamed through the occasional gap in the stone wall, also providing a glimpse of the outside world. Somewhere within the caverns, water trickled.

Eden suppressed a shiver. The temperature inside the caves had dropped significantly.

A thunderous boom echoed down the passageway behind them. The muffled voices came again, followed by another crash. It sounded as though the men were trying to barge their way through.

Simeon wandered ahead, unconcerned. "They won't get through that," he muttered. The lamp swayed in time with his lumbering gait. "That door has kept out —"

Another crash resounded down the passageway. This one was followed by a crack.

Fifty feet further on, the passage curved to the left. An imposing wooden door, studded with iron, blocked their way. The light from Simeon's lamp danced across slimy-looking walls.

"Take this," Simeon said, passing the lamp to Baxter. Baxter accepted the lamp and Simeon tapped down his habit in search of something.

Another splintering crash reverberated down the passage. It sounded as though the old wood was finally giving in. Eden spun around, expecting to hear the door crash open and the pounding of running feet. For a few moments, no sound came.

Simeon removed a large key with something of a flourish. He stepped up to the door and slid the key into the mechanism. The key minced against the grimy tumblers. The lock groaned and then clicked open. Simeon heaved the door, which creaked heavily on ancient hinges.

Simeon indicated for Baxter and Eden to step inside. They did as they were told, the lamp held high by Baxter. Strange shadows danced across the slimy walls.

The room behind the door was nothing more than a cell, around twelve feet square. A pile of stained blankets lingered in one corner. Water trickled down the rear wall, before disappearing through a crack in the ground. The whole space smelled of damp and decay.

Eden spun around just in time to see the heavy door slam shut with surprising speed. The wood crashed into position, sending a cloud of dust into the air.

"No no no!" Eden shouted, leaping toward the door and seizing hold of the flimsy handle. She pulled hard, but the door didn't move. She heaved the door again, her feet slipping across the floor.

"Now I'll see how important you are," came Simeon's lilting voice from the other side of the door. A small hatch slid open in the center of the door and Simeon peered through. "I wonder what those men will pay to see you."

"But, wait!" Eden screamed. "What do you need with money up here?"

"Everyone needs money," Simeon said, shrugging. "Some people just lie about how much they need it."

Simeon slammed the hatch. Eden and Baxter listened to the sound of his retreating footsteps.

34

"WHAT'S GOING ON OUT THERE?" Archibald Godspeed bellowed, leaning out through the door of the Toyota.

The men turned from the door which they'd been trying and failing to break through for what felt like several minutes. Godspeed didn't understand how something that looked so old could withstand so much punishment.

"Sir, stay in the vehicle," the one-eyed man said. "We will be through in a couple of minutes, but it's paramount that you stay out of sight until we're sure we have visual confirmation on the tomb."

Godspeed grumbled back inside and slid the door closed. Of course, the man was right. If Eden realized he hadn't died on the country estate back in England, then she would disappear and the tomb would be lost. Godspeed thought about Helios' threat again. He needed to find that tomb, and fast.

Godspeed settled backed into his seat and removed a handkerchief from his pocket. He swept it across his forehead, removing several beads of sweat. *At least it's cooler in here*, he thought, holding his hand in front of the air vent to check that the air conditioner was still working. A trickle of cool air slid lazily over his fingers. He pulled his shirt away from his sweating chest. The sooner they had these blasted tablets found, and get somewhere cool, the better.

Godspeed peered out through the windscreen as the men prepared themselves for another run at the door. So far, the decrepit wood, blistered and stained from years in the hot sun, was putting up quite a fight. Godspeed mused that in any other situation, it might even be amusing. That was the problem with men like these two — they used their biceps first and their brain cells second. If Godspeed were out there, he would be searching the Land Cruiser's tool kit for something they could use to pry open the hinges or dislodge the lock. It was clear that the bull-in-a-china-shop technique just wasn't working.

"Let them try, though," Godspeed said out loud, flexing his shoulders as the sweat finally began to recede. *It's not like they'll have any secret escape tunnels. They'll have to come out soon enough.*

The men took a step back, levelled their meaty shoulders at the center of the door, and prepared to charge.

"It's like watching rhinos out in the Serengeti," Godspeed said, remembering a hunting trip he'd taken there several years ago. All off the books, of course. But people will do anything for a few thousand — including smuggling a hunting party into a national park to allow a wealthy man with an inferiority complex to shoot defenseless animals.

The man on the right nodded and they both charged toward the door. A heart beat before they reached the blistered wood, the door swung open.

. . .

"Hello there, how can I help —" Simeon said, swinging open the door. His eyes sprung wide, almost bulging from his head as nearly half a ton of bones and muscle charged his way. He tried to step backward, but not quick enough. One of the men collided with Simeon's shoulder, sending him into a spin. The thug tripped, his hands windmilling, searching for something to grab hold of.

The monk tumbled backward. His feet slipped out before him, smashing his tailbone hard against the jagged floor. He looked up at the brute still flying toward him, arms flailing uselessly. The big man struck Simeon's legs and tumbled, his heavy body crashing hard into the ground beside Simeon.

The other thug charged forward, his feet slipping and sliding as he tried to gain his balance. He slid toward the far wall, and, resting two hands against the slippery rocks, finally managed to stop his forward motion. The centuries-old cave had other ideas, however. Due to the buildup of grime over hundreds of years, the man slid slowly, unceremoniously down into a pile on the ground, his hands and chest covered in the gunky residue.

Simeon took a deep breath. His lungs wheezed at the effort. His bottom ached, and the back of his head throbbed along with the beating of his heart. Nothing seemed to be broken though, thankfully.

A slow clap echoed through the monastery.

Simeon struggled to turn, acting much like a turtle on its back, and saw a shadow filling up the doorway. Although this one was much less imposing than the Goliath brothers Simeon had just encountered, the man certainly towered over Simeon while he was lying on the floor.

"Good work there," Godspeed barked between hoots of laughter.

"We've got access to the monastery, sir," one of the men groaned.

"We'll set up a perimeter," the other said, scrambling to his feet.

"No," Godspeed bellowed. "I've had enough of you two playing Action Man. From now on we're doing it my way." Godspeed marched into the monastery and kicked Simeon hard in the ribs. "That starts with this guy telling us what he's done with our friends."

"I SHOULD HAVE KNOWN NOT to trust him," Baxter snarled, pacing around the tiny space like a caged animal. The light from the oil lamp danced with each step he made.

"Just stop," Eden said, spinning around to face him.

"Stop what?"

"Just stop walking around for a second, you're making me dizzy. Plus, if that light goes out, we'll have nothing."

Baxter begrudgingly stood still.

"So, what? The monk isn't as pious as we first thought," Eden said, playing the situation down. "At least we know what he's going to do now."

"We do?" Baxter said, whirling to face Eden. The lamp light dimmed with the movement.

"Give me that," Eden said, holding out her hand.

Baxter handed the lamp over.

"We know that our man of the cloth is going to try and get whatever he can, before leading whoever was in that car right to this door." Eden paced over to the wall and placed the lamp in a nook, doubtless carved into the damp rock for that very purpose.

"I'm pretty sure they're more likely to shoot him than give him anything for his trouble," Baxter replied.

"Exactly, so either way, we're going to have those two knocking on this door in a few minutes time."

"Which doesn't seem to help a great deal." Baxter strode across to the door and gave the wood a shove. The door didn't even move.

Eden grinned at Baxter's frustration.

"What?" Baxter barked.

"This is one of those situations where brute force isn't the answer. You could push at that door all day and get nowhere."

"What do you suggest then?" Baxter said tersely.

"Look at the door," Eden said. "It looks to me as if it were designed to keep people out, rather than keep people in."

Baxter turned and squinted at the wood. He shrugged in silence.

"Look at the hinges," Eden almost shouted. "They're on the inside. If you wanted to keep someone in, you'd mount the hinges on the outside. Have you got that knife?"

Baxter slid out the knife they'd relieved from the men in the alley back in Baalbek.

"You can fly a plane, but have no idea how to hang a door. Typical," Eden huffed, grinning. Using the knife, she jimmied the pin from the hinge at the top of the door, and then repeated the process with the bottom one. The heavy door groaned as the hinges no longer took its weight.

"Now pull this," Eden said, indicating the edge of the door that was free of its bindings. Baxter did what he was told, and the door scraped along the rutted ground. "Quietly," Eden hissed.

Together they heaved the door from the frame and lowered it to the stone floor.

"Impressive stuff," Baxter whispered.

Voices, distorted by reverberation, echoed down the passageway.

Eden grabbed the lamp. "Now we just have to get past them," Eden said, beckoning Baxter toward the voices.

"I think we can do that," Baxter said, slicing the knife through the air. "Let the fun begin."

35

"You would not want to hurt an old harmless man of faith, would you?" Simeon whined. In truth, he knew the answer. It had come a minute ago with the first kick to the ribs. Now the old man was bruised and battered, and with a stream of blood running from his nose.

"I care about one thing, and one thing only," Godspeed growled. "Finding Aloma's tomb. If you tell me where it is now, we will let you go with the use of your legs."

"But, but, I do not —" Simeon howled. A boot crunched into his knee. He wasn't sure if it was broken, but it hurt like hell, heaven, and everything in between. He tried to mutter out a prayer, spraying blood and spit through broken lips.

Godspeed looked down at the crumpled man, assessing his every move. Maybe he didn't know, but it paid to be sure.

"I do not know, but I think they do." Simeon pointed a shaking hand down the passage.

"What do you mean?" Godspeed barked. "It looked to me like you were showing them something."

"No... no... I locked them in the cell at the end of the hall. I was going to try and get some money for their capture. I have to eat and... and..." Simeon removed a large key from beneath the folds of his habit.

Godspeed grinned and then shook his head. He snatched the key from the old man. "You were trying to make a quick buck or two out of this? You have no idea what you've gotten yourself involved in." He turned to face his men. "Kill this loser and then go and check on the prisoners." Godspeed looked around the cave which made up the inside of the monastery. He crinkled his nose as the stench of the place tried to invade his senses.

He tapped the key in the palm of his hand several times, a plan formulating in his mind. "We will keep them here for a day or so. That should get them ready to talk."

Before the men could answer, Godspeed turned and strode out into the sunlight. He inhaled a welcome lungful of the fresh outside air, crossed to the Land Cruiser, and climbed into the back. Croft and Stone could make sure the prisoners were secure, and then head out of here for the night. Forty-eight hours in a cell should be enough to get Eden singing like a budgie.

Godspeed settled back into the seat and folded his arms. They would have the location of the tablets within the next two days, he was sure of it. He imagined the call he would make to Helios.

"Yes, I have the location sir. She gave us a little run-around, but once I got her cornered she started to see the benefits of sharing her knowledge."

Helios would say something complementary and then ask about his men.

"Lost in the fight, I'm afraid." Maybe Godspeed should see to that himself. He didn't think Helios would really care. The man had all sorts of other things to worry about. "Your men were pretty good at the brute work. Not much between the ears, though."

A bright light flashed inside the monastery, dragging Godspeed back to the moment. He sat bolt upright and gripped on to the seat. He peered closely through the wind-screen. Roaring orange flames danced from beyond the monastery's open door.

EDEN AND BAXTER stalked down the passage toward the source of the noise. Eden held the lamp low, her hand cupped around the flame to mute its glow as much as possible.

Baxter slid the knife away, for now. Only useful in close combat, it was better that it stayed out of sight until their quarry was within striking distance.

Nearing the end of the passage, Eden slowed. She stepped carefully across the damp cobbles and peered around a corner.

Simeon was slumped against one of the walls. Blood was smeared across his face, and he moaned softly. She felt pity for the old man, before reminding herself that the guy had tried to screw them over. Simeon hadn't cared about their fate one bit.

Two large men stood over him, talking in whispers. Eden recognized them instantly but forced herself to stay concealed for now.

Eden glanced through the open door. An SUV sat about twenty feet away. To get away, they would have to stop the men returning to that vehicle.

The man on the right slid out a gun and levelled it at Simeon. "You have one more chance to survive this," he hissed at the monk. He sounded like the same man she had heard talking in her father's office, the man who had poured fuel throughout the house and then left it to burn. Eden glanced down at the oil lamp in her hand, an idea forming. She stepped back behind the rock wall and checked the lamp's fuel level. It was almost full.

"Yes. I can help you. I will tell you anything you need to know," Simeon muttered.

"We need to know the location of Aloma's Tomb." The man took a step back, his finger curling around the trigger.

"I do not know it right now, but I am sure I can find out. There are records, and I can ask around," Simeon spoke quickly, trying to get the words out before his time was up. "I know many people who can help. I will make it my life's work. Together we will find this." Simeon tried to struggle to his feet.

The man kicked him back down to ground, as though the monk was weightless.

"Not good enough," he barked. "I need proper answers. Not all this nonsense. I don't have time for this."

Eden watched the tendons in the man's forearm tense. His finger depressed the trigger, a hair's breadth from ending the monk's life.

Eden crouched, ready to attack. Baxter watched her closely and prepared himself too. The time to fight or run was now.

"Over here!" Eden shouted, charging from behind the cover of the wall.

She threw the lamp hard as she ran. It spun through the air, the flame dancing and flickering, on the edge of being extinguished altogether.

Both men spun around. The one with the gun fired off a shot without first taking aim. The bullet thronged through the air, ricocheting several times off the hard rock walls.

The lamp continued to twirl through the air toward the men.

The second man drew out a gun too and raised it toward the intruders.

Simeon watched the scene from the ground, his eyes bulging from their sockets. His bloodstained fingers scrabbled across the rock floor.

The lamp collided with one of the men. It crashed into his chest, extinguishing the flame and shattering the glass. The man fanned at the thing, slapping it to the side. The lamp smashed to the floor, skittering uselessly across the rock. Oil from the lamp pooled across the ground. The thug slid a thick hand across his chest. Other than soaking his shirt with oil, the lamp had done no damage.

Charging forward, Eden and Baxter registered the scene. Both men were armed with guns. Between them, they had one knife. That won't stop me giving it a good go, Eden thought. What part these men had played in her father's death, Eden didn't know, but they had been involved. She would stake her life on that.

Eden leapt forward, swinging into a jumping scissor kick before the oil-soaked man could take aim. She swept her right foot through the air, slamming it into the thug's ribs. The man grunted and shifted back a few inches, but remained upright.

Regaining his balance, he took aim at Eden. The gun howled several times, the sound deafening in the enclosed space. The bullets hit nothing but air. Eden jumped into a crouch and attempted to sweep the man's legs out from underneath him. Her shin struck his leg beneath the knee. Pain seared up Eden's leg as though she'd just kicked a tree. The man smiled down at her, tilting his head to the side.

Eden rolled to the side moments before another flurry of hot metal came her way.

On the other side of the cave, Baxter leapt toward the other man. A hail of bullets zinged past him, causing his ears to buzz in protest. He sprang for the gun, looping his left arm around the thug's right, preventing him from taking aim. The man fired another two shots. The recoil sent a vibration through Baxter's shoulder.

Baxter slammed two neat punches into the thug's jaw. His head whipped back twice, and blood oozed from a cut on his cheek. Baxter slid out the knife and plunged it forward.

The thug saw the glinting steel and reacted quickly. A ball of bone and muscle — the man's free fist — struck Baxter's hand with the power of a freight train. The knife flashed downward, scoring a line across the thug's abdomen through his shirt, but doing no actual damage. The thug sneered in pain, and crushed Baxter's hand further. The knife dropped uselessly to the floor.

The man locked eyes with Baxter, his gaze hard. The thug spat, a globule of blood, phlegm, and two teeth splattered down beside them.

Baxter tried to land a punch to the man again, but this time the thug was ready. He slapped Baxter's hand away and then sent a fist hard into Baxter's stomach. The air lurched from his lungs. Baxter tried to keep hold of the thug, but while he was struggling to breathe, the man pulled his arm away and pushed Baxter across the room. Baxter stumbled, finding his footing a moment before tumbling to the ground. The thug, now two feet away, drew the gun up and aimed it squarely between Baxter's eyes.

"Try that again," the thug snarled, leaving no doubt that the next shot would find its mark.

Several feet away, Eden sprang back up into her fighting stance. The thug with the gun was off center now, giving her a few fractions of a second to make her move. She leapt forward into another kick, this one aimed at the gun. Disarming this man would seriously level the playing field.

"Stop what you're doing, or your friend will die."

Eden heard the voice and froze. In all the commotion, she'd not even considered how Baxter was faring with the second man. Her momentary pause was all the thug needed. He took a step backward, out of her reach, and brought the gun to bear. Eden glanced beside her. Baxter stood still, beads of sweat running down his face, looking squarely at the nose of the gun.

"I'm afraid this fun has to end," the man in front of Baxter said, sneering. "We've wasted too much time, and now —"

Eden wasn't listening. Surreptitiously, she watched Simeon lying in the cave's shadowy recesses.

Simeon slipped a box of matches from deep within the folds of his tunic.

Eden glanced at Baxter. He too watched the monk.

The thug continued speaking. He was in no rush to finish the job. Eden assumed that, right now, she and Baxter were more valuable to him alive.

Simeon carefully pushed open the box of matches, his hands shaking. Concentration knitted his brow.

Eden willed the monk to hurry up.

Simeon struck the match against the side of the box. The small flame flared, lighting his bloodstained face in a soft glow. Simeon held the match upside down, letting the flame grow. When the whole match was consumed with fire, he flicked the match across the cave.

For a few moments nothing happened, and then bright

light flooded the cave. The pool of flammable oil which had spilled from the lamp flared into a ball of fire. The flames ran across the floor, consuming half the space. Thick black smoke engulfed the room. The flames flared up and across the oil-soaked clothes of the thug who had been struck by the lamp. The man wailed and dropped the gun. He slapped at the flames with a hand. Within half a second his body was consumed by fire.

Eden launched towards the thug, now distracted by his burning friend, and landed a fist on the side of the neck. It connected just where she'd intended, and the big man crumpled to the floor. He wouldn't be out for long, but half a minute should be enough.

The flames roared higher, filling at least half of the cave. The pounding noise of combustion filled Eden's ears. She squinted through the smoke and locked eyes with Simeon, who now cowered right at the back of the cave.

Eden darted across the cave, side stepping the flames. She helped the monk to his feet and together they hustled towards the door. The guy had set them up, and then had saved their lives. Fair trade.

36

THREE-QUARTERS OF A MILE AWAY, a Jeep Wrangler pulled up beside a dust-covered Volvo. The Jeep crunched to a stop, almost obscured by an enormous pile of stone. Under the hot midday sun, the valley was deserted. Any visitors to the region or workers in the nearby farms would be sheltering for at least the next two hours.

The Jeep's door swung open, and Athena climbed out. Used to deployment across the globe, the wall of heat didn't faze her. An experienced operative, Athena had worked in some of the most inhospitable conditions Mother Earth could muster.

Athena assessed the scene. A mile further up the gravel path, a cloud of smoke drifted skyward. Whatever Helios' other man was up to, he wasn't being subtle. Athena, on the other hand, had subtlety down to a fine art.

She padded across to the light blue Volvo 114. The car was common on the roads of Lebanon, and as such made a good choice for anyone looking to remain unseen.

Reaching the car, she dipped into a crouch. Her mission

today was a simple one. She moved in close to one of the front wheels, reached around the wheel and found the point where the brake cable attached to the pads. She removed a small electronic device from her pocket and fastened it to the cable. It took her a further two minutes to repeat the process three more times.

Athena stood and surveyed the Volvo. It looked just as it had when she'd arrived. She brushed the dust from hers knees and jogged across to the waiting Jeep.

She started the engine and powered off in the direction from which she'd come, a cloud of dust billowing up behind the Jeep's thick tires. With the road here only leading in one direction, she would see the Volvo and its occupants very soon.

GODSPEED WATCHED, frozen in the back seat of the car. He couldn't believe what he saw. A few seconds after the flickering flames roared inside the monastery, Eden and Baxter ran out through the open door. The pair darted across the courtyard and then sprinted hard down the access road. It looked as though they wanted to put as much distance between the monastery and themselves as possible.

Godspeed glanced at the keys dangling in the Toyota's ignition. Without even considering whether his men were alive or injured, he wondered whether he should give chase. He could easily catch up with them in the Toyota. But then, when he had caught up with them, what would he do? They were supposed to think he'd died several days ago. At some point they would find out the truth, but was this the right moment? He didn't know for sure.

He watched them descending the steep road for several seconds, his mind flitting between options. His lips twisted together in thought and his hands clenched in the seats beside him. This whole plan felt as though it were falling apart at the seams. Godspeed exhaled slowly. Each time he felt as though he were getting ahead, getting closer to the prize money offered, something happened, and he was back to square one.

The phone in his hand buzzed. Godspeed glanced down at it. An unrecognized number appeared on the screen.

Godspeed's stomach tensed. There was only one person this could be. Helios. He would have to answer it. If Helios called, you answered. That was the only way.

Godspeed watched Eden and Baxter disappear around the first bend and wondered how Helios could always call at the worst possible time. Godspeed exhaled heavily, ran a hand across his face, and then thumbed the answer button.

"It sounds like things are getting away from you." The voice Godspeed was really starting to dislike boomed from the speaker. He gritted his teeth. "Are you sure you're still up for the job?"

"I've got a handle on it," Godspeed growled, his gaze narrowed toward the direction in which Eden and Baxter had disappeared.

Godspeed looked up at the monastery as the pair of thugs appeared at the door. One of them, his clothes smoking and skin burned, hobbled toward the Toyota. The other helped his colleague. Godspeed shook his head slowly, watching the men.

"That's not what it looks like to me," Helios replied.

Godspeed shuddered at the words. Did Helios have someone watching them? He always seemed at least one step ahead. Godspeed turned and looked around the valley. He saw no one.

"You have forty-eight hours, Godspeed," Helios barked.

"Find me this tomb, or the deal is off, and I'll deal with you myself." The line went dead.

37

EDEN AND BAXTER sprinted back toward the Volvo. The temperature in the valley had risen in the last hour, causing heat currents to dance through the still afternoon air. Sunlight radiated off the Volvo's scratched body work.

Panting and covered in sweat, Baxter reached the driver's side and swung the door open. Heat poured from the vehicle. Even the plastic door handle was too hot to use comfortably. He winced and glanced down at his hand, then caught sight of Eden smirking at him.

"That'll be the least of your worries," Eden said, yanking open the passenger door. She swept her hand across her face and flicked off the sweat.

"We need to get moving," Baxter said, looking back up the gravel track toward the monastery. The building was out of sight now, but a wispy column of smoke snaked into the sky.

Eden nodded. "The fire will slow them down, but it won't stop them. I'm getting to know these two now. They don't give up."

Baxter went to climb into the driver's seat.

"I'll drive," Eden said, moving around the car.

"Like you said, there's no time," Baxter stated, sliding into the driver's seat. He started the engine and put the fans on full. The Volvo's air conditioning system had packed up many years ago.

Eden scowled and dropped into the passenger seat. She reminded herself that when this was over and done with, she could go back to being totally independent. She didn't need Baxter, but right now he was useful to have around. Two pairs of eyes were better than one, and he had proved very capable.

Baxter crunched the Volvo into gear and accelerated down the track, spraying dust and gravel in its wake. He shifted up a gear. The car slid from side to side on the narrow trail.

"Calm down," Eden said, shooting him a look. "If we come off the road, we might as well hold a welcome party for them."

Baxter grunted and reduced his pressure on the gas.

Eden glanced behind them. No one was following them for now. She turned her gaze back to Baxter. His eyes moved with practiced ease from the road to the rearview mirror. The Volvo rumbled and bumped across unforgiving potholes.

Eden twisted her neck and stretched out her arms. Her body ached after the escapades of the last few days. What was worse than the physical pains of the search, though, were the doubts that constantly swarmed through her mind. There were thousands of tombs spread across the Lebanese countryside. The more she thought about it, the more Eden realized they could traipse around the country for months, or even years, without anything jogging her memory. They were clutching at straws in the most frustrating way. But, right now, clutching at straws was the only thing they had.

"We've got company," Baxter muttered, his voice dragging Eden back into the present. He peered in the rearview mirror.

Eden spun around and looked at the road behind them. Sure enough, the black Toyota sped down the slope from the monastery. Eden watched the vehicle slide around a corner and accelerate. She gripped the seat hard. These guys were really starting to get on her nerves.

Baxter accelerated and the Volvo fishtailed from one side of the track to the other. He flung the wheel hard to the right just in time to stop them leaving the track altogether.

"We can't outrun them in this," Eden said. "We'll need to think of something else." Eden fished her phone from the car's central console and pulled up a map of the surrounding area.

The main road, a single strip of tarmac running in both directions, appeared up ahead. Baxter floored the accelerator. The Volvo growled, bumped up on to the asphalt and, the tires now finding grip, accelerated hard.

Eden glanced through the rear window again. Despite its superior handling on the unpaved road, the Toyota was still some way behind.

"At this pace, they'll be on us in a few minutes," Eden mumbled, scrutinizing the map on her phone. "We can't outrun them, but we could get out of their way."

They slalomed around two tight bends as the road began to climb. Baxter handled the Volvo with ease now on the open road.

Verdant rows of vines flashed past on both sides of the road. Eden looked out at the neat and carefully maintained lines. The change in the landscape in less than a hundred miles surprised her. It seemed unfair that people here were surrounded by luscious fields where fruit and vegetables grew with ease, while others lived in the arid desert landscape of the mountain regions.

"There's a small vineyard about half a mile up on the left," Eden said, turning her attention back to her phone. "It looks like they've got a couple of barns, that sort of thing. If we get off the road in time, we might be able to hide out there."

"Roger that," Baxter barked, his focus never leaving the road ahead. The Volvo rattled and shook as the speed continued to climb.

"Just there," Eden said, pointing through the windscreen. A hundred feet ahead a sign advertised St Charbel's Vineyard. Two large trees overshadowed the track leading up to the vineyard.

Eden spun around and checked the road behind them. The Toyota had yet to appear around the bend. She muttered to herself, gripped the seat, and wished she was driving. Not doing anything, not being in control, was the hardest part.

Baxter, his knuckles whitening on the steering wheel, waited until they were almost upon the turning, then stamped on the brake and spun the wheel. The Volvo shuddered into a skid, sliding hard across the road.

Eden gripped onto the seat, the muscles in her arms and legs tensing.

The Volvo spun, turning the surrounding farmland into a blur through the windscreen. Finally, the tires found their purchase, and the car lurched forward. Baxter spun the steering wheel and eased off the brake. The Volvo bounced from the asphalt and on to another grit-covered farm track.

They rattled down the track for a hundred feet and

pulled between a collection of buildings. Two large barns occupied one side of the yard, and on the other, several tractors and other farm machines waited.

Baxter reversed the Volvo out of sight behind the barn.

Eden jumped out of the car before it had even stopped moving. She ran across to the barn and peered around the wall. The cloud of dust they had aggravated on their way up the access road drifted slowly back toward the ground. From the road, less than a hundred feet away, they would be completely obscured.

Baxter killed the engine and climbed out too. He padded to the barn's far wall and looked out beside Eden.

Eden peered through the gap left by a missing board in the barn's wall. Giant barrels were stacked from the ground to the roof. She turned back and watched the road, her heart thumping hard. She surveyed the scene, looking for their best means of escape should the Toyota head their way. Splitting up and running between the trees, she decided, would be their only option. At least that way the men would have to pursue on foot.

The vineyard around them was silent, outside work having stopped for the hottest part of the day.

Somewhere up the hillside a bird cawed. To Eden, hiding behind the wall of the barn, it sounded like a warning.

Then the sound of an engine reverberated through the silence. The growling grew louder as the vehicle reached the top of the hill. Then, the engine began to slow.

38

ARCHIBALD GODSPEED CRINKLED his nose as though the action would stop him smelling the air inside the Toyota. Since Croft and Stone had climbed back into the car, Godspeed couldn't stop thinking about the strange scent. It was an unusual mix of lighter fluid and barbequed meat.

Godspeed, perched in the back of the vehicle, looked from Croft to Stone, and back again. How it had transpired that a beaten-up old clergyman, and a pair of inexperienced treasure hunters, had managed to get the jump on them, Godspeed couldn't figure out. If these really were the best men Helios had at his disposal, then The Council needed to up their recruitment game.

Croft dug the small first aid kit out of the glove box and started to clean up one of his many burns. He would need more sophisticated treatment than that... starting with a shower, Godspeed thought.

They reached the main road and Stone bumped the Toyota up on to the asphalt and swung the wheel to the left. The SUV accelerated evenly on the smooth road and within a few moments they were whizzing past farmland on both sides.

Leaning back into the seat, Godspeed reflected on what Helios had said. The conversation had riled him. Helios had spoken to him as though he were over here on holiday, not crammed in the back of an SUV tearing around the country with a pair of knock-off Action Men.

Stone accelerated again as the road straightened out for a couple of miles. Godspeed peered out through the windscreen, leaning forward on his knees. The road in front of them was clear of traffic in both directions.

"That's strange. They were not more than a mile ahead of us." Godspeed searched the road for any sign of the Volvo.

"They must have stepped on it as soon as they got to the road," Stone replied, his tone of voice leaving no doubt that he didn't appreciate Godspeed's interruptions.

"In that old rust-bucket? No way."

Stone's one working eye narrowed on Godspeed in the rearview mirror.

"We saw them turn left, so they must have just got a —"

"Wait, stop!" Godspeed shouted, crashing his hand down on the Toyota's central console.

Croft and Stone exchanged a glance. Stone sighed and reluctantly slowed the SUV. They crunched to a stop.

"Back up, back up," Godspeed yelled.

"Sir, this really isn't —"

"Just do it!" Godspeed's face took on the same tint as Croft's burned skin.

Stone clicked the SUV into reverse and pulled them back a hundred yards.

"There, look!" Godspeed pointed wildly at the asphalt in front of the SUV. Sure enough, a pair of long rubber skids streaked down the road. The skids ceased just before a small farm track.

"Those marks look fresh. They drove up here at high speed to get away from us and then turned into that track."

Croft and Stone exchanged another glance.

"If they didn't, this will cost us time," Croft said, his voice little more than a grumble.

"Just do what you're told," Godspeed shouted. "Turn up that track now. We need to finish this thing."

EDEN LISTENED CLOSELY. The sound of the approaching engine dimmed almost beneath audible levels.

She gripped the wall of the barn tightly. The muscles in her arms and legs tensed, ready for fight or flight.

Then, slowly at first, almost stealthily, the nose of the black SUV crept into view.

Eden darted backward, out of sight, crashing into Baxter.

The engine growled again.

Eden's pulse vibrated in her throat. Slowly, carefully, she leaned out around the edge of the building.

Her stomach whirled when she registered what was happening. The Toyota turned toward the vineyard, then bumped down from the asphalt and shuddered down the rutted track toward them.

"I thought they would go straight past," Eden hissed, almost apologetically.

The Toyota bounced closer down the lane.

"Maybe that only works with stupid bad guys in the movies," Baxter muttered.

The track leveled out on the approach to the yard and the Toyota picked up speed.

Eden quickly analyzed the scene. Grape vines led away

from the farm buildings in both directions. Although the Toyota blocked their only means of escape in the car, that didn't mean they were caught yet.

"There are only two of them, right?" Eden asked.

Baxter nodded.

"We need to draw them out separately, lose them amongst the vines and then circle back this way. Make sure they split up. If we can be back here before they realize what's going on, we'll just drive away."

"But what if they —" Baxter tried to argue, but Eden darted from their hiding place and out into the yard.

The SUV crunched to a stop beside the large barn doors as the driver saw Eden. The man threw open the door and leapt to his feet. He shouted, and groped for his weapon, but Eden charged away toward the first row of vines. The man started after Eden in something of a panic. He knew that once she was out of sight amid the vines, she would be difficult to find again.

Still concealed behind the barn, Baxter shook his head slowly. Whilst Eden's plan was predictable, it may just work. Simple was good, right? Baxter watched Eden disappear behind the first row of vines and then ran out into the yard.

The second man, his burned skin now blistering into painful welts, was less quick on his feet. He struggled painfully from the passenger seat and lumbered after Baxter.

Baxter turned and led the man in the opposite direction.

Running in an all-out sprint between the vines, Eden glanced behind her. In full bloom, the vines were thick, leaving a clear path of just two feet between them. Branches whipped at Eden's face as she ran. The vines were dense, too, obscuring the parallel rows to each side. As Eden had hoped, it was the perfect place to get lost.

The thug, now almost fifty feet behind, pounded hard up the gentle incline. He was gaining on Eden easily. Eden suspected he had some kind of elite military training, with days and days of torturous running. She probably wouldn't be able to outrun him, but then again, she didn't need to.

Eden put on a burst of energy, increasing the distance between them, and then shot a look over her shoulder. The man ran with his gun loosely gripped in his hand. He hadn't attempted a shot yet. Eden suspected he wasn't there to kill her. Not before he found out the location of the tomb, at least.

Eden reached a lane climbing up the hill and darted to the left. For now, she was out of sight. She sprinted up the hill as fast as she could, then stopped. Her heart beating savagely hard, and sweat pouring, she turned to face her pursuer. A moment later, the man appeared from the vines. He saw Eden and slid to a stop. A giant bead of sweat ran down his forehead. Before the man could raise his gun, Eden darted to the right and between the vines again.

Eden counted out five steps and then dropped to the ground. Pulling her hands in tight, she rolled beneath the vines. Branches clawed at her face, but she forced herself through, emerging in the row further down the hill.

She repeated the process again, pulling herself under another two rows of the vines. Eden rose into a crouch and ducked in close behind a particularly bushy part of the plant. Purple grapes hung like fists, ready for picking.

Just a few feet away she heard the man's lumbering footsteps. She listened closely, not even daring to breathe. The footsteps thundered past Eden a few feet away on the other side of the vines.

She waited a few moments as the man continued to run.

Then, silently dusting herself off, she turned and headed in the opposite direction.

Reaching the lane, she peered around the edge and into the next row. Fifty feet away, the thug ran in the wrong direction. Soon enough he would realize his mistake, but by then she would be on the other side of the vineyard.

Baxter led his pursuer between the vines in the opposite direction to which Eden had disappeared. He ran hard for the first two hundred feet and then glanced over his shoulder. His pursuer was clearly struggling with the pain of his burns and was already losing ground. The skin on one side of the man's face was red-raw. The clothes across his chest were burned through and the skin beneath, puffy and blistered.

The snap of gun tore through the air, sending a barrage of hot metal in Baxter's direction. Baxter dropped to the ground as the bullets thumped through the air just an inch above him. It was clear this man didn't care whether Baxter lived or died. But then again, Baxter didn't know where the tomb was. To these men, he was expendable.

The thug struggled up the incline a hundred feet behind Baxter. Fortunately, too far for an accurate shot, Baxter thought, climbing to his feet and sprinting on. Two more rounds sailed wildly past him.

Baxter reached a lane which cut diagonally through the vineyard. He ducked out of sight and considered his options. Another row of vines led down a gentle slope ahead of him. The lane rose steeply to the right and dropped away to the left. His pursuer was now less than fifty feet away but struggling with the incline.

Further up the lane sat a tractor, as though abandoned when the vineyard workers got too hot. Another bullet sailed his way as Baxter sprinted toward the machine. The thing must have been fifty years old, its hood rusted and blistered from several decades of good service. Baxter raced to the rear of the tractor, putting the machine between himself and his assailant. He looked inside a small trailer, attached to the tractor's towbar. The trailer contained two large coils of wire, used to secure the vines, as well as a selection of tools. Although there was nothing that he could reasonably use as a weapon, an idea formed in Baxter's mind. He seized one of the wire coils and tested it between his hands. It was strong yet flexible.

Another shot hammered through the air, ricocheting off the tractor and thumping away amid the vines. Baxter ducked behind the vehicle.

His pursuer stepped out from between the vines, gun raised. He took a step toward the tractor, scanning the vehicle for the shot he needed.

Hidden behind the trailer, Baxter worked quickly. He looped and then secured one end of the wire around a hook on the back of the tractor. Then, using the other end, he made a large noose.

"There's nowhere for you to go," came his pursuer's voice.

Baxter peered out from behind the trailer. The man had lumbered up the slope and was now less than fifty feet away. Baxter suspected the man just wanted to get this job done and get his injuries seen to.

"Okay, you've got me," Baxter called out, holding the wire noose behind his back. "Don't shoot, I'm coming out."

The man straightened up, attempting to stop his hands shaking. Baxter noticed the man's trigger finger tighten, ready to put a bullet in him as soon as possible.

Swallowing hard, his throat dry from the heat and the exertion, Baxter stepped out from behind the trailer.

"I'm not armed," Baxter said, taking two steps forward. "Don't shoot me. I can tell you where the tomb is."

The man didn't move. Baxter suspected the man had instructions to leave him with numerous bullet holes as soon as possible. Baxter took another step forward. He glanced at the tractor and saw exactly what he was looking for. Baxter jumped in behind the tractor and seized the brake lever. He pushed the button and forced the lever downward.

The man fired a pair of rapid shots. One clanged into the tractor's grill and another flew wide.

Slowly at first, the tractor rolled forward. Sheltering behind the wheel arch, Baxter gave the thing a shove. The tractor picked up speed, rattling down the rutted track. Still walking behind the wheel arch, Baxter watched the man's confused expression morph into one of amusement as he easily stepped out of the path of the slow-moving machine.

Baxter put his back against the vehicle and shoved it again. It was rolling at a walking pace now but accelerating with every inch of movement

"Nice try," the thug said, taking another step back out of the way of the moving vehicle.

Using the man's focus on the moving tractor as a distraction, Baxter crossed behind the trailer and darted out of sight two rows up the hill from the man. The assassin continued to aim his gun at the tractor, growing more frustrated that he couldn't get a clean shot at his quarry.

The tractor rumbled past the thug, picking up speed. Baxter leapt out from between the rows, now almost behind the thug. He threw the wire noose across the man's shoulders, forcing his arms to his sides. Then he pulled the cable tight and looped it around one more time. As the wire pulled taut behind the lumbering vehicle, Baxter watched the man's eyes bulge wide. He fired off several shots in panic, each one thumping into the dirt.

The tractor sped up now, rumbling over the bumpy ground. The wire tightened more around the man. His face contorted into a mask of shock, fear, and confusion. The thug ran a few paces after the tractor to stay on his feet, then fell over and bumped heavily down the track.

"Bye," Baxter shouted, raising a hand in a wave. He watched the brute slide down the hill in a cloud of dust for several seconds, before turning back toward the yard.

Pacing back between the vines, Baxter heard another noise above the now distant rumbling of the tractor. He slid his phone from his pocket and stared in unbridled shock at the screen. Eventually shaking himself into action, he held the phone to his ear.

39

EDEN CUT QUICKLY BACK between the vines, doubts growing in her mind. Although she'd escaped the thug, he was still nearby. Right now, they needed to get back to the Volvo and put some serious distance between them.

Maybe, Eden thought, she should have found a way to stop him following them permanently. Maybe she should simply have killed the man. She was sure she could physically do it, but had it really come to that? Was she really a cold-hearted killer?

What would her father do? Eden wondered. She suddenly froze. A chill ran through her body. She knew there were parts of her father's life that she didn't yet understand, but he wouldn't kill anyone. Would he? Two weeks ago, she would have answered with an ironclad no. Right now she didn't feel so sure.

She shook herself back into the present and paced between the vines. That was the problem when things were personal. Everything shook you down to the roots. Nothing seemed certain anymore.

Eden reached another track. She approached carefully and

looked both ways. Vines stretched in uniform lines, running in both directions. Luscious fistfuls of purple grapes hung ripe and low. Nothing seemed out of place. Eden paused, listening for the approaching thud of footsteps. Other than the gentle breeze whistling through the vines, everything was silent.

Then, carrying ethereally on the air, she heard a voice. A man's voice. Eden ducked into a crouch, ready to fight or run, and listened. From this distance, she couldn't make out the words, but it sounded as though the conversation was one sided. As though he was talking on the phone.

Eden hurried silently toward the noise. She padded across the track and ran on her tiptoes between the vines opposite.

The voice came again. It was closer now.

"Yes sir, understood," came the voice.

Eden froze, listening. A few seconds of silence followed, and then footsteps thudded away. Eden ducked down and, as silently as she could, pushed herself beneath the vines. Near the ground, the leaves were thinner and without too much effort, she peered out into the neighboring row.

Eden inhaled, almost gasping. She forced a hand against her mouth to stop any sounds coming out.

Baxter paced back toward the vineyard's buildings. He pushed a small phone, which Eden had never seen before, into his back pocket. At the end of the row, Baxter paused and looked around as though expecting someone to greet him, then he set off down the hill toward the waiting Volvo.

Eden struggled back through the vines and stood up. She scowled, confusion welling through her. Why would Baxter have a secret phone? What was it he wasn't telling her?

She felt the tectonic plates of recent events shift beneath

her feet again. She rubbed her hands together, thinking. There were forces at work here which Eden didn't yet understand.

She walked slowly back toward the Volvo, her thoughts running at a hundred miles an hour. She could confront Baxter about the call, but that would give him the opportunity to lie. Right now, she thought, she could use this as an advantage.

Ultimately, it didn't matter if she trusted him or not. Right now, they were working toward the same thing, so it made sense to do it together. Eden remembered a case a few months back when she'd found herself working alongside the infamous Adriana Villa. In the end, Eden's not trusting of Adriana had gotten them out of a sticky spot with a Parisian police inspector.

Eden turned down the lane and jogged in the direction of the yard. Just because she was going along with him didn't mean she couldn't make her own plans.

Baxter started the Volvo as Eden approached.

"How did you get on?" he asked, as Eden swung open the door and climbed in beside him.

"I sent him on a wild goose chase. You?" Eden scrutinized Baxter for any sign of dishonestly.

"Yeah, I had to let him go," Baxter said, almost grinning. "Poor guy." Baxter swung the wheel and pulled out into the yard.

Eden glanced back at the Toyota sitting in front of the barn.

"Hold on," Eden said, swinging open the door again. Before Baxter could argue, she jumped out and ran across to the barn. She pulled open the side door and slipped inside. As she'd seen through the crack in the wall, giant barrels of wine were stacked right up to the ceiling. There were about twenty in each stack.

Grinning to herself, Eden crossed to the stack of barrels on the far side.

Eden was certain of one thing now; if she didn't start playing dirty, she wouldn't get to the bottom of this. People were getting hurt here, there was no getting away from that. Eden just needed to make sure she wasn't one of them.

Eden crouched down and heaved out one of the wooden struts holding the bottom barrel in place. The barrels wobbled for a moment, as though wondering whether or not to fall. Eden stepped forward and pulled out the second strut. Again, the barrels wobbled and settled back into a precarious balance. She frowned and paced to the far end of the stacked barrels. She stood behind the stack and shoved. The giant pile of wood and wine groaned and wobbled. Eden heaved again, shoving the pile as hard as she could. An ear-splitting roar echoed through the barn, shaking the wooden walls. Dust fell from the ceiling, and the ground beneath Eden's feet shook.

The barrels groaned and slipped forward, slowly at first. The first barrel hammered to the ground, followed by a second. Then the stack lost all its structural integrity. The barrels started tumbling forward, bursting through the vast barn door. Light streamed in, cutting a beam through the dancing dust. More barrels rumbled and fell, tumbling over each other like a spilt bag of giant marbles.

Eden stood back and watched the barrels tumble out into the yard, cracking and spilling their contents all over the SUV.

She brushed her hands together and strode outside, reached the waiting Volvo, and turned. The Toyota now sat beneath a pile of broken wood, with several barrels still balanced on top.

"Sorry," Eden said, slipping back into the passenger seat, "I just needed to finish something."

Baxter shot Eden a glance and powered the Volvo back toward the main road.

40

Archibald Godspeed ducked into the rear footwell of the Toyota, peering carefully out through the window. Eden and Baxter ran across the yard, leapt into the Volvo, and then started back in the direction of the road.

Godspeed muttered to himself. Helios had told him that Croft and Stone were the best; so far they'd failed at every turn. If they never found these blasted tablets, it was all Croft and Stone's fault. If Helios sent Godspeed down for this, he was sure as anything taking those two useless mounds of muscle with him.

Godspeed clenched his fists and instinctively looked around the vehicle for his weapon. He longed to go out there and riddle Eden and Baxter with bullets.

But then again, Godspeed thought, exhaling and trying to ease his frustration, that wouldn't get him any closer to the tomb. That girl was most likely the only person on the planet who knew where the tablets were. Godspeed reminded himself that the tablets were his ticket back to fame and fortune. With the money Helios was offering, Godspeed could live the life he deserved, and then some. No more scrabbling around in the dust, as he felt he had been doing for the last decade.

Godspeed peered at Eden and Baxter as the Volvo bounced past him. From where he cowered, ensuring he stayed out of sight, it looked as though they were smiling. Godspeed sneered. The time would soon come for him to wipe away those smiles forever. As soon as they had sight of the tomb, he would leap out and claim the discovery for himself. It was a simple strategy, but one in which he trusted implicitly, frustrating though it was.

"He who laughs last, laughs longest," Godspeed hissed, the idiom taking on a new and sinister meaning.

Twenty feet down the track, the Volvo screeched to a stop.

Godspeed watched closely, his brow twisted in confusion.

A door swung open, and Eden jumped out. She turned and ran back toward the SUV. Godspeed's pulse quickened and his eyes bulged. If she discovered him hiding, the plan would be forever ruined. She would give up now, never finding the tablets. Or, perhaps, Godspeed would just have to kill her right there, right then. He could tell Helios it was an accident, or that he had nothing to do with it.

Godspeed thought about this for a moment, discounting it almost immediately. No riches lay that way.

Godspeed slid even lower into the footwell as Eden approached the Toyota. He readied himself to leap forward and grab the gun he knew was stored in the glove box. He could put a bullet or two between those pretty eyes before she even knew it was him.

Eden reached the rear of the Toyota, but didn't stop. She ran straight past the vehicle without so much as a glance inside.

Godspeed let his breath out slowly.

Eden ran up to the barn, which towered over the Toyota. She heaved open the door and disappeared inside.

"What's she up to?" Godspeed muttered. He had expected them to make a run for it straight away.

A crash echoed from inside the barn, shaking the decrepit structure. The noise was quickly followed by another, even greater crash. This time, the vast doors of the barn swung open.

Godspeed watched, frozen in position.

Several large barrels, free of their supports, rolled out of the barn, across the yard, and smashed into the side of the Toyota.

Hands covering his face, Godspeed ducked a moment before the first of the barrels collided with the side of the vehicle. Windows shattered and cracked, scattering shards of glass throughout the vehicle. One of the barrels split apart, covering the vehicle in wine, both inside and out.

More barrels followed, rolling across the roof, shattering glass, and bending the vehicle out of shape. The Toyota shook as it weathered the impacts.

Finally, when the booming collisions had stopped, Godspeed peered out to see Eden running back toward the Volvo. She leapt in and the car headed off in the direction of the main road.

Godspeed looked around at the Toyota; several windows had broken, and the inside of the car was slick with wine. He tried to open the door, but the impact had twisted it out of commission.

He glanced at himself in the rearview mirror. Wine dripped across his face. He scowled again and thought about how much he would enjoy killing Eden Black.

41

EDEN AND BAXTER CRUISED ALONG, the Volvo growling reluctantly. After a few miles they slowed through a small village. A handful of buildings crowded beside the road. From the passenger seat, Eden glanced into a small restaurant. The tables were now filling up for the evening. Clouds of smoke rose industriously from the cookers. Eden's stomach rumbled so loud that she assumed Baxter must have heard. It had been six hours since they'd eaten. A few miles further on, the town of Tannourine Al Faouqa offered their best chance of finding a comfortable bed for the night.

Eden turned and scrutinized the road behind them. Beyond the cloud of dust kicked up by the Volvo, the road was clear. Her worries momentarily allayed, she turned back and looked at the road extending out in front of them, curving out of sight.

"They won't come after us again tonight," Baxter said, obviously trying to reassure Eden.

"Maybe, although a few days ago we didn't think they would come after us at all." Eden studied Baxter's expression from the corner of her eye. He stared ahead, almost nervously.

A tanker chugged out into the road two hundred feet ahead. It turned and crawled along in front of them, coughing out clouds of thick black smoke.

"They're getting desperate," Baxter said, finally. "That must mean we're close."

"They think we're close," Eden corrected. "We don't even really know who they are."

Baxter put his foot on the brake to ease in behind the tanker. The brake pedal sunk down to the floor. Something clunked from the Volvo's engine. That wasn't unusual. Each time the Volvo started it was a small miracle.

Baxter took his foot off the brake and then applied it again.

"Is there a problem?" Eden said, watching Baxter's movement. She glanced from the tanker ahead to the speedometer on the dash. The Volvo hadn't slowed down. In fact, it picked up speed as the road stepped down toward the town.

A knot of fear tightened in Eden's chest.

"The brakes," Baxter said urgently. "The brakes aren't working."

Eden sat up straight and looked around, her hands uselessly gripping the dashboard. Panic surged in her chest. She caught her breath and focused.

Baxter pushed the brake pedal again. Something crunched within the Volvo's guts. The car didn't slow.

Eden's eyes bulged. She glanced around, trying to read the situation.

The tanker was less than a hundred feet ahead now. Eden could clearly see the blistered metal. The tanker moved up a gear, sending another cloud of smoke belching into the sky.

The gradient of the hill increased, and the Volvo picked up speed. The car rattled furiously as they sped down the rutted concrete.

Baxter gripped the wheel and forced himself to focus. He took his foot from the brake completely and then applied it again. The pedal moved, crunching as it usually did, but nothing happened. He tried twice more. Nothing made a difference.

Eden tried pulling up the handbrake, yanking the flimsy handle skyward as aggressively as she could. The Volvo continued to accelerate.

Eden glanced at the dashboard. They'd just passed fifty miles per hour and the needle continued to rise.

Baxter gripped the steering wheel even harder. The muscles in his forearms stood out. His wide eyes searched the roadside.

Eden took a deep breath, tasting the tanker's exhaust fumes, sucked in through the vents. A long bead of sweat ran down the back of her neck.

Baxter gripped the wheel and swung them out into the oncoming lane. At this speed, he had to heave the wheel, one hand over the other. If he could overtake the tanker, then at least they would have more time to figure out how to stop. The hulking shape of another truck lumbering up the hill came into view. The truck sounded its horn, a deep growling warning to get out of the way.

Baxter gritted his teeth and pulled back in behind the tanker. The great rusty rear of the vehicle filled the windshield now, less than fifty feet away. Liquid seeped from the tanker, marking a slick line on the road.

The Volvo shuddered, rattling hard, shaking Eden to the

bones. She gripped on to the seat, readying herself for the inevitable impact.

Baxter clutched the wheel as tightly as he could, struggling to keep them on a direct course. The car whipped from right to left. The color drained from Baxter's knuckles.

Thirty feet ahead, grit sprayed up from the tanker's heavy tires and spattered across the Volvo's windscreen, tapping morse code at an impossible speed.

Baxter swung the Volvo one way, and then the other, looking for options. The rear of the tanker loomed ever closer, towering over them now.

Eden saw a large mound of something, gravel, or dirt maybe, at the side of the road. An idea formed. "That way," she shouted, pointing at the pile.

Dust covered the windscreen now. The deep, sonorous blast of the tanker's horn filled her mind.

The idea was dangerous, but with the tanker just fifteen feet away, it was the only chance they had.

Seeing the mound too, Baxter swung hard on the wheel. Tendons stood out on his arms and neck, like steel cables beneath his skin.

The Volvo wobbled, as though destined to continue on its path. And then, just as the tanker's vast shape filled the entire windscreen, the Volvo leapt from the road.

For what felt like several seconds — although in reality it was less than one — the Volvo flew through the air. Baxter held the wheel straight, locked on their forward course.

Eden held on tight in the passenger seat, powerless.

Baxter hammered the horn with his left hand. Two people jumped out of the way, just in time.

The old car crunched down onto the uneven ground, sending shudders through Eden's whole body. Baxter ducked, his head bouncing off the roof.

Baxter struggled painfully to keep the car going in a straight line. He aimed it, knuckles shaking on the wheel, at the mound they'd glimpsed from the road.

Thirty feet ahead lay the giant pile of gravel. A group of men stood nearby, shovels now resting on the ground beside them. A tractor and trailer idled nearby.

Baxter pounded the horn again, the feeble bark almost drowned out by the shuddering Volvo as it smashed across the uneven ground.

The men noticed the careering Volvo at the last second and dashed for cover. The Volvo trembled on, panels flapping open and metal crunching.

The pile of gravel loomed closer. Eden's mouth set into a snarl. They needed to hit the gravel straight on.

Baxter clenched his teeth, struggling to hold the careening car on an even keel.

Eden glanced beyond the pile. The land descended into the patchwork of fields.

Baxter twisted the wheel slowly. The tires screamed, kicking up giant clouds of dust and sending torrents of grit one way and then the other.

The workers turned, tracking the Volvo, their eyes wide.

The gravel loomed high above them. The sky disappeared, blocked out by the mound.

42

EDEN, waiting for the impact, clamped her eyes shut. A noise shook through them, shuddering the car as though the ground was falling away. The sound crunched, then boomed, then bellowed against Eden's eardrums. The Volvo decelerated impossibly hard, forcing Eden and Baxter against their seatbelts. Eden's head and arms whipped forward, almost tearing her muscles. Then it felt as though they were thrown backward. The sound drifted away. Eden's ears buzzed.

Eden opened her eyes slowly. She flexed her muscles, feeling for areas of pain. The seatbelt dug in hard across her chest. Other than that, she was fine.

She turned her attention to her surroundings. The first thing she noticed was that the Volvo lay in almost-total darkness. The second, arriving more slowly, was the smell. Spending much of her time in the countryside, Eden knew the aroma. It wasn't often this strong, though. As her eyes adjusted to the crack of light seeping in through the rear windscreen, Eden understood why. She had never before been completely submerged in the stuff. She saw it pressed against the windows all around the car, its strange, tangy smell seeping through the vents. Cow dung.

Eden exhaled slowly for several seconds, letting the relief and tension flow from her body. Moments ago, she had been considering the pain of the collision with the tanker. Cow dung was far preferable to that.

"That was close," Baxter whispered from the seat beside her. He unclipped his seatbelt and stretched.

Then, the Volvo shuddered backward. Eden turned and tried to see through the dirt-covered rear windscreen. The car shifted back again, this time a few feet. Dung fell from the rear windows and the evening light streamed in.

Eden could see through the back now. The Volvo had been hitched up to a tractor. The tractor engine grumbled, and the Volvo slid another two feet back. More dung fell from the windows. Eden noticed a crowd of people standing around, observing the strange spectacle. The tractor's engine growled again, and the Volvo juddered backward, free of the dung.

A man rushed forward and pulled open the passenger door. Speaking in a language Eden didn't understand, he helped her stagger to her feet.

"I'm sorry," Eden said, smiling, "do you speak English?"

The man turned back to the waiting crowd. He shouted several commands, and a young woman was brought forward. The woman had long, flowing black hair and large almond-colored eyes. Eden guessed she was in her mid-twenties.

Another man helped Baxter out of the driver's seat.

"My uncle worry, you okay?" the woman said, slowly.

Eden nodded, further relief washing through her. "The brakes, they wouldn't work on the hill."

The woman tilted her head. "Sorry?"

"The car could not stop." Eden enunciated each word slowly, smashing one palm against the other to demonstrate. "Broken."

The woman translated and the rest of the crowd shuffled in to hear, nodding and whispering.

The uncle spoke again, translated a few seconds later by the young woman.

"My uncle's friend fix for you. You eat food with my family. Please. It is our custom. My name is Aisha," the woman said, smiling.

Eden smiled in return and introduced herself. Aisha spoke to the assembled group, introducing Eden and Baxter to them. Countless smiles and nods came their way.

Eden explained that she couldn't put them to any trouble, but they were both whisked away to a house just a few hundred feet from the car. Eden and Baxter were told to sit at a table overlooking the yard, and beyond that, the road.

Aisha disappeared inside, returning with a tray of tea, served steaming hot in small glasses. Eden took one and sipped from it greedily.

"You lucky," Aisha said, shuffling a chair alongside Eden's. "They only put that pile there yesterday. It makes our crops grow."

A large woman clattered toward them from the house, carrying several plates of food. She laid them across the table. Eden felt her stomach swell in happiness as flat breads, salads dripping in oil, humous, stuffed leaves, and tightly rolled kebabs were brought forth.

Countless members of the family shuffled around the table, sitting on whatever they found.

"Eat, please," Aisha said.

She didn't have to ask twice. Eden dug in, savoring each of the unique and distinct flavors, as well as the sound of conversation she didn't understand and the warmth of the fading sun on her face. She glanced up at Baxter; he was doing the same. Eden found herself smiling slightly. Although the man hardly spoke, she enjoyed his company. He was calm, resourceful, and logical — perhaps a good person to have on the team after all.

43

AFTER DINNER WAS FINISHED, and the empty dishes cleared away, Baxter went to see if he could help the men fix the car. Eden had insisted many times that they should leave it until the morning, but the men — via Aisha's translation — refused.

Eden laid back in the chair and sipped yet another cup of steaming tea. She watched a man hose down the Volvo. Several others, including Baxter, poked around under the hood with another of Aisha's uncles, who ran a local repair shop.

Night had fallen, thick and heavy. In the distance, the lights of the town glinted dully. A car rumbled down the road, washing the scene in ghostly light before fading away to nothing. Insects zinged and chirped in the undergrowth.

Eden took another sip of the tea. Right now, with the Volvo out of action, there was nowhere she could go, or nothing she could do. She tried to relax, but couldn't stop her mind working on overdrive.

"It's a beautiful place," Eden said, catching Aisha's eye. "Have you always lived here?"

"Yes." Aisha nodded. "My family worked the farm for many generations." Aisha lifted the tea to her lips and looked out toward the horizon. "What are you doing here?"

Eden took a deep breath and considered her answer. "I lost my father recently and this was one of his favorite places. My father and I came here together when I was young. I suppose I'm trying to reconnect with him, in a way."

Aisha nodded. "I lost my father too, long time ago. He was in the south of country, to buy something for the farm, I think. Then war broke out and he was killed on the road. He was coming home when he was killed, we think. Although we will never know for sure."

Eden reached out and placed her hand over Aisha's. The other woman's skin felt warm and smooth. The two women shared a few moments of silence.

The Volvo's engine roared to life and a cheer rose from the assembled men. The mechanic in charge barked instructions and several of the men bustled away to fetch various tools.

"Do you think you'll stay here forever?" Eden asked, her voice brightening. She rubbed at her eyes.

"I think so," Aisha said. "Although part of me would like to move to the city. I feel very selfish saying that. We are well looked after here. We are never hungry, and that is a lot to be grateful for. I do wonder, though, what it would be like to live out there." Aisha waved her hand vaguely toward the horizon.

"I can understand that," Eden said, turning to the horizon too. "I tried living in the city once, but I didn't like it. It was the opposite for me, too much noise, too much going on. I like the quiet. It helps me concentrate." Eden pictured her RV, deep in the English woodland. She hoped the wildlife she'd spent several months feeding through the winter would be alright without her there to fill the trough.

Men continued to bustle around the Volvo. Aisha's uncle, a torch in hand, shuffled beneath the car. Baxter stood back watching, his arms folded. The mechanic's legs stuck out from beneath the vehicle, his disembodied voice demanding a different tool every few seconds.

"What city would you like to live in?" Eden asked.

Aisha wondered for several seconds.

"We have many great cities here in Lebanon, and of course there are others around the world. I think the favorite that I have visited, though, is Byblos. My father took us a few years before, you know. I was only a child, but I loved it. I'll go back one day."

Eden nodded.

"Have you been there?" Aisha's voice lightened in excitement.

"I'm, uh, I'm not sure," Eden said. "I last came to Lebanon when I was very young. I can't remember exactly where we went."

"You must go before you leave. It is very historic and on the shore of the Mediterranean. They say it is growing very much with tourists." All traces of sadness had disappeared from Aisha's voice now. "I have some photos, let me show you."

"Sure, that would be great," Eden said, smiling. Aisha climbed to her feet.

Aisha hurried inside and Eden turned her attention to the car below. The mechanic continued to work on something beneath the chassis, as the sound of metal striking metal clanged through the air. Eden wondered whether Aisha would get this sort of reception from strangers, should she ever visit England. With a pang of regret, she doubted it.

Before leaving she would give Aisha her contact details so that she could personally repay the kindness in the future.

"It's such a wonderful city," Aisha said, padding back through the door. She sat down and placed a photo album on the table between them. Aisha flicked it open, revealing several sepia-toned photographs. In the photographs, Aisha was a child of only eight or nine. In the top picture, she held the hand of a tall, tanned man as they walked along a beach. Palm trees curved across the sand, and water lapped lazily across their bare feet. The photograph was a perfect snapshot in time, neither of the subjects knowing their lives would soon be torn apart by senseless conflict.

"Your father?" Eden pointed at the photograph.

Aisha nodded, flipping to the next page.

In the next picture, the young Aisha stood with her mother — a woman no older than Eden was now — looking up at an ancient building. Eden examined the picture carefully, not the young woman and her child in the center, but the building behind them. Something chimed deep within her memory.

Aisha skipped to the next photograph. Aisha and both her parents stood on a hill overlooking the town, the sea glimmering in the distance.

Eden looked at the photo slowly. Her smile dissolved into a gasp of astonishment. Her hand shot to her mouth. She blinked twice, expecting the photograph to change. It didn't.

"Wait, wait," Eden blabbed, scrabbling at the bag by her feet. She pulled out the photograph of herself with her father. Eden looked from one picture to the other. The same jagged coastline. The same buildings. The same curved road.

She looked hard at Aisha. "I need to know where this photo was taken."

Aisha rummaged around inside the house and returned some minutes later with a street map of Byblos. She spread it out on the table before them. The yellowed paper cracked and split with the movement after more than a decade of no use.

"This city has been around since 5000 B.C.," Aisha said, glancing playfully at Eden. "I don't think it will have changed too much since I was a child."

Eden smiled, then examine the map. Her heart pounded a steady rhythm, her senses primed and focused. All previous thoughts of her relaxing evening had disappeared with the discovery. Could this be the lead they had been waiting for?

Eden laid the two photographs beside the map. She followed the coastline, curving in the background, and tried to imagine it laid flat on the map.

"That is the Citadel," Aisha said, pointing at the blocky silhouette of a building in both photographs.

"That means these must have been taken from some-where around here," Eden said, circling an area with her finger.

"The photos are taken from high ground too," Aisha said. "That means it can not be this bit over here." Aisha pointed at an area on the map.

Eden leaned in close and examined the map. Aisha was correct. According to the tiny gradient lines, there was only one area from which the photograph could have been taken. The road's switchback curves showed just how steep the gradient was.

A shout rose from the Volvo. Eden and Aisha glanced up at the men. The mechanic slid out from beneath the car, and another helped him to his feet. The mechanic then climbed into the driver's seat and started the engine. The car rolled forward several feet and then crunched to a stop. Baxter shared high-fives with several of the men.

"It looks as though your car is okay now," Aisha said, smiling.

"Thanks to you," Eden said, locking eyes with the woman. "And thanks to you I now know where I need to go. How can I ever repay you for this?"

Aisha thought for a moment, looking for the right words. "Why do you need to go to Byblos?"

"I want to go to some of the places I visited with my father," Eden said after a pause that was slightly longer than convincing.

Aisha smiled sweetly and nodded. "When will you leave?"

"As soon as possible." Eden examined the dark sky. "If we leave now, we'll be there before dawn."

Aisha's expression dropped. Eden considered telling her the true nature of their visit but decided she couldn't. With merciless forces at play, telling Aisha about the tomb may put her in danger. That was not something Eden could stomach.

Eden's throat suddenly felt dry. She took a sip from the now cooled tea.

"In different circumstances, I would ask you along for the ride, but this is sort of a personal thing. You understand?"

Aisha nodded. "You take this." Aisha pointed at the map, then picked up a pen and scribbled a few words in the map's yellowed margin. "Get in touch whenever you get home."

"Thank you," Eden said, touching the other woman's hand. "We will speak again."

Ten minutes later, Eden and Baxter slid back into the Volvo's worn-out seats. Eden wound down the window. Baxter had volunteered to drive the first shift.

"Please ask your uncle again if I can pay him for fixing the car," Eden said to Aisha.

Aisha translated. Her uncle, arms crossed over a wide chest, shook his head.

"No need," Aisha said, shaking her head too. "I hope to see you again."

Eden smoothed down the map on her lap. "Me too."

The Volvo chugged to life, Baxter spun the wheel, and, testing the brakes just to make sure, turned back in the direction of the road.

As THE VOLVO II4 groaned toward the road and turned left, Helios stepped out of the house. He crossed the yard and laid his hand on the back of Aisha's chair. The young woman sat up straighter in the chair. Her gaze became hard and focused.

"You were flawless as ever Athena. Did she figure it out?" Helios said.

"Just like you said she would," Athena said, dropping into her own accent.

The Volvo's taillight merged into the darkness.

"They're on the way to Byblos now?"

"Yes. She had the picture, like you said she would." Athena stood and paced to the edge of the yard, and looked out at the farm. "She figured out where the photo was taken very quickly. I think she's sharper than you give her credit for."

"Oh, I know she's sharp." Helios fished a packet of cigarettes from his pocket. He shook one out and placed it between his lips. "There's a lot riding on her being sharp right now, believe me."

Athena turned and looked at the man, his face hidden by the shadow.

"Did she invite you along for the ride?" he said, lighting the cigarette.

Athena shook her head. "She said it was a personal sort of thing."

Helios nodded. A cloud of grey chamomile-smelling smoke streamed skywards. "I thought she might. No matter. We know where she's going."

44

THE JOURNEY through the central mountains of Lebanon, mostly on single track roads, was long and arduous. Baxter drove for the first few hours. Unable to sleep, Eden watched with a stoic-like focus as the Volvo's weak lights swayed from one rocky hillside to the other. Now with a suggestion as to where the tomb was located, Eden's mind ran on overdrive. She wondered constantly whether this could really be the place her father had brought her all those years ago, or if it would be another dead-end.

"Are you worried about what we might find?" Baxter's voice broke the silence for the first time in several hours. Eden glanced at him.

"I'm not sure. I haven't really thought about what I'll do when we get there. Just finding the place seems like the most important thing right now."

Baxter nodded, slowing for an upcoming corner.

"What do you think we will find?" Baxter asked.

"My dad told me the tomb was empty, so I think it'll be empty."

"He told everyone that it was empty because he was afraid of the chaos the truth might cause."

"You're asking how I would feel if I found out that he had lied to me?" The sentence hung unanswered for several seconds.

"Yeah, I suppose I am," Baxter said after a long pause.

Eden turned and peered through the rear windscreen again, something she'd done every few minutes for the duration of the journey. No lights pierced the darkness behind them.

"He did what he had to do in the situation. If he chose not to tell me, then it was for a good reason. I was very young at the time and wouldn't have understood. Also, if I'd known what was there, that could have put me in danger." Eden swallowed a ball of emotion. She would deal with her emotions when the time was right, but not today.

Baxter nodded. "For what it's worth, I think you're right. He obviously did everything he could to protect you. I think it will be empty too. At least, I hope it will be."

"Why? Don't you want to find the tablets and spread the word about this whole thing?"

"Sure, but getting one hundred thousand delicate and top-secret stone tablets out of the country won't be easy."

Eden barked out a tiny laugh. The sound pierced the serious mood in the car.

"Why's that funny?"

"I don't even know. You're just so practical all the time. If the tablets are there, we'll find a way to get them out. You're totally right, of course. Anyway, pull over, it's my turn to drive."

Baxter slowed the car to the side of the road, and they swapped over.

"It's no simple thing," Baxter said once they were cruising again a few minutes later.

"I know. How many could we fit in that little plane of yours?"

"The Cirrus has a payload capacity of a kiloton. I don't know how heavy the tablets are, but I bet it's ten times that."

"Then we will have to do ten trips. Don't worry about it. As I say, they won't be there, anyway."

Baxter didn't look so sure but didn't press the issue any further.

"We're almost there," Eden said an hour later, as they crested a hill and got their first sight of Byblos squatting beside the Mediterranean Sea. The blue light of the burgeoning dawn radiated across the heavens, bathing the hillside in a milky pre-dawn glow.

"Let's have a look at that map." Eden killed the engine and climbed out of the car. She stretched her aching arms and legs. Whilst she was getting pretty attached to the ancient car, she had to admit that it wasn't the most comfortable ride. Actually, she thought, kneading her lower back, she'd probably have been more comfortable sitting on the road itself.

Baxter climbed out of the passenger seat and stretched too.

Eden gazed out toward the sea, glittering beyond Byblos's jagged skyline. A cool breeze drifted in from sea, refreshing Eden from the sleepless night. Villas and hotels peppered the surrounding hillside; some glistened in bright whitewash, others still showing their structural concrete. A brightly painted sign on the side of the road in English and Arabic boasted that a nearby cocktail bar had the best view of the city.

It was strange, Eden thought, that one of the oldest cities

on the planet was trying to reinvent itself for tourists. It seemed to her, for a moment, slightly unfair that nothing was immune to capitalism's desperate ravages.

Baxter pulled out the map and laid it across the hood. Eden examined the map and followed the road with her finger until she saw their exact location. They were just a few hundred feet from the spot in which the photograph had been taken.

"Bingo," Eden said, stabbing the map with her finger. "I knew it wasn't far."

"Do you recognize anything yet?" Baxter asked.

"Not yet, but it'll come, I think." Eden glanced across the road at a narrow farm track leading up into the hills. "I hope," she added. "We need to get the car off the road, as someone might recognize it." She pointed at the farm track.

Baxter nodded and then refolded the map.

Her muscles protesting, Eden slipped back into the car. She started the engine and drove up the rutted track. After a few hundred feet, she turned and parked the Volvo out of sight between a shed and an overgrown bush. A tree had grown through the shed's roof, suggesting the place wasn't often used.

Eden hauled the rucksack over her shoulders and headed back toward the road. Baxter walked silently beside her, searching their surroundings for any threat.

Eden was looking for something quite different. She examined every detail of their surroundings, hoping that something would unveil a long-forgotten memory. Overhead, the sky lightened further.

They passed a fueling station, an orange light glowing from its canopy. A car chugged up the hill.

Then something happened.

To Eden, it felt as though she'd stepped away from

reality and into a dream world. She looked around, wide eyed. A four-story apartment block stood on one side of the road, and on the other side a small, raised area looked out over the city. Eden rushed forward. Memories flooded forth. Her heart beat at twice its normal rate.

She ran across to the railing. With the first light of dawn warming her face, and the sea breeze tickling her skin, Eden knew for certain that she'd been here before. She absorbed the view, as though it was nourishment. The buildings of the town stretched out before her. Ancient walls rubbed shoulders with modern concrete tower blocks. Several cranes stood like skeletal fingers sticking up through the earth.

Eden dug the photograph from her bag. She looked down at the image and then up at the view. Sure enough, they were the same. A smile lit Eden's face and her eyes sparkled.

She looked down at the photograph again. Her eyes moved from the image of herself as a child to her father beside her. She glanced at the space beside her now. The smile drained from her face, and she clenched the photograph.

Eden was now more certain than ever that her father had died because someone wanted to keep these manuscripts a secret. Her jaw clenched and her expression hardened. Now she was going to find them and make sure, once and for all, that they failed.

45

EDEN TURNED from the horizon and examined the hillside. Memories spooled through her mind. She remembered clearly that the photo had been taken on the morning of the day they'd opened the tomb. Just an hour before.

Everything after the opening of the tomb was a blur. Something was wrong, but Eden did not know what. She had been just a child, after all. Her father had whisked them away from the site, and within a few hours, they were on the plane back to England. If something had been wrong that day, Eden was about to uncover it.

Baxter stood silently off to one side, watching Eden with curiosity. "You recognize this place, don't you?"

His voice almost surprised her. "Yes, this photo was taken right here. The tomb was somewhere up there." Eden examined the hillside above them. Several modern buildings now dotted the barren landscape. She looked from one building to another, a pang of fear growing. For all she knew the tomb could now be beneath tons of concrete.

Eden shook the thought away and focused on her memories.

"We walked up to the tomb from here." She poked at the photograph. "The walk didn't take long, a few minutes maybe. That way, I think." As though in a dream, Eden crossed the road and headed for a narrow trail which climbed directly up the hill. She had no specific memory of the rocky path, but something about it seemed familiar. Dust and gravel slipped beneath Eden's feet as she scaled the incline.

Baxter walked a few paces behind.

They passed a modern villa, dug into the hill on the left.

Eden looked around, struggling to take it all in. Somehow, strangely, it was as though she was back there. She was ten years old again, she and her father, trying to change the world.

She stopped, turned, and looked back at the town. Dawn was breaking quickly now, washing away reds and blues in favor of daylight. A few hundred feet below, the road snaked downward.

A semi-constructed villa sat fifty feet to the right, surrounded by metal fencing. Piles of bricks, a concrete mixer, and various other building supplies littered the area.

Eden didn't think the site of the tomb could be much further. She turned back toward the hill and examined the track above her, hands resting on her knees.

Recognition chimed again. Above the construction site, several trees twisted out of a small cliff. Eden examined their misshapen trunks and gnarled bows, obviously stunted by the rocky ground and harsh sea winds. Despite the tough conditions, thick white blossoms hung from the branches.

"The white blossom of the trees was thick and the sun strong," Eden muttered, repeating the first line of the diary which Godspeed had read to her.

The blossoms on the trees, that had to be it. The trees were the marker to the tomb. Hiding in plain sight, ignored by everyone who didn't know what they were looking for.

"There! That's it!" Eden shouted, springing into action. She clambered off the track and half ran, half crawled up and across the rough land toward the trees. She leapt over several large rocks, losing her footing on a patch of uneven gravel. Her knees struck the ground, but Eden didn't even notice the pain. She clambered on, using her hands and knees to pull herself up the steep slope.

Baxter watched her go for a few seconds, before giving chase. He picked his way forward more carefully.

Finally, Eden reached the trees. She was out of breath and covered in dust. Stepping on to a small, flattened area, Eden looked up at the cliff face and the twisted trees. The cliff was about twenty feet high and formed of the same orange-grey stone that dotted the landscape. The trees, defying gravity, sprung from the craggy rocks and twisted skyward. Insects buzzed around the blossoms, which hung thick from each bow, almost covering the entire face of the cliff.

Eden stepped toward the cliff, searching for further evidence she was in the right place. She pushed one of the branches aside, exposing the cliff face behind. Blossoms fell to the ground and insects buzzed angrily. Eden tried again, frantically pushing branches aside to check every inch of the cliff.

Doubts grew in her mind as she worked her way along the cliff wall. She'd only been ten years old at the time. Maybe coming back here was too much to ask.

Baxter stood behind, watching her calmly.

Pushing the final bough aside, Eden gasped. A symbol had been carved into soft rock. It was the symbol which

Eden felt had been following her around the whole time. The Key to the Nile.

Eden stared at the symbol for several moments. She was in the right place, she had to be. She examined the rock face but couldn't see any obvious entrance to the tomb.

She let go of the tree and stepped forward to touch the rock. The tree swung back into its previous position, obscuring the symbol.

Eden seized the bough and pulled it away from the cliff face. The branch cracked and a flurry of small rocks fell away from the cliff. Eden looked up at where the tree grew from the cliff above her. A small hole had appeared.

She pulled the bough again and more rocks fell, widening the hole. Eden let go of the bough and scrambled up the gap. She peered inside but couldn't see anything. She cursed herself for not bringing a torch.

She pulled several more rocks away, enlarging the hole. When the hole was about a foot square, she pushed her arm inside right up to the shoulder. The cave went back as far as Eden could reach.

At that moment, a bullet zinged through the air, ricocheting off the rock beside her.

46

THE ROTORS of a Hughes 500 light utility helicopter pounded through the air. The pilot skillfully navigated the machine, staying close to the surface of the Mediterranean Sea so as not to attract attention.

Up ahead, the Balonia sat at anchor, bobbing slowly on the calm waters. The pilot eased off the throttle, slowing the chopper. Lights blazed around the yacht, illuminating her multiple decks.

The chopper slowed until it hovered above the Balonia's rear deck, turning the surface of the surrounding water white in the powerful downdraft. The pilot lowered the small craft until it touched down smoothly, barely even sending a vibration through the yacht. The engines whined and the rotors slowed.

The helicopter's rear door slid open, and Helios climbed out on to the deck. He strode across the deck and slipped inside the yacht. Once inside, he peeled off his jacket and crossed to where the secretary sat behind a bank of screens.

"Good evening, sir." The secretary was the first to speak. "How was your trip?"

"Fine, thank you. Is there anything I need to be made aware of?"

"Another report on the use of computer-generated artwork," the secretary said.

"I'll read through that tomorrow. Is there anything urgent? If not, I think I'll call it a night."

"Yes, Uriel made contact."

The tiredness which Helios had felt a few minutes before instantly dissipated. "That is very unusual outside the normal meetings of The Council. Did he discuss with you the nature of the call?"

"He said you would probably know already." The secretary tapped at the computer, bringing up details of the call.

"I'll return his call now. Patch it through to the conference room, please." Helios strode across the room and pushed through the soundproof glass doors of the conference room.

"Helios, thank you for returning my call." Uriel's deep voice came from speakers built into the walls. "I know it's against protocol to speak outside of the meetings, but I felt the exposure of these tablets gave us just cause. When we spoke in Switzerland, you said that this was under control. Am I to assume that's still the case?"

Helios took a deep breath of the heavily conditioned air. His fists clenched and he scowled. "You are absolutely to assume that. I have some of The Council's best men on this and it will be brought to a successful conclusion in the next few hours."

"Yes, that's what you said last time," Uriel continued. "I am sorry to push the matter, sir, but I feel that something of this magnitude needs to be dealt with by The Council, not just by you."

Helios brought his fists down heavily on the conference

table. "Please rest assured that if I need help from The Council, I will ask for it. I am the leader of this organisation and I take threats to our anonymity in the most serious way. As I have already said, I have a small but effective team on this, and they are on course to recover the tablets in the next few hours. When they do, the tablets will be taken to a secure facility where we can assess the threat they pose to The Council. It is all under control."

"Of course, sir," Uriel said, his smooth voice sounding unfazed by Helios's anger. "I look forward to the conclusion of this problem, and being able to congratulate you as the man who neutralized it for the benefit of The Council."

"Absolutely. Now, Uriel, if there's nothing else I have more pressing concerns to deal with."

Uriel's voice faded, and two beeps sounded through the speakers to signal the line was closed.

Helios strode out on to the deck. The lights of the coast were just pinpricks in the distance from here. He leaned on the railing and looked down at the inky water lapping against the side of the yacht. He was playing close to the wind now, he knew that. He wouldn't expect someone like Uriel to understand. Uriel didn't see the bigger picture. He didn't see what else was at stake.

Helios knew that sometimes, to win the war, you had to lose a battle or two along the way.

47

THE GUNSHOT ECHOED up the hill and rolled back down again. Shards of rock splintered, covering Eden in debris.

Eden pulled her arm from the hole and dropped to the ground. The gun roared two more times. Slugs sailed mere inches above Eden's head and thwacked into the cliff. She flattened herself against the ground, her ears ringing.

Baxter flung himself to the ground beside her. Together they listened closely.

The sound of running feet drew closer.

Eden rolled over, then scurried across to a large rock and peered down the hillside. Three figures scrambled at speed toward them. Two were large, young men, muscles rippling beneath casual clothes.

"It's them," Eden hissed, recognizing the men who had been chasing them for what seemed like weeks. The man who had been burned in the fire now had bandages wrapped around one hand and both shins. The skin on his face looked raw. He moved more slowly than his colleague, obviously still in a great deal of pain. The one-eyed man, who had so far escaped injury, charged ahead, raised his gun, and fired two more shots.

Eden ducked in behind the rock as the shots thudded into the cliff somewhere above her.

Eden looked out around the rock again. The pair of thugs had a third man with them now. He was older and dressed much more formally. He had closely cut grey hair and his face was reddened with exertion. His shoes slipped over a loose pile of rocks, almost tripping him over.

With a physical shockwave moving through her body, Eden recognized the man. Her hands clenched, digging into the soil of the gravelly trail. Her tongue dried up in her mouth. She glanced at Baxter, unable to speak for a long moment.

Another gunshot screamed up the hillside, tearing Eden from her disbelief. She pushed herself down against the ground, and the bullet cruised above her head.

Eden looked at the man again, now just thirty feet away. She could see him clear as Baxter beside her.

Baxter recognized him too. His expression paled.

"I didn't know," he whispered to Eden. "I promise you. I didn't know."

The older man took another step forward, and then paused. He was out of breath from the climb.

Eden's eyes were locked on him, still disbelieving. The last time Eden had seen the man, he was bleeding out from a bullet wound in an English forest. Fear flowed into confusion and then back to fear.

"Stay where you are," Archibald Godspeed shouted. He took several deep breaths. "If you stay still, my men will not shoot you. Run, and you will die."

The men charged forward in unison.

Eden glanced up the hill behind her. The hillside was

open for several hundred yards in all directions. She could run, but without cover, would be an easy target.

She peered back at the Key to the Nile symbol carved into the rock. Suddenly the pieces fell into place. She had been set up from the beginning. What greater motivation was there than explaining the death of a loved one? Godspeed knew that. He'd played her from the start, all so that she would lead them here.

Eden glared at Baxter, wondering whether he was part of the setup too.

The three men reached the ledge. The man with the scarred face was first and took aim at Eden. Eden sat up and locked eyes with him, but didn't run. Trying to escape now would result in several bullets coming her way. She figured that at least one of them would find its mark.

A few seconds later, the burned man limped up onto the ledge and swung a kick at Baxter. Baxter swung to the side and blocked the man's shin with his forearm.

The thug grunted and pulled back for another attack.

"Not yet," Godspeed interrupted. "You'll get to inflict all the pain you want on these two when the job is done." Godspeed leaned forward on his knees and heaved several labored breaths.

"Too many cigarettes, old man?" Eden said, fire burning in her eyes.

"Shut up," Godspeed barked.

The thugs took a step back, one with his weapon trained on Eden, the other on Baxter.

Godspeed sucked in another great gasp of air.

Watching the man, the pathetic excuse of a man, rage bubbled through Eden's body. She stood up, the thug's gun following her all the way.

"Did you really have to kill him?" Eden spat, her voice somewhere between anger and grief.

Godspeed took another breath, his lips curved into something of a snarl. He nodded slowly. "You're clever, I'll give you that. But then, with a father like yours, that's no surprise."

Eden dropped into an instinctive fighting stance. Her hands balled into fists. It took every bit of strength she had not to leap at the man. She longed to tear him limb from limb, even if she died in the process.

"And all those other people? The pilots and crew on the plane. How could you do that?" Eden shouted.

Godspeed shrugged. "Once again, you're asking the wrong questions. But, this is important." He indicated the tomb. "Far more important than the lives of five, ten, even one hundred people."

Eden fumed. She heard Godspeed talk but didn't understand the words. He had calmly arranged the disappearance of her father's plane — what could be his justification for that?

"For hundreds of years these tablets have been a secret. You may think that keeping the world stable is easy. I can assure you, it's not." Godspeed took a step forward and pulled back the branch, revealing the Key to the Nile. He shook his head and smiled.

"At the hospital too," Eden said. "Your men killed that nurse."

"Collateral damage." Godspeed shrugged. "People die every day. Maybe one day you'll understand that." Godspeed turned and considered Eden, then his gaze turned to Baxter. "I must say that I am disappointed with you, young man. You tried to double-cross me, but alas, you have failed."

Eden turned toward Baxter.

"Oh, he didn't tell you?" Godspeed said. "Baxter here was working with your father. Feeding him information, trying to get one step ahead. I'm afraid I've been on to him for some time. He even tried to tell your father not to get on the plane, but for some reason old Winslow wouldn't listen." Godspeed chuckled in a manner that expressed no humor. "That was your father all over, really. He knew he should have just left these tablets alone. But he was just far too stubborn, which ultimately led to his death. I was fond of him really, the silly man."

Godspeed removed a handkerchief from his pocket and dabbed his forehead. The sun was up over the hills now, and already beating down upon them.

"What I explained back at the house was all true, these documents really would change the world. Irrefutable evidence that the history our religions and governments are built on is wrong."

"People deserve to know the truth." Eden spat the words.

Godspeed laughed, tilting his head toward the sky. "The apple really doesn't fall far from the tree." His laughter faded into an expression of seriousness. "I don't think you understand how fragile peace in this world is. People have gone to war, killing hundreds of thousands of people, for different interpretations of the same text. Can you imagine the impact of a manuscript that belittles the whole thing? No. We are going to take the tablets away now to somewhere they'll never be found, and the world will live on." He turned to face the hole in the cliff.

"How are you going to move ten thousand tablets?" Eden asked. "These guys look pretty capable, but you struggled to make it up the hill."

Godspeed grinned. "Don't worry. I have a team on standby. I'll make the call as soon as I've made a visual identification of the tablets. The tablets will be out of the country by nightfall." Godspeed pulled a gun from beneath his jacket. "But I'm afraid, young Eden, this is the end of the road for you. Thank you for showing me the way, but I'm sorry to say your services are no longer required." Godspeed levelled the gun at Eden's chest.

Eden stared down the gun's barrel, and then up at the man who had been leading her through this sorry mess since the beginning. Something suddenly seemed so wrong. This definitely wasn't how it was supposed to end. She gasped a breath of the warm morning air. She tried to swallow, but something clogged her throat.

"It's a shame a young life must end this way. Especially someone like you with so much promise. But, like your father, you just don't see the bigger picture." Godspeed's finger curved around the trigger.

An image of her father swam into Eden's mind. It wasn't him as she remembered him recently, but him when they were here together all those years ago. For a moment, as clear as though it were right in front of her now, she saw the expression on her father's face as he'd rushed them away from the tomb.

The tectonic plates of memory shifted in Eden's mind, causing a seismic shift in her thoughts. The epicenter was the look on his face all those years ago. Something hadn't been as he'd expected. The plates settled and suddenly things made a little more sense. Eden blinked several times as a realization emerged from the mist.

"These tablets need to disappear, and so does everyone who knows about their existence." Godspeed took a step forward, the gun raised.

Eden's lips moved as though she wanted to say something. Then, she smiled.

Godspeed froze, not expecting the expression. In a moment of stillness, Eden knew what she was doing, and she knew exactly what they'd find inside the tomb.

"Wait," Eden said, her voice barely more than a whisper. "I want to see what's inside the tomb. Let me see the tablets. You owe me that at least."

Godspeed tilted his head to the side, considering Eden carefully. "Fine," he said, finally, then he pointed at the cliff. "Open that up."

48

THE THUGS TUCKED their guns away, crossed to the cliff face, and started pulling away big chunks of rock.

Eden watched them, her mind racing. She glanced at Baxter beside her. He stood rigidly upright, his expression pale. She couldn't quite believe Godspeed's allegations that he'd been working with her father and had been set up to come here just like she had. She wanted to talk to him about it, but not with Godspeed in earshot.

The men struggled together to pull away several large rocks, dropping them in a pile to the side of the opening.

Eden gazed into the dark, yawning hole. It was now over three feet across. She felt as though she knew what they would find inside, but a grain of doubt tied her stomach in knots.

Godspeed's eyes flicked from the cave to Eden and back again. He was clearly excited about what they were to discover. Eden wondered whether he really did intend to keep this quiet. A man like Godspeed would surely want to tell the world about what he had done. He would want his name in newspapers around the world.

Godspeed's gun never wavered from its focus on Eden's chest.

Eden turned slowly and gazed down the slope. A construction site fifty feet below was their nearest shelter. They could run now while Godspeed was distracted. Maybe they would cover enough distance in the time it would take him to notice, so he couldn't land a clean shot. It was dangerous though. And, then she wouldn't get to see what was, or wasn't, inside the tomb. Eden's curiosity overrode the thought. She turned and watched the men heaving stones away with their bare hands.

"Why now?" Eden asked, drawing Godspeed's attention.

Godspeed turned to face her, a smile lighting his face. "For years your father had been threatening to expose the tablets. He'd known about them for over two decades but said he was waiting for the right time."

"His lecture at Cambridge," Eden interrupted. Her father was due to give a lecture at the prestigious university next month. While many of the world's top experts in the field would be in attendance, the lecture would also be streamed around the globe. The last such lecture, by an expert in artificial intelligence, had garnered tens of millions of views in the first six months alone.

Godspeed nodded. "That's what I feared. In a forty-minute speech, he would have thrown the world back into the dark ages. That couldn't be allowed to happen."

"We're in," shouted one of the men. They pulled away a large piece of rock, exposing the full width of the opening. The Key to the Nile stood undisturbed on the left. Large, jagged rocks lay strewn across the ledge in front of the opening.

Eden studied the opening, roughly hewn into the rock.

The indentations of the tools were still visible, even after several thousand years.

The thugs stood almost entranced by the opening. They hadn't even glanced at Eden and Baxter in several minutes. One of them dug a torch from a bag and together they stepped toward the hole.

"No," Godspeed snapped, turning his attention away from Eden. "I'll go first." Godspeed lunged forward and seized the torch, his eyes wide. "I've been waiting so long for this." He moved toward the tomb with the slow reverence of a religious awakening.

Eden watched as Godspeed disappeared inside the tomb, followed by his men. She glanced down at the construction site below. They could be there in twenty seconds and then back at the Volvo in a couple of minutes. She spun back to face the opening, Godspeed's light sweeping through the darkness inside.

Eden rubbed the back of her neck. A knot formed in her stomach. Her legs and head begged her to run, but her heart longed to see what was inside the tomb. The men moved deeper inside the tomb now. Eden took a half step forward, then turned back and looked toward the safety of the construction site below them.

She turned to Baxter. His eyes were fixed on the opening, no doubt debating the same dilemma she was.

If she ran now, Eden knew, she would never get to see what was inside the tomb. This was her only chance to find out what her father had discovered all those years ago. Her one opportunity to see if her theory was correct.

She steeled her resolve and stepped toward the opening. She paced across the ledge, stepping carefully over the rocks. Then, taking a deep breath, she stepped inside.

The air inside the tomb was cold and damp. Beyond the entrance, it opened up into a large cave.

Baxter shuffled in behind her.

Eden stepped over and touched the wall. The space had been carefully and painstakingly carved through the solid rock, thick enough to preserve the contents for thousands of years. She glanced up, and in the sweeping light of Godspeed's torch, saw that the ceiling curved into a dome high overhead. The workmanship involved in the construction showed that the person buried here had obviously been of some importance.

A raised stone slab sat in the center of the room. Eden walked over to it. Strands of tattered fabric and a heap of dust outlined the shape of a human figure. Eden studied the shape carefully. A gust of wind swept in through the open door, scattering the dust across the floor.

"What? Where are they?" Godspeed's voice boomed through the cave. "Winslow told me they would be here."

The light swept more frantically now, examining every inch of the cave.

Eden looked closely at the remains of the body and noticed something out of place. Beneath one strand of the tattered fabric sat an object which had no business in an ancient tomb at all. Eden reached down and picked it up. She studied it quickly. Grinning, Eden realized she had been right. It was time to go.

Slipping the object inside her pocket, she turned and charged for the door.

49

Eden and Baxter were barely through the opening when Godspeed's voice boomed from behind them. "They're getting away. She's set us up. Get her back here now."

Godspeed's words were quickly followed by the sound of boots thumping over the rocks.

Eden's feet dug into the ground as she ran full pelt. Her arms pumped through the air, pushing her onward. Buoyed by what she now knew, hope flared in her chest.

Beside her, Baxter did the same, trying to put as much distance as he could between them and his former employer.

Eden reached the edge of the ledge in two strides and leapt down the hillside. The ground came up to meet her, a shock wave jarring through her knees. She half ran, half slipped her way down. Rocks skittered from beneath her, threatening to throw her off balance.

The men tore down the slope in pursuit. Eden sensed they were behind but couldn't tell how far. She didn't dare turn around.

The man with the burns, struggling to keep pace,

paused and raised his gun. He took aim at the fleeing pair and squeezed the trigger. Two bullets whizzed through the air, narrowly missing Eden and Baxter before thudding harmlessly into the ground some way off. He grumbled and set off again, picking his way down the slope as quickly as he was able.

Eden swung to the left, only just avoiding a knot of tangled bushes, their leaves covered with dust from the construction site just thirty feet away.

She focused on their destination, trying to ignore the men behind. A temporary steel fence surrounded the skeletal concrete structure. A dormant crane towered above, its cables hanging still. The site was empty, the workmen having yet to start their day's work.

The ground levelled off ten feet from the steel fence. Eden's soles found grip on the solid ground and accelerated. She lunged for the fence. Her body slammed into the wire, threatening to tip the whole thing over. She looped her fingers across the top and hauled herself up and over. Jumping down on the other side, she risked a look back at the men.

The leading man was twenty feet behind, but gaining. The other lagged behind, picking his way more carefully down the slope.

Baxter joined her a second later. "This way," he shouted, pulling them toward the building. Eden and Baxter jumped through a glass-less window frame and dashed up a concrete staircase. Reaching the first floor, they peered back at the hillside. The first man jumped over the fence in one slick movement.

Watching him charge toward the building, Eden's feeling of dread returned. These men were armed, she and Baxter were not.

"Come on, we're not here to look at the view," Baxter shouted, racing up the curving staircase.

Eden set off behind him. A few seconds later, they emerged from the staircase and stepped out onto the roof. Still in the middle of construction, metal rebar spiked upward where the concrete of the next floor would soon be poured. The motionless crane towered over them. Bricks lay stacked up in various piles and electrical cables ran across the floor.

A plastic-covered scaffold tower shrouded one side of the building. The dirty, torn plastic rippled in the breeze. Beyond which, in the distance, the center of Byblos hunkered beside the shimmering Mediterranean.

Footsteps hammered up the stairwell behind them.

Eden ran to the edge of the floor and peered over. Thirty feet below, an empty swimming pool sat waiting to be filled.

"Over here," Baxter said, beckoning her toward a large box on the far side of the floor. He rummaged through and pulled out several tools. Eden looked at the tools doubtfully.

"You want to make some furniture?" Eden said, looking at the saw and the hammer which Baxter held out toward her. "They're not really going to help against them." Eden nodded toward the stairs behind them, from which their pursuers would emerge at any moment.

Eden scurried toward another large toolbox and emptied it out across the floor. A selection of screwdrivers in various sizes crashed to the concrete.

At that moment Baxter let out an almighty cry. Eden whipped around just in time to see the leading man launch himself from the scaffold tower and seize Baxter around the neck. The man's thick arm closed around Baxter's neck before he even knew what was happening. The man's one good eye contracted until it was little more than a slit.

Baxter fought, attempting to wedge his hands beneath the arm of his captor. The other man was strong and gripped Baxter like a vice.

Baxter swung a fist over his shoulder, striking the man on the cheek. The thug grunted in pain. The second swing missed entirely. Baxter jabbed an elbow into the man's stomach, getting a similar reaction, but no reduction in the pressure.

Panic now rising through her, Eden grabbed a claw hammer from the box and leapt to her feet. She held the hammer down beside her, the claw pointing forward, and dropped into a crouch.

"Let him go," she snarled.

"Or what?" the man spat, taking a step backward. His thin lips twisted into a snarl.

Eden lunged forward, swinging the hammer at the side of the man's rib cage. The man took a step backward, pulling Baxter with him.

Baxter, already weakened by the lack of oxygen, struggled again. He swung out and tried to land a punch on his captor. He hit nothing but air.

Eden repositioned herself to swing the hammer again. A laugh welled on the man's lips. Eden's blood pressure increased as she watched the last bit of color drain from Baxter's face. The thug pulled Baxter backward with relative ease now.

Eden lunged forward again, this time aiming for the man's knee. Again, he stepped easily out of the way.

This time the man laughed out loud, the noise chilling Eden to the bone.

And then, as if it wasn't bad enough, the laugh was joined by another.

Eden turned to face the second man, her stomach

turning to lead. Despite his burns, the second thug walked from the staircase, grinning. Clearly revenge was on his mind.

Eden snarled, an animal instinct taking over.

"Stay where you are. This is the end of the line," the burned man said, stepping toward Eden. He drew his gun from its holster and raised it at Eden. "I get the feeling I'm going to enjoy this."

Both men laughed again.

Feeling a wave of responsibility, Eden turned to look at Baxter. Surprisingly, Baxter's eyes were locked on her, his lips twisted in a faint, knowing grin. Then Eden noticed the slightest metallic glimmer from his hand.

The knife, Eden realized all at once. Baxter had kept the knife they had taken from the man back in Baalbek. He'd clearly kept it concealed this whole time, in preparation for something like this.

Baxter slowly moved the knife into position. Then in one swift thrust, he jammed it deep into the man's side. The thug roared in pain, the look of menace in his eyes dissolving into one of agony. The thick arm slackened from around Baxter's neck. Baxter ducked and leapt forward, sucking greedy breaths of oxygen into his lungs.

The man with the gun now distracted, Eden seized her opportunity. She leapt toward the man, now reeling with the knife sticking out of his side. She swung the hammer, striking the huge thug on the thigh. Then she doubled back, swung again, and struck him on the neck. Both strikes hit home. The man fought out blindly, whipping his arms around in a sightless panic.

The man with the gun shouted, but not wanting to hit his partner, no bullets came.

Eden launched into the man, pushing him hard. He

stepped backward to correct his balance. His hands wind-milled through the air. The thug attempted to step back-ward again. His foot struck nothing but air. His eyes bulged with the realization and his arms swung uselessly. The other man rushed forward in an attempt to save his friend.

A sickening scream echoed through the concrete build-ing, followed by a dull thud.

Eden peered over the edge. The thug lay at the bottom of the water-less swimming pool. His legs were twisted up behind him, his face set in a mask of terror. Blood poured onto the concrete all around him.

Baxter, his breathing now recovered, snatched up a scaf-fold pole and ran toward the remaining thug. Distracted by his attempts to save his friend, the man didn't notice Baxter's approach. Baxter swung the bar low. It cracked hard against the man's ankle, shattering bone. The killer crumpled to the floor. Baxter raised the bar again and struck the man on his flank. A rib cracked. The man grumbled.

The thug spun around and leveled his gun at Baxter. He squeezed off a shot, missing Baxter by inches.

Baxter froze, the metal bar raised above his head. The gun's single eye looked up at him, square in the face.

Baxter shifted an inch backward. The man followed his move. This was a point-blank shot, unlikely to miss.

The man spat a globule of blood and phlegm to the concrete.

"I've been looking forward to killing you," the thug snarled, struggling up on to his feet. "Try to move now, and let's see what happens."

From twenty feet away, Eden watched in silent shock. The tendons in the thug's hand contracted as his finger tightened around the trigger. His hand shook slightly as he breathed through the pain.

Baxter's Adam's apple bobbed. For the second time in two minutes, he blanched of all color.

Eden looked around, frantically searching for something. From her distance, there was little she could do.

The man's finger tightened around the trigger.

Eden looked up at the crane towering above them. A large steel beam hung from a giant hook, swaying gently above them. Eden studied the crane. She had used one before to break into a penthouse apartment in London. She had spent hours researching that one though, working out how to move the gantry into the required position. This crane looked as though it was operated via a remote control which dangled on a cable near the tower.

Eden scurried silently across to the tower and seized the control. It looked pretty simple to operate. There was an up and down lever and one to change the position of the gantry. She turned the key, and the system whirred quietly to life. Eden played with the controls. Far above her, the motors hummed, and a mechanism creaked. The giant steel beam drifted effortlessly through the air.

Eden analyzed the beam's position. She nudged the control slightly to the right. She looked from Baxter, to the man, and then up at the beam. Her hands tingled with the pressure of getting this right. Too far one way and she'd hit Baxter, too far the other way, she would hit nothing. Eden took a calming breath and then, with all the force she could muster, pulled the lever. The crane whirred and the giant beam dropped through the air.

"Baxter," Eden shouted. "Move!"

Baxter glanced up. Time seemed to slow down.

Eden watched wide eyed, her heart missing at least two beats.

Baxter ducked and then launched himself backward. A

moment later, the beam shot through the air inches from where he'd stood.

The thug glanced up as the heavy beam cast its thin shadow across his face. His lips strained into a cry of pain, although the sound never made it out.

The beam hit its mark with a deafening clang and the destruction of bone. The building shook with the impact. The crane continued to whirr and hum, cables spooling across the steel and the hook. Blood flowed from the now-obscured body.

50

As THE FOREMAN for a construction company specializing in luxury villas, Sami hated being late for work. As part of his job, he was expected to be first on site and last to leave. But with his wife preparing for the birth of their third child, whilst still having to take care of the other two, it was rarely that easy.

He pulled the company-issue Jeep to a stop outside the site's main gate and stood. He stepped across to the gate and dug in his pocket for the keys. He had just ten minutes to get things ready for the men to arrive. If they arrived and he wasn't ready, company money would be wasted, and that would make somebody further up the chain very unhappy. They were already behind schedule.

Extracting a bunch of keys from his pocket, Sami set about selecting the one he required. Just as he found the key, his phone shrieked above the sound of the Jeep's radio.

"Never again," he muttered to himself, pacing back to the Jeep.

Two minutes later, with what sounded like the end of the world averted, he returned to the gate. He unlocked the padlock and pulled back the bolt. The gate swung open revealing the villa, the town beyond nestling at the foot of the hills, and a man and a woman standing inside the site. The woman raised a gun and smiled.

Sami took a step backward, his eyes locked on the two unexpected people.

"Sorry," Eden said, pulling the keys out of the stunned site foreman's hand. "And I'm afraid we're going to need to borrow your car. I'll pay for it, don't worry."

The foreman tried to speak, his mouth opening and closing. Sami shook his head and threw his fists into the air, and then after shouting a stream of expletives in every language he knew, let his hands fall to his side.

Eden jumped into the Jeep's driver's seat. She started the engine and they roared off down the hill.

"Should I feel bad about taking that guy's car?" Eden asked as they bounced town the track toward the main road.

"Nah, I wouldn't worry about it." Baxter grinned, rifling through the glovebox. "It's a company car. They'll be insured to the max. He'll have a new one in the morning. Anyway, it's unlike you to care."

"I don't know what you mean," Eden said, faking shock. "I'm not a monster." She flung the wheel to the left as they hit the main road. The tires screeched and the Jeep slid for a few seconds before finding grip on the tarmac and powering them forward.

"What's the plan now?" Baxter asked.

"We get out of here by the quickest way possible. Then you're going to tell me everything," Eden said, overtaking an old Mercedes with mis-matching doors. A vehicle coming the other way slid to a stop, sounding its horn.

Baxter swallowed nervously. "Okay," he said, sounding as though the situation was very far from okay. "I'll find us a way out first." He dug a map from the door pocket and opened it across his lap.

They pulled up to a junction with a small row of shops on one side.

Baxter glanced down at the map, tracing their location with his finger. "Take the 51 southbound. We'll be in Beirut in a few —"

A colossal crunch vibrated through the Jeep, cutting Baxter short. Glass shattered. Metal whined and twisted. Tires screeched across asphalt as the car spun 180 degrees.

Eden's ears buzzed and hummed. She gripped the shuddering steering wheel with all her strength, attempting to control the Jeep's slide. Metal crashed against metal.

They slammed into a parked car, sending the alarm into a high-pitched frenzy. Then another sound filled the Jeep. The howl of a weapon, combined with shattering glass.

"Get down," Baxter shouted, pushing Eden down behind the steering wheel.

Another shot pounded through the Jeep, shattering the windscreen.

Eden blinked several times. She swept a hand across her forehead. She was shaking. She tried to speak, but the words didn't make sense. She reached up and tore the rearview mirror from the windscreen. Another shot zipped through the Jeep, narrowly missing her hand. She took a deep breath. With the ringing in her ears, everything else felt as though it was happening underwater.

Eden held up the mirror and surveyed the scene behind them. A large black SUV had driven clean into the back of them, shattering the rear windscreen and twisting the Jeep into an unrecognizable mess. A man leaned from the driver's door of the SUV behind. Eden recognized him instantly.

"It's Godspeed," she said, a tremor in her voice.

Baxter glanced behind them, his face ashen.

Godspeed climbed down from the SUV. He approached the Jeep, the gun trained on Eden.

Eden tried her door. The parked car which they'd collided with had wedged it closed. She threw her whole weight against it. The door wouldn't budge.

Godspeed rounded the rear of the Jeep. In a few seconds he would have a clean shot of both Eden and Baxter in the front seats.

"Drive," Baxter whispered, his voice horse.

Eden looked down at the dashboard. With her ears buzzing and her senses disorientated, she hadn't noticed that the Jeep was still running.

Godspeed took another step forward.

Eden slipped the Jeep into gear and thumped her foot down hard on the accelerator. The Jeep growled, shuddered, and then issuing an almighty scraping noise, finally started to move.

51

Godspeed stalked around the Jeep with the gun raised. All ideas of subtlety long forgotten. He didn't care who saw him now. The thoughts of his potential fame and fortune slipping away, nothing else seemed to matter.

But there was still a chance he could get what he wanted. Eden knew where the tablets were, that he was sure of. He would catch her, and he would make her talk.

There was, after all, only so much pain someone — anyone — could endure.

He peered through the side window. Eden and Baxter cowered in the front seat, like lambs to the slaughter, awaiting their inevitable fate.

The thrill of the hunt buzzed through him now. They were his prey, and he was the predator.

Godspeed took another step forward. He would shoot that traitor Baxter, first. Then he would get Eden. She would give him the answers he needed, then he would kill her too.

The Jeep's engine howled like an animal in duress. The gear box clunked, and the car groaned forward, shredding bits of metal, glass, and rubber. Fuel sprayed across the road. The car growled away, dragging bits of hanging chassis across the asphalt.

Godspeed groaned and emptied the rest of the magazine into the rear of the Jeep. A tire hissed and the Jeep dropped to one side. Another stream of fuel sprayed from the vehicle.

They wouldn't get far, Godspeed thought, lowering the gun. He stood still, watching the Jeep lumber around a corner.

When the Jeep had disappeared from his sight, Godspeed turned back toward the SUV. A group of people had stopped to watch the commotion. One teenager filmed him with a smart phone. Godspeed didn't care. His cause was greater than any of them, and now it was personal. She had made it personal.

He strode back to his vehicle. The Toyota hadn't fared so well in the collision and the whole front end was crumpled up. That didn't matter. There were plenty of other vehicles he could requisition to complete the mission. Helios would make it worth his while — of that, he had no doubt. The Toyota was already a wreck after several barrels had rolled across it. He climbed in. The windscreen was cracked in countless places now, slightly distorting his view of the outside world. He ejected the spent magazine from his gun and grabbed another from beneath the passenger seat. He pushed two more into his back pocket.

Godspeed climbed out of the SUV and stalked up to the car waiting behind him. He yanked open the driver's door and placed the gun against the driver's temple. The young man nodded, burbling incoherently, and scrambled from the car.

Godspeed slid into the driver's seat and sped off after the Jeep.

Just two minutes later, he slammed on the brake. A

flurry of protesting horns sounded from the vehicles behind, but he didn't even notice. As he'd expected, they hadn't got far. Less than a mile from the site of the collision, the Jeep sat abandoned by the side of the road. A growing puddle of fuel pooled around the smashed-up vehicle.

Godspeed pulled to a stop beside the Jeep and climbed out. He tucked the gun out of sight beneath his shirt. The Jeep had stopped by the entrance to the Old Souk, an ancient part of the city with crisscrossing passageways and hundreds of people milling around the shops and restaurants.

Perfect, he thought, feeling the gun beneath his shirt. *It's time to hunt.*

EDEN AND BAXTER peered out through the dirty front window of a small clothes shop. They saw Godspeed tuck the gun beneath his shirt and stride in toward the souk, his mouth set in a line of grim determination.

"I told you," Eden said. "Leave it thirty seconds and we'll head the other way. There must be a bus station nearby. By the time he realizes we're gone, we'll be a hundred miles away."

Baxter nodded and pretended to examine the garments on display. The shop keeper eyed the pair suspiciously.

Thirty seconds later, Eden pushed out through the door, Baxter following closely behind. "This way," Eden said, leading them back toward the main road.

Eden rushed up the road, looking around frantically. Her senses were on high alert now. Godspeed had crept up on them before. She didn't want that happening again.

The pair turned a corner, and suddenly sirens screamed through the air. Eden froze, her eyes locked on the road ahead. They had been seen at the site of a double murder up in the hills, and stolen the Jeep as a getaway car. The site foreman would have given a visual description of them with ease. What's more, with the police chasing them out of Baalbek, it was likely to assume Godspeed had a contact in the force. For now, Eden decided, the police were with the bad guys.

"Change of plan, this way," Eden said, pulling them down a side street. A pair of police cars squealed past and stopped either side of the Jeep. Four police officers piled out with their guns raised.

Eden and Baxter hurried down the side street. After fifty feet, they slowed to a walk, stepping in with the early morning shoppers. The wailing sirens and raised voices of the police officers merged with the idle chatter of shoppers. Restaurants lined one side and trees with pink blossom overhung the other. In any other situation, it would have been a great place to holiday. Not today. Not with Godspeed somewhere very close by.

They rushed round a corner. Eden glanced around, tense. Her legs begged to run, but she kept her pace slow and languorous. They needed to look like tourists exploring the ancient city for the first time. They turned another corner and into an even narrower street. Large sheets of fabric hung above, sheltering merchants and shoppers from the dazzling sunlight. Shops occupied both sides of the street. Eden and Baxter rushed on, ignoring the bright-eyed traders who beckoned them toward their wares.

The souk was getting busier, with groups of locals and tourists streaming through the narrow passageways. Eden and Baxter stepped in behind a large family, moving slowly from one stall to the next. Eden scrutinized their surroundings. She couldn't see Godspeed anywhere. Although on the outside she tried her best to look calm, tension raced through her veins within. Right now, they were on the wrong side of the predator-prey equation. Eden didn't like it one bit. For a moment, she pictured the dead animal heads mounted on the walls of the Godspeed manor house. At least those poor creatures didn't know what was coming for them.

Eden and Baxter pushed on down the street, scanning every doorway and passage for signs of their foe. They emerged from the souk onto a small cobbled plaza. Four roads ran in different directions. They looked from one to the next slowly, considering their next move.

"What do you think?" Eden asked.

Large palm trees dappled shade over customers sat in the corner cafes, drinking coffee and smoking in the morning sun. A large 4x4 chugged past, rumbling over the cobbles.

"That way, I think." Baxter pointed to the right. "I remember seeing a marina on the map. If we get there, maybe we can get someone to take us down the coast."

"Good idea." Eden nodded. "Godspeed and the police will expect to catch us on the roads on the way out of town. With luck they won't even consider the sea."

They scuttled away from the plaza and in the direction of the marina. Eden hoped that Baxter's sense of direction was up to the challenge. After several minutes in the twisting medieval passages, she couldn't be sure.

They turned again, this time into a street which was even narrower than the one before. The back of a large hotel loomed up on one side and a brick wall ran down the other. Twenty feet further on, the road turned hard to the right. With no people wandering this far from the souk, Eden and Baxter upped their pace to a jog without looking suspicious.

Eden remained on full alert, searching the windows above for any threat.

They slowed as a dilapidated car rattled past. When it was out of sight again, they picked up their pace.

"It's just this way," Baxter said. "Right after the —"

The rapid-fire crack of a pistol cut Baxter off mid-sentence.

Eden hauled them both behind a parked car. Two slugs bounced harmlessly off the concrete, clanging into something high above their heads.

"He's here," Eden said, barely above a whisper. She froze in position, afraid that even the slightest movement would draw more fire.

Baxter nodded, wiggling on his stomach, and peering out beyond the rear tire. He saw the man looking around the corner up ahead.

"Twelve o'clock, about twenty feet. We'll have to go back."

"In English, please?" Eden quipped, knowing full well what Baxter meant. They might be in mortal danger, but Eden knew if it came down to it, she would go down joking.

Baxter ignored the comment and looked back the way they'd come.

"The next turn is about thirty feet back. It doesn't look good. He's got us covered."

The rear wall of a large building occupied one side of the road, and a solid brick wall loomed up on the other.

"We will look like Swiss cheese by the time we get there."

Baxter turned back to face Eden. "Alright Houdini, you got a better idea?"

"Sure." Eden pointed at the top of the wall. "We go up."

52

HOLDING the gun just inside his jacket, Godspeed leaned against the wall and tried to look casual. To the disinterested observer, he aimed to give the impression that he was waiting for someone or enjoying the sunshine. He'd seen many people doing the same thing during his time here, so didn't think his presence would raise questions.

He glanced around the corner again. The pair had scurried behind a parked car, like the rats that they were. He'd been tracking them for the last few minutes, waiting for them to walk into one of the market's less busy areas. Although he didn't particularly care if innocents died in the crossfire, he didn't want to raise alarms again. Sure, Helios had some arrangement with the local police, but Godspeed didn't want to put that to the test. The local force had been as good as useless so far.

Godspeed checked the gun again. It was a shame he didn't have his hunting rifle. With that, he could get a clean shot from several hundred yards. They would only know he was nearby when one of his rounds left its mark.

Things weren't looking too bad, though, Godspeed

reflected. Cowering out of sight, there was nowhere his prey could go without stepping straight into his line of fire. All he had to do was wait. Wait, and prepare for victory. Checkmate.

Without taking his eyes off his prey, Godspeed fished a packet of cigarettes from his pocket and planted one in the corner of his mouth. He could wait for as long as it took.

Twenty feet away, Baxter peered around the rear of the car and saw Godspeed exhale a cloud of smoke. Baxter fumed. Of all the jobs he'd had, working for Godspeed was by far the most frustrating. Baxter watched the man, hiding in plain sight, examining the scene, and waiting for their move. Baxter wished he had a weapon of his own. If he had a weapon, he'd be able to finish this in moments.

Godspeed removed the gun from beneath his jacket and aimed at the car. Baxter darted back behind the vehicle. Godspeed's distant laugh echoed down the street. The older man was playing with them, and once he was certain they were unarmed, he would just walk toward them and shoot at point-blank range.

Baxter swallowed. It wasn't a good position to be in. They needed to move, and fast.

Eden looked up at the top of the wall above them. It wasn't high, maybe twelve feet from the cobbles. Standing on the parked car, or lifting each other up, they could be up and over in less than a few seconds.

"You go first," Baxter said, his voice a low growl.

"No, we'll go together," Eden countered.

"Absolutely not. I'm taller than you. It'll be easier for me to get over there."

"You also make a bigger target."

Baxter thought for a moment. "If we go together, he's got more chance of hitting us."

Their faces just inches apart, Eden caught Baxter's stare. The eyes that she first thought were cold, now brimmed with kindness. Eden couldn't explain it, although she liked it. She broke the stare and looked up at the wall.

"Okay. On my count." Eden readied herself. Baxter placed his hands beneath her foot. Eden counted down from three and sprung up. With Baxter's help, she reached the top of the wall with ease. She threw her elbows across and heaved herself up.

The gun popped several times. Slugs thwacked into the wall. Eden felt bricks shatter across her legs. She heaved herself up, swung her legs over the wall, and thumped down to the dusty ground on the other side. Two more rounds of hot metal boomed into the bricks behind her, just a moment too late.

Baxter glanced up at the wall. Dust and debris rained down on him from where Godspeed's bullets had ricocheted off the bricks. The shots had missed their mark by just inches as Eden had kicked herself over.

"That was close," Eden hissed from across the wall.

"Too close," Baxter replied, peering around the parked car. Godspeed was now waiting, the gun leveled and ready. This time, it was going to be closer still.

The muscles in Baxter's jaw stood out in determination.

A rumbling engine roared up close behind him. Baxter glanced over his shoulder. A truck, almost filling the road completely, thundered toward him. The vehicle swayed as it passed over uneven cobbles.

Baxter watched as Godspeed slipped the gun back beneath his jacket. The man clearly didn't want to make another public scene.

Baxter took his chance. He launched to his feet and jumped. His hands reached out for the top of the wall. His fingers curved around the stone, clawing at their sandy surface.

A cacophony of noise reverberated from behind him. The gun howled. The truck's brakes whined and then the engine noise dropped.

Bullets slammed into the wall, peppering Baxter with debris. With great effort, he heaved himself upward and then rolled across the wall.

The gun popped several more times. A white-hot pain surged through Baxter's leg. Baxter gasped and suppressed a cry. He forced his mouth closed and threw himself down from the wall. He crashed to the ground in a cloud of dust, knocking the air from his lungs.

Baxter lay still for several moments, then sat up and forced a deep breath.

He struggled to his feet, using the wall for support. He gasped great lungsfuls of the dust-filled air.

The truck's engine fell into silence.

Eden pulled Baxter to his feet, wheezing and spluttering.

"We need to go," Eden said. "The driver of that truck will call the police."

Baxter straightened up using the wall to help him stand. A sharp pain jarred through his ankle. He gritted his teeth.

Eden bent down and pulled up the leg of Baxter's trousers. The material was already soaked in blood.

"You've been hit," she said, examining the wound. Blood seeped slowly from a two-inch gash just above his ankle. Eden tenderly passed her fingers across the wound. "The bullet has gone straight through. It's just a flesh wound. A paper cut, really."

"Lucky, hey?" Baxter grinned through the pain.

"It could definitely have been a whole lot worse. I would ask if you can walk, but you don't have a choice. Let's go."

Baxter hobbled forward. "Sure, nothing will stop me." Baxter looked around for the first time since jumping over the wall. A giant sand-colored building reared up in front of them.

"We're on the grounds of the citadel," Eden said. "This way."

Baxter limped across the dusty patch of land at the citadel's perimeter, then hastened up an incline and onto a stone path. A monolithic sand-hued wall reared up before them, almost blocking out the sun.

Eden stared up at the battlements towering somewhere above them.

Two sharp pops thundered through the air. Slugs whizzed above their heads, slicing into the ancient rock. Shards of dust and rock rained down from the wall.

"We need to move," Eden said, pulling Baxter behind a section of wall. She led them toward an archway through which a group of camera-toting tourists had just disappeared. "I think it's time we got out of here."

53

ARCHIBALD GODSPEED STOOD on the roof of the car and squeezed the trigger until the gun clicked empty. The shots hit nothing but the ancient stone, showering his quarry with dust. Eden and Baxter ran out of sight behind the ancient battlements. A group of tourists moved idly around the citadel, unaware of the noisy action hidden by their audio guide headsets.

Godspeed ducked down behind the wall. Desperation coursed through his veins and anger clouded his vision. He cursed the ineffective weapon. He cursed Croft and Stone, now lying dead at the building site up in the hills. He cursed Helios and his so called "easy job." He had hoped to be in possession of the tablets by now. He should be on the way to handing them over to Helios and receiving his reward. The fame and fortune Godspeed desired — no, deserved — drifted ever further out of his grasp.

He looked down at the gun. Sure, he was improvising now, but it wasn't over.

He glanced over the wall and saw Eden and Baxter scurry away into the citadel.

Godspeed didn't know how, but he was sure that Eden had played him. She knew where the tablets were, and she had led him to the wrong place on purpose.

When he caught up with Eden this time, he would drag her somewhere quiet and cause her serious pain until she told him everything she knew. She knew something, and she would tell him — Godspeed would stake his entire potential fortune on that.

Godspeed glanced back at the truck, still idling behind him. The driver cowered low, sheltering behind the door. He ejected the spent magazine and let it fall to the floor. He pulled a fresh one from his pocket and slid it home. The gun clicked reassuringly. He loaded a round into the chamber and leveled the weapon at the driver. He didn't want any witnesses. No more reports to the police.

The driver visibly quivered, his eyes locked with Godspeed's.

Godspeed squeezed the trigger twice and watched as the quivering stopped. Blood bloomed across the driver's shirt.

Godspeed tucked the gun away, heaved himself over the wall, and dropped down to the dust on the other side.

54

_____

EDEN AND BAXTER dropped their pace and merged in behind a group of tourists. Hushed voices echoed from the vaulted ceiling. Eden looped her arm around Baxter, helping him walk without too much of a limp.

The group turned and clattered up a stone staircase toward the castle's battlements. Eden and Baxter pushed on through the shadows of the citadel's interior. They were heading directly through the building, hoping to emerge on the other side, which would just be a short walk from the marina.

The further they walked, the darker the castle's interior became. Water dripped against stone somewhere nearby, its echoing thud filling the space like a heartbeat. Eden looked up but couldn't even make out the arched ceiling, curving somewhere overhead. Her heart missed a beat with every thump and creek from the ancient structure. She remained horribly aware that every one of those noises could be Godspeed coming to finish the job.

"There must be a way out down here," Baxter whispered.

His voice sounded loud in the enclosed space, almost startling Eden.

Baxter's pain had subsided somewhat with the movement. Having sustained many much worse injuries in the past, he was confident the wound wouldn't overly slow him down.

"There's got to be," Eden agreed.

Eden took another careful step. She could barely see the uneven, slippery stones beneath her feet now.

They stumbled on in silence for what felt like several minutes. Other than the occasional light hanging from the ceiling, complete darkness reined.

"I think we should go back and try the other way," Eden said finally.

Baxter grunted but said nothing.

Then there was movement somewhere. A flurry of footsteps. A hissing, sibilant noise. A dull crack boomed, and then echoed a thousand times. Eden spun around. She made out movement in the shadows, but nothing else.

Then, slowly at first, Baxter slipped from her grasp. Eden tried to grab hold of him, but he was too heavy. He slipped, unresponsive, thudding somewhere to the floor.

Eden gasped. Her hands groped around for something, anything. The countless echoes of multiple sounds reverberated around the space. Eden looked one way, and then the next, seeing nothing but darkness.

She crouched down and felt around the floor for Baxter's shape. He lay still in the gloom, his face pressed against the cold, wet rocks. Panic rose like a physical ball in Eden's throat.

Then Eden heard another breath. This one didn't sound like Baxter's slow inhalation. The short, sharp breaths came closer.

Eden felt Baxter's chest. He was breathing and the beat of his heart still throbbed.

A voice hissed through the gloom. A hand seized her arm.

"Enough messing around," Godspeed hissed. "Now you're coming with me." He pulled Eden up and pushed the gun hard against her ribs.

Eden tried to pull away, but Godspeed pressed the gun against her more firmly. Right now, in this enclosed space, she couldn't fight. Godspeed would put a bullet in her back before she'd even broken free.

"This way," Godspeed directed, walking her back the way they'd come. Eden walked stiffly, her eyes wide with fear. She slowed down a little. Godspeed grunted and pushed the gun's barrel even more aggressively into her back.

Eden thought about Baxter, lying on the cold, damp floor somewhere back there. At least he was still breathing.

Eden squinted as the opening loomed up ahead of them. Godspeed quickened his pace and shoved Eden out into the blazing sunlight. She closed her eyes to slits, colors dancing across her vision.

"Wait," Godspeed barked, his fingers digging into her shoulder. He took off his jacket and draped it over his arm, hiding the gun. "I'm a very good shot," he hissed. "If you try to run, I'll put a bullet in your spine."

"You're a good shot?" Eden spat in return. "I've seen no evidence of that so far. Are you sure that thing's even pointing the right way?"

Godspeed growled and shoved Eden again. They passed a group of tourists coming the other way. Godspeed took a step toward Eden and cracked the butt of the gun hard against her ribs.

Eden winced at the not-so-subtle reminder that Godspeed was in control.

The path descended at a steep angle away from the citadel and toward the exit. Eden dragged her feet, slowing, and glancing over her shoulder. Godspeed frowned. Eden looked up at the citadel standing brutish and monolithic behind them. She thought about Baxter thumping to the cold wet stone somewhere within that building. Godspeed's strike had been so accurate that Baxter hadn't even cried out. Eden's stomach tied itself into a knot of fear.

Godspeed pushed them through the exit and out into the city.

For several minutes, they shuffled down a tree-lined street. Godspeed moved in closer each time a car or person passed.

Eden's mind sped, trying to think of a way out. Whether Godspeed was a good shot or not didn't matter, he was directly behind her. All he had to do was squeeze the trigger and a lump of hot metal would sear through her body. Eden cursed herself for not having super-human fighting powers. If she really were Lara Croft, a backward jumping scissor kick would lay him out for good.

Finally, they paced down a ramp and on to the marina. Music drifted from a restaurant and lively conversation babbled from a group of men sitting on a wall. A mix of pleasure boats and fishing craft bobbed on light swells. The marina was protected from the sea by a long harbor arm. The concrete wall jutted out into the sea, leaving a small gap for boats to come and go.

Eden took a deep breath. The combined smells of sea and the day's catch brought back memories of childhood seaside trips. Eden thought of her father, and the man behind her who had deceived them both. Anger bristled through her body, causing her to stand motionless.

"Move," Godspeed growled.

Eden swallowed the pain, grief, and fear. She rubbed a hand across her face. It wasn't over yet. She wasn't beaten yet. She would stay alive and keep fighting. Keep fighting until the very end.

Godspeed walked them along the waterfront, examining each boat in turn. They passed a group of men, smoking cigarettes and resting on their motorcycles. He paused beside a speed boat with two chunky outboard engines.

Godspeed shouted at the men resting on their bikes. He spoke in fluent Arabic. Whilst Eden was far from fluent, she had been attending lessons. She got the gist of their conversation.

One of the men threw down his cigarette and sidled across the quay. Keeping Eden in his sights, Godspeed shuffled away. The two men spoke in hushed tones. He peeled several notes from a wad in his pocket and exchanged them for a set of keys.

The knot of fear in Eden's stomach tangled into a ball.

"It's time to go," Godspeed stated, pushing them toward the boat. "Get in."

Eden's feet remained fixed to the floor. She looked toward the men, but they were both facing the other way. Her muscles tensed to steel. The cold pressure of the pistol pushed harder against her ribs.

"Now," Godspeed snarled.

Still, Eden didn't move.

All pretense of normality gone, Godspeed seized Eden's arm and forced her toward the boat.

"No, stop," Eden grunted, pushing against her captor.

Godspeed shoved her hard. Eden fell from the quay and

stumbled into the boat. She caught hold of the seat to prevent herself from falling overboard. With one hand, he undid the rope and tossed it into the boat. Then he jumped in, scrambled to the controls, and started the engines.

The outboard motors grunted to life, churning the harbor's water into foam. Godspeed pushed forward on the throttle and the sound of engines intensified into a growl. The boat pulled away from the quay.

Eden watched as two feet of open water stretched between her and land, then four, then eight. Eden looked back at the quay. The muscles in her legs tensed. As a competent swimmer, she could easily make it across the marina and attempt to dive out of sight. She bent her legs in preparation.

The boat accelerated further. Clouds of grey fumes billowed from the engines, mixing with the spray of the sea.

Eden glanced back at Godspeed, maneuvering the boat adeptly with the gun in one hand. Even if she jumped, there was no cover nearby. She could only hold her breath for so long and when she surfaced, Godspeed would still be there, gun in hand.

Eden turned and gripped onto the seat, suppressing her instinct to flee. For now, she would have to stay put.

Godspeed spun the wheel and the boat swung around the wooden bow of a tourist cruiser just entering the marina. The canvas awning of the slow-moving craft flapped and snapped in the breeze.

Godspeed aimed the bow of the speedboat at the open sea and accelerated. The engines whined, as water foamed and bubbled in their wake. The acceleration pushed Eden back into the seat. The speedboat's bow tilted skyward as they skipped across the swells and troughs of the sheltered waters. On the open sea, visible beyond the harbor arm, breakers foamed like charging stallions on the crest of each wave.

Godspeed turned and locked eyes with Eden. His lips twisted into a victorious snarl. Feelings of intense hate flared through every one of Eden's senses and synapses. She hated this man for what he had done to her father, and what he was about to do to the world.

These tablets were humankind's chance to learn the truth. Eden believed, as her father always had, that access to knowledge was a human right, as much as water and food. The bigger hatred that burned inside her, though, the one that boiled the blood in her veins, was being powerless. Eden stared back at the man, knowing that while there was still a pulse in her body, she would fight for what she knew was right.

"People deserve to know," Eden whispered, her voice lost beneath the noise of the speedboat and the sound of another engine whining somewhere behind them. The other engine coughed, choked, and then rose to a loud, constant hum.

The arrogant sneer drained from Godspeed's thin lips as he saw what was happening on the quay behind them. His jaw set forward, he turned, shoved the boat into its highest register, and gripped the wheel.

Eden glanced behind them, her feelings of powerlessness suddenly melting away.

55

COMING BACK TO CONSCIOUSNESS, Baxter didn't know where he was. He groped around, looking for some indication of his location. The damp and slimy rocks on which he lay offered nothing in the way of indication. He closed his eyes and opened them again, almost expecting light to flood into his retinas this time. Nothing happened.

After several seconds of breathing hard, the confusion began to dissipate. He remembered the impact to the back of his head. Moving his hands slowly, he explored the back of his skull with his fingers. The area was sore but didn't seem to be bleeding. His head throbbed as though it were stuck inside a kettle drum.

His confusion drained away further, bringing with it the aching of his ankle. He ran his fingers across the broken skin, not quite remembering how he had ended up in this position.

As though someone had just switched on a light, the memories appeared fully formed in his mind. Baxter sat up straight.

"Eden," he mumbled, his tongue feeling too thick for his

mouth. The words rebounded from the stone walls and came back his way tenfold. The room spun around him, threatening to knock him flat again. Baxter felt the contents of his stomach boil as though they were fighting their way out. He swallowed, forcing away the urge to vomit.

When his nausea had passed, Baxter examined the space. From some distant glint of light, he could see he was there alone.

"Eden," he said again, his heart sinking. "Godspeed," he muttered, his voice taking on a darker tone. In a moment of clarity, Baxter knew exactly what had happened. Godspeed had found his way into the citadel. He'd followed them into the passage, incapacitated Baxter, and gotten away with Eden.

The thought of Eden being in danger acted like a shot of adrenaline to his heart. A feeling of intense power surged through Baxter's veins, forcing him to his feet. Having worked alongside Godspeed for several months, Baxter knew how depraved the man could be. Lava ran in his veins at the thought of what Godspeed might do to Eden.

Using the wall for support, Baxter turned and struggled toward the dim light. After a few steps, the room stopped spinning and his breathing settled, from short clawing gasps, to the deep, steady rhythm of a war horse.

Reaching the mouth of the passage, Baxter stumbled out into the dazzling sunlight. He paused, scrutinizing the scene. The reason the citadel had been built on this site was obvious; it afforded the occupant an unbroken view of the bay, nestled in the middle of which was the marina. Baxter squinted. Several boats of different designs bobbed on the swells, their colorful flags snapping at their masts.

Somehow Baxter knew Godspeed would head the same way as they'd planned. Godspeed may have a contact within the police force, but that wouldn't stop them from closing the roads in pursuit of the killers from the building site. Plus, if the police got Eden, that would prevent Godspeed from getting his answers. The sea offered the only way out.

A group of tourists walked toward the citadel's entrance. Noticing Baxter, bleeding and bruised, they stopped chattering and hurried in the other direction.

Baxter didn't notice, his eyes locked on the crystal-topped water of the marina, fear bubbling in his throat.

Baxter pushed himself into action and set off at a sprint toward the marina. Once or twice, a spell of dizziness threatened to knock him off balance, but Baxter kept upright and moving forward. He shoved past another group of tourists making their way up the hill. He increased his speed, his shoes slapping at the road in time with the ferocious beating of his heart. Long years of service had trained him for this. To push everything from his mind in pursuit of the mission. Except this time, it felt strangely different. The mission wasn't an object, it wasn't something decided in secret rooms by men in suits. The mission was a woman. Baxter's pace increased at the thought of Eden. It was a mission he fully intended to complete.

Two minutes later, sweat streaming down his face but as focused as he'd ever been, Baxter reached the waterfront. He paused, then looked one way and the other. He analyzed the scene. The boats he'd seen from the citadel bobbed peacefully. Tied securely to the quay, they weren't going anywhere. Baxter looked further down the waterfront. Music streamed from a nearby restaurant. A group of men on motorbikes smoked and chatted.

Then Baxter froze. A hundred feet down the quay he saw Godspeed, gun in hand, leap into a small motorboat. Without a thought, Baxter set off at a sprint. He reached the place where Godspeed had been in a few seconds flat, but he was too late.

Godspeed maneuvered the boat out into the channel, leading to the open sea. Baxter squinted, trying to get a better look at the craft. Rage bristled through his body. Sure enough, in the back of the speedboat, crouched like an animal and ready to attack, sat Eden.

Baxter's mind sorted through solutions to the problem. He assessed the craft lashed to the quay. All were slow touring craft; none could match the dual-outboard motors of the speedboat. Baxter watched Godspeed, angling the boat toward the end of the harbor arm, and an idea formed.

Baxter spun around and charged for the group of men smoking on their motorbikes. The nearest one was a classic Royal Enfield in black, with the key still in the ignition. He reached the bike in half a dozen strides and pushed the man from the saddle.

Baxter leapt across the saddle, started the engine, toed the bike into gear, and gunned the throttle. The engine whined, sputtered, and then roared into reluctant service. The worn tires spun for a few moments, sending clouds of gravel flying in all directions, before finding purchase. The bike lurched forward, accelerating hard.

The man, who a moment ago had been smoking a cigarette and lounging against the bike, scrambled to his feet. He leapt forward, but his fingers swept through the air inches behind Baxter's back.

Baxter shifted gears and then pulled back harder on the throttle. He glanced out at the accelerating speedboat. Godspeed was pushing the boat as hard as it would go, just moments from the open water. The speedboat's strong engines churned the water in their wake, sending great waves out to the marina's edges. Boats bumped against the quay and pulled impatiently at their ropes.

Baxter looked back at the road just in time to swerve around a group of men loading buckets of fish into a van. He pulled the bike into a skid and leaned into the corner. The tires shrieked, leaving big streaks of rubber on the concrete.

Baxter straightened up and accelerated again. He glanced out at the speedboat. They were still moving at speed. Godspeed's expression was a mask of determination. The harbor arm was just thirty feet away from the boat now. Baxter examined the structure. The speedboat would have to pass within a few feet of the arm, after which it would be out in the open sea.

Baxter tore back on the accelerator, shooting past half a dozen parked cars. Two men, ambling down the quayside, leapt out of the way just in time. Baxter wasn't certain, but he thought he'd heard one of them topple and splash into the water.

Baxter turned the bike hard to the right, leaning at an almost impossible angle. The tires shrieked and slid across a patch of gravel. Finding grip at the last possible moment, the bike shot out on to the harbor arm. The concrete was rougher here, and Baxter struggled to control the bike. He stood up and leaned forward, forcing his weight onto the front wheel.

Several fishermen, rods curving into the water, watched the bike roar past. Their heads spun in unison like a pack of meerkats.

When the bike was under control, Baxter glanced at the speedboat. The craft lurched from the water, as though trying to take off. Giant fans of spray and smoke billowed up behind the craft. Baxter focused on Godspeed and then Eden.

The end of the harbor arm was just twenty feet away now. The sea's glittering canvas beyond beckoned him on.

Baxter pulled back on the throttle again, this time leaning back and forcing the bike on to its rear wheel. He accelerated hard, fighting to keep the bike balanced. The engine screamed and cried, pounding down the concrete. Baxter's eyes flicked from the boat to the end of the harbor arm.

He shot past the point of no return. Now he had no choice but to power the bike on and into the water. The thought steeled his determination and he pushed on harder.

The bike rumbled across the concrete, the tattered suspension barely keeping the shockwaves from Baxter's arms.

And then the concrete ran out.

56

EDEN HELD HER BREATH, her eyes bulging in disbelief. She gripped on to the seat with aching muscles. Everything seemed to be happening at once. The speedboat roared toward open sea, shuddering over larger waves, threating to swallow the small craft. At this speed, each swell was as hard as rock and shook Eden right through to her solar plexus.

Then, Eden watched open-mouthed as the motorbike took to the sky. It happened in front of Eden's eyes, as though in slow motion. The bike continued its forward trajectory, defying gravity, for what felt like an age. Then, the front tire tilted downward, and the bike spun toward the water.

Baxter, with the grace of a gymnast, stood on the seat in mid-air and kicked the bike away. The bike shot from the path of the speedboat with only inches to spare.

Baxter sailed through the air. He lifted his feet into a crouch, ready for impact. His expression was one of unusual calm, like a painting of a renaissance warrior.

Baxter landed hard inside the boat, knocking Godspeed from the controls. The gun flew from Godspeed's grasp and disappeared beneath the waves. The boat hit a wave and with no one at the wheel, lurched hard to the right. The wall of the harbor arm loomed over them, perilously close.

Eden saw the danger and leapt to her feet. She yanked the wheel to the left, pulling them back out toward the sea. The boat rocked violently, almost threatening to flip over on the bigger waves. The speedboat thundered on, passing the harbor arm.

Baxter and Godspeed struggled to their feet. Godspeed glanced around looking for his weapon.

Baxter didn't wait. All injuries forgotten, all pain buried deep beneath years of training, he swung out at the older man. Baxter landed several good punches on Godspeed's face and neck. Godspeed stumbled backward. Baxter followed, his weight tilting the boat at an angle.

They smashed through a wave, the impact threating to split the boat's fragile body in two. Spray splashed up over the bow, soaking Eden at the controls. Eden yanked the throttle backward. The engine's roaring died down and the speedboat levelled out.

Baxter grabbed Godspeed, twisted the man around, and looped his arm around the man's neck. Godspeed's hands shot to Baxter's thick forearm a moment too late. Baxter squeezed. Godspeed's eyes bulged and a gurgling sound came from his throat.

Eden killed the engine completely and turned to face the brawling men. Color drained from Godspeed's face. The speedboat tipped this way and that, threatening to throw them overboard.

"No, stop!" Eden shouted, leaping across to Baxter. "You'll kill him. Don't!"

"You don't get it, do you?" Baxter said, his steely eyes locking with Eden's. There was a look of madness within him that Eden hadn't seen before. "This guy will never give up. He doesn't know how. He will do anything he can to reinstate his family name. There is only one way to stop —"

"You are not a killer," Eden said, putting her hand on Baxter's shoulder. "We will find a way. My father knew a lot of influential people, and we will find a way to make sure he faces justice."

Baxter's grip softened slightly. Godspeed gasped a greedy breath of air, his fingers clawing at Baxter's bicep.

"If you kill him now, then you're as bad as him," Eden shouted, pain and grief running through her veins. "I want the world to see what's on those tablets. I need the world to see that. He killed my father for that. But we are not stooping to his level." She pointed at the older man, her vision blurred with sea water, tears, or both. "This man is a monster. I believe you're so much better than that."

The anger drained from Baxter's face and his muscles visibly relaxed. He dropped Godspeed, who collapsed into a gasping heap on the floor of the boat.

Then, for the second time in two minutes, everything seemed to happen at once. Baxter stepped forward, and the big arms which had a moment ago been squeezing the life from a man, enveloped Eden. The grey eyes, the color of Brighton's winter sea, which had been rimmed with rage, were now soft and calm.

Eden took a deep breath. Baxter's smell mingled with the sea in a heady, intoxicating concoction. For the first time, possibly ever, she felt fragile, beautiful, and she loved it. Her body melted into his. She looked up at his angular face, now shadowed with stubble.

"There's something I need to tell you," Baxter whispered. "I've felt awful that I haven't been able to tell you all this —"

Suddenly every muscle in Baxter's body stiffened. The sudden change almost forced the breath from Eden's lungs. She pulled away and looked at his face. His mouth was set in a circle of surprise, his eyes wide. He fought for breath. Baxter's lips quivered, as though he could no longer control them.

Eden stepped backward. She lifted her hands to her face.

Baxter staggered forward.

Protruding from Baxter's back, just below his left shoulder blade, extended the handle of a knife.

Baxter turned back toward Eden, each movement labored.

Godspeed crawled away like a cowering animal.

Baxter's steel eyes locked with Eden's. Again, he took her in his arms, but the strength and longing of a moment ago had already drained away, flowing and seeping like the blood that was now pooling on the floor.

"What... what did you need to tell me?" Eden said.

"No time now," Baxter said, his voice a whisper. "You'll find out soon. You've got a..." His face contorted into a grimace of pain. Tendons in his neck stood out. His breathing became weak. "You've got a job to do," he hissed finally.

"No," Eden said. "We'll do it together. We will get back there. You'll be fine."

"Listen to me," Baxter hissed. "I saw you pick something up in the tomb. You know where the tablets are, don't you?"

Eden nodded.

"You find them, and you finish this."

Eden leaned in and hugged him. Then the strong arms held her at arm's length.

"You finish this for good," Baxter whispered.

Then Eden was falling backward, out of the boat and toward the sea. The water rushed up and consumed her, filling her ears, and blurring her vision. Eden struggled upright just in time to see Baxter push the throttle. The boat powered away.

Eden took a deep breath.

Baxter paced to the back of the boat, the knife still sticking from his back, and picked up Godspeed as if he weighed nothing. Holding the older man beneath an arm, Baxter returned to the controls. He swung the boat back around to face the harbor arm and then increased the speed.

Eden watched it all as though it were a dream. The boat lanced forward, its bow bouncing across the waves. The harbor arm reared up before them, a great rib of concrete protruding from the sea. Spray arched out, spitting angrily behind the twin outboard motors.

Godspeed squirmed and wriggled, trying to escape Baxter's grip. Baxter's arm stayed locked like a vice, trapping the man. Godspeed struck out, thumping Baxter several times. Baxter didn't even seem to notice, his eyes locked on the impenetrable wall of concrete before them.

Eden bobbed, the water lapping around her neck. She watched as the speedboat slipped into the shadow of the harbor arm. The engines thrust onward, powering them forward.

Then, there was a crunch and a crash, followed by the splintering of wood. Eden tried to look away, but she couldn't. The engines gurgled and then bawled. The fragile boat broke in half, debris slamming against the wall like firewood. Howling flames replaced the roaring engines. Starting with the craft's fuel tanks, the fire soon ripped through the craft incinerating wood, plastic, and rubber.

Several people rushing across the harbor arm gawked at the wreck. A few reached for their phones and called for help, although it was clear there was no life to be saved below.

The inferno consumed the debris and tore up against the concrete. Burning fuel gushed out across the surface of the water, flickering across the waves. Thick black smoke rose into the sky in a pillar that must have been visible for miles around.

Eden watched for several seconds as the larger parts of the speedboat sunk beneath the water. She touched her lips and thought about their soft embrace. Then she turned and swam toward an abandoned stretch of coastline.

57

Brighton. Ten days later.

EDEN CLIMBED out of the taxi and pulled her coat tightly around her. It always surprised her how quickly the temperature could change at the end of the summer. One day you were basking in the balmy heat, and the next, you were sheltering from freezing rain.

She thanked the driver and crossed the road in the direction of Brighton Cemetery. A pair of seagulls cut through the wind, shrieking their somber tone as they went.

Eden's phone vibrated in her pocket. She slid it out and glanced at the screen. She'd received a message from her contact in India, reporting that the remains of Saint Frances Xavier were back in the Basilica of Bom Jesus where they belonged.

Eden smiled weakly. At least her efforts to rescue the stolen relic from Gatwick Airport hadn't been in vain. It felt like the first good news she received in ages.

The contact said that they would send a picture as soon as they were able.

Eden put her phone away, walked through the cemetery gate and climbed the hill quickly. Reaching the top, she turned. Thick trees surrounded the large cemetery, masking the sound and sight of the city. Up here amid the trees, Eden thought, it felt like another place altogether. It felt far away from the snarling traffic and the churning sea. Maybe that's why her father had chosen it.

Eden thought about the last time she was here. The day she had buried her father. It hadn't even been that long ago, but so much had happened.

She felt the first drops of rain and looked up at the brooding sky. It had been raining then too and now it was threatening to do the same. Maybe the great deluge was in fact returning again.

Eden flipped up the collar of her coat and walked through the cemetery. Seeing her father's headstone for the first time, she slowed. He had made all the arrangements for the burial himself, including the design and inscriptions of the headstone. With her trip to Lebanon, Eden had yet to see it. The newly carved headstone's ornate and classical design glimmered against the other dulled graves. Time and weather would soon see to that.

Eden stood at the foot of the grave and read the inscription. It was simple. Her father's name was followed by the dates of his birth and death. There was no inscription, only a symbol. It was a symbol which Eden had seen night and day for the past several weeks. The Key to the Nile.

Eden's eyes lost focus and she wiped her face.

She slid her hand inside her pocket. She drew out the object which she'd found inside the tomb in Byblos. It was an object which, on the surface of it, had no business being in a six-thousand-year-old tomb in Lebanon. But it was there for a reason, Eden knew that.

She examined the object closely, turning it over in her hands.

The object was a simple box of matches with a Victorian painting of Brighton's beach on the front. She pushed the box open as she had dozens of times and inspected the matches inside. Eden had seen boxes like this frequently in the tourist shops that lined the streets of the city. But why such an item would find its way to an ancient tomb in the hills outside Byblos, she had no idea. She had spent hours considering the find, looking at it in every way she could think, but to no avail. It was in times like this that she really missed her father. He would have figured it out in moments. It was a riddle. A mystery. An enigma. One that clearly led her back to Brighton, although she had no idea why.

A large drop of rain hit the box, splashing from the waxy surface. Eden rubbed at the box with her sleeve. The surface felt oily. Eden looked down at it. The image of the seafront had smudged slightly, staining her sleeve but showing a blank surface beneath. Eden's vision suddenly snapped into focus. She looked up at her father's grave, exhaling slowly. For some reason, and not for the first time, she felt as though her father was very close indeed. It felt as though they were sharing a joke.

The rain fell more heavily now, running down Eden's face and matting her hair against her skin. She didn't notice at all as she stared back down at the box of matches in her hands.

Eden rubbed the box again. More paint smudged and then came away. Using her sleeves, that were now thoroughly wet through, Eden rubbed slowly, systematically, at the box of matches. With each drop of rain, the picture cleared a little bit further. Soon she could make out some text beneath the image. One word, or two, had been written on the box before the image had been carefully painted over the top. It was the work of a master craftsman. Possibly made by someone who's life depended on secretly passing around information.

Growing frustrated, Eden gave up with her sleeve and scraped away the waxy paint with her fingers. Within a few minutes, she was staring down at two words. They were two words she recognized. A name.

Horsam Rassam.

Godspeed's words streamed back through her mind.

"The diary was first discovered in 1876, by two men, George Godspeed and Horsam Rassam. Coincidentally, Horsam Rassam is buried in the same cemetery as your father."

Realization hit her like a punch to the gut. She almost dropped the matchbox. Her mouth fell open and she swayed back on her heels. Rassam was buried here, in this very cemetery. She looked around wide-eyed, as though she'd just observed a miracle. She looked back at the symbol on her father's headstone, shaking her head slowly. From beyond the grave, her father had led her here.

Eden smiled down at the grave and set off at a run.

Whilst the cemetery was vast, she knew Rassam would have died in the late 1890s. That meant that she could discount large areas of the site. Eden also figured that if the tablets were going to be stored in his tomb, then he wouldn't have a grave, but a mausoleum. She had seen such structures in an overgrown section at the cemetery's far side.

Eden ran past lines and lines of modern graves, her feet sliding over the wet grass. She reached the cemetery's overgrown far corner and paused. Rows of decrepit gravestones leaned against the far wall, overrun with creepers and vines.

The path narrowed until it was just a worn-down patch of dirt curving between the trees. Raindrops thumped through the canopy overhead. The hulking masses of the mausoleums were visible now, looming amid the undergrowth. Eden stomped through knee-high grass to inspect the first two. A sickening feeling rose in her stomach at the thought that she might be walking over a grave or two. With nature now the ruling force in this part of the cemetery, there was no way to know for sure. She whispered an apology to the deceased and picked her way forward slowly.

She inspected the first mausoleum. It was constructed in now moss-covered stone. Ornate carvings curved above a thick iron door. She checked the inscription on the door. It was the mausoleum of the Jones family and last used in the late 1880s. She was in the right place, but not exactly.

Eden moved on, padding gently through the undergrowth. Something rustled beneath a tree, startling her momentarily before she saw a fat squirrel charge up the trunk. Eden approached several more mausoleums. She checked the name of the family and the dates carefully. None could have been Rassam.

Then, after almost an hour of searching, Eden saw something at the very far side of the cemetery. A mausoleum set away from all the others. The construction looked different too. With turrets and a steeply pitched roof, it looked like something out of a gothic horror novel. Eden pushed her way through a nest of curling brambles, ignoring the pain as they scraped and scratched at her legs. The walls of the mausoleum were moss-covered and crumbling in places.

From twenty feet away, Eden paused and examined the building. If she could see the name from here, then she may not need to go any further. She squinted, scrutinizing the stone above the door. A symbol sat in the place where words were usually carved.

A bolt of electricity shot through Eden's body.

There, above the door, was the symbol she'd been following around for the last few weeks. The Key to the Nile.

Eden rushed forward, pushing the brambles away. She reached the thick metal door and ran her hands across its blistered surface. Sure enough, Rassam's name was carved into the stone.

58

Tracing her here was easy, he thought, following the trail of grass which now lay flat. But that wasn't surprising, as she didn't have reason to think anyone was following anymore. She'd left that behind in Lebanon.

It always paid to be careful though, he thought, ducking behind a tree as Eden turned a corner up ahead.

In truth, he had gotten quite used to following her. It felt as though he knew what she was going to do before she did. That was only natural, though, he thought.

The only danger of her seeing him today was the lack of other people around. He thought she'd almost glimpsed him a couple of times back in Byblos. But because he'd turned his back at the right moment, or knelt to tie a fictional shoelace, she'd not thought anything of it.

Out here, though, in this deserted cemetery, there was no one else about. Noticing another person here would attract attention.

He peered around the tree and watched her stalk further into the undergrowth. Rain padded softly against the canopy of the trees above him. He would wait in the dry a little longer, he thought. After all, he had a pretty good idea where she was going. Probably a better idea than she did.

EDEN HAD FOUND IT. Rassam's mausoleum. Just a few hundred yards from where her own father was buried.

Suddenly, the hairs on the back of Eden's neck bristled. It felt as though someone was watching her. Eden swung around, her eyes searching the bushes. Raindrops tapped through the leaves above and dropped heavily to the ground. A pair of pigeons cooed and chattered somewhere overhead. No shapes moved between the trees. No gun-toting men ran her way. She couldn't see anyone. In fact, she hadn't seen a single person since arriving at the cemetery.

"Get a grip, Eden," she whispered out loud. Godspeed was dead, Baxter had made sure of that. No one was chasing her now.

Eden turned back to the door. An ancient, rust-covered padlock sealed it closed. Eden pushed against the metal. It swung open a couple of inches before the lock jammed. Eden crouched down and examined the stones around the door frame. The mortar had crumbled away, leaving several of the stones loose. She eased one out slowly. The stone was carved into a point at one end like a readymade hammer. Eden rose it above her head and struck the padlock. On the third strike, the ancient metal crunched and fell open.

Eden unhooked the padlock and then eased the stone back into position.

The door shrieked as she shouldered it open. A thin beam of light swept through the room, lancing through cobwebs which hung as thick as ropes from one wall to the next. Eden drew out her phone and clicked on the light.

Eden's first thought was that the mausoleum was much

smaller than the tomb they'd found in Byblos. A sinking feeling swept through her.

Eden stepped inside, pushing cobwebs out of the way, and panned the light from one side to the other. The mausoleum was about twelve feet square, with a large stone casket in the center. The walls were constructed from bare stone and the roof with timber and slate.

There was no way that thousands of stone tablets could be hidden in this small place, Eden thought, her excitement draining. Maybe this was just another wrong turn in a journey full of them. She slumped to the ground against the large stone casket in the center of the room. She dug out the matchbox again and looked at it closely. But what else could it mean?

She looked around the mausoleum. There was just no way several thousand stone tablets could be concealed in a space this size. She was back to square one.

Eden's thoughts were interrupted when the casket behind her slipped an inch backward. She jumped to her feet, her heart pounding. She spun around and examined the casket. She calmed slightly, realizing that no long-dead archaeologists were reaching out to get her. But the casket had definitely moved.

Eden trained the light down on the stone floor. She could see from the lighter color of the stones, that her leaning on the casket had caused it to slide about an inch toward the far wall.

Eden rubbed a hand across her face to remove the cobwebs. She thought through this new discovery and examined the floor again. The casket had definitely moved. Eden slid the phone back in her pocket and pushed against the casket. At first her feet skidded against the moss-covered flagstones, but once she found grip, the casket moved easily.

It slid with an ease that belied its size. It felt as though the whole thing was mounted on hidden wheels.

Eden heaved, looking down at the floor. Two more inches of flagstone were revealed. Then, a deep void came into view. Eden gasped, at first not believing what she saw.

She pushed on, widening the gap. The damp smell of wet earth streamed through the hole. When the gap was about three feet wide, Eden stood up and caught her breath. She stretched her arms and then pulled her phone out of her pocket. She crawled to the edge and peered inside.

Eden inhaled in shock, almost choking on the thick, dust-filled air. Her heart pounded at double speed. There was another room beneath the mausoleum. She couldn't work out how big the room was because it was full of large, flat stones piled in tall stacks.

Eden reached in and took one from the top. She examined it closely. Both sides of the stone were covered in a scrawling language she didn't understand. Eden knew exactly what she'd found.

It was the lost diary of Aloma.

59

ALEXANDER WINSLOW DUCKED back out of sight as his daughter appeared at the door of the mausoleum. Her face was set in an expression of wide-eyed shock, and between her hands she clutched one of the tablets.

He recognized the tablet, although he'd not seen them for several years.

Having discovered that Aloma's tomb was empty in 1998, there was only one possible place Winslow could think the tablets would be. Making people think that the tablets were still in Byblos, well, that was a classic piece of misdirection. After all, who would have believed that a world-changing artifact had been in a cemetery in Brighton for over a century.

After the discovery in 1998, Alexander Winslow had come all alone to this corner of the cemetery and found just what he was looking for. As much as he'd wanted to shout his discovery to the world, he knew then that the time wasn't right. Back then the old guard was still strong. People weren't ready for change.

He peered out from behind the tree and watched Eden

refasten the door. Eden tucked the tablet beneath her coat, flipped up her hood, and stomped back through the undergrowth.

Now, Winslow predicted, people were ready for change. In the last few years, he had watched protests sweep the globe. From human rights, environmental issues, to equality, now everyone had a cause to fight. The younger generation were asking questions of their leaders, and the usual nonsense answers weren't holding up.

People were ready for change, and he planned to give it to them.

A smile spread across Alexander's grizzled face as Eden disappeared into the swaying undergrowth. Well, Eden would give it to them, really.

A fission of sadness shuddered through Winslow's body. He longed to speak to his daughter, to hug her, to spend time with her in the way a father normally would. Right now, though, that just wasn't possible. It was far too dangerous for them both.

Without him, Eden could do this. She could find the answers people wanted. She could expose the secrets that had been kept undercover for so long.

There was a battle going on, but this time it wasn't fought in the muddy fields of a far-off land. This was a battle of truth and freedom, fought in the mind of every human on the planet.

A cold breeze pushed through the undergrowth, hissing through the trees, and shuddering down Winslow's spine. He pulled the black scarf more tightly around his neck.

Right now, he would be Eden's guardian angel. He would keep her out of harm's way as much as possible. He would show her the path to uncovering the things she needed to. He would work behind the scenes, making sure the right people showed up at the right time. He would give her access to his contacts, who would provide the perfect platform to spread her message.

With him gone, she had a fresh chance to lead this change.

Looking wistfully in the direction of his own grave, Alexander Winslow pulled a pack of chamomile cigarettes from his pocket. Sometimes, he thought, the best thing to do was to get out of the way and let the next generation lead the fight. He stuck a cigarette in the corner of his mouth and lit up, and then checked his watch. Time was short. Eden had a big event coming up. She just didn't know it yet.

Glancing at the sky, Alexander Winslow pulled his coat tightly around himself and headed off between the trees.

EPILOGUE

Cambridge University. One month later.

A BUZZ of excitement electrified the air at Cambridge University's Lady Mitchell Hall. Disregarding the University's rules, the venue's five-hundred-person capacity had been expanded at least two-fold. People stood at the back, in the aisles, or wherever space was available.

The small television crew checked and re-checked their equipment. They spoke via ear radios with the vision mixer stationed in a van outside. With today's lecture, the pressure was on. Several thousand people were planning to watch from other venues around the world. And, if the content of the lecture was as intriguing as everyone predicted, it could be watched for years to come. A ban on audience members using their own cameras also meant the official crew's footage would be carried by major news networks around the world. Mistakes could not be entertained at this level.

A grey-haired professor in the front row turned and scrutinized the crowd behind him. His eyes moved slowly behind the lenses of his thick glasses.

"I know what you're thinking, they never turn up like this for our lectures," said his colleague, sitting beside him.

The professor guffawed and pushed his glasses further up his nose. "I've not seen it as busy as this since the Lennon concert." The Lady Mitchell Hall had been the venue of John Lennon and Yoko Ono's first public concert together over fifty years ago.

"That's a bit before my time," the other man said, grinning wolfishly.

Exactly on schedule, three black Range Rovers pulled up to the hall's rear entrance. A gaggle of waiting journalists rushed around the corner, only to be pushed back by police officers.

The doors of the Range Rovers at the front and rear swung open and eight private security personnel climbed out. Four disappeared inside the venue, while the other four set up a perimeter around the vehicles.

Several minutes passed as another security check of the venue was carried out. Finally, the doors of the central vehicle swung open. Two more security agents climbed out, one carrying an aluminum briefcase. Eden followed.

Unaware she was the subject of a security operation of this size, Eden stretched and looked around nonchalantly. Her hair was pinned up high. Although her blue trouser suit felt restrictive, she'd been told frequently that it "looked the part."

With a glance over her shoulder, and offering the faint outline of a smile to the howling press gang, she followed the guards inside.

Nearly fifteen minutes later, Professor Richard Beaumont climbed to the lectern. A silence settled over the hall. Hundreds of people held their collective breath.

Professor Beaumont cleared his throat. The sound echoed through the venue's multiple speakers.

"As part of our Pushing Boundaries Summit, Alexander Winslow was supposed to speak here today. The content of his lecture was a closely guarded secret, but it had been said that it was going to be, how shall I say... explosive. We were all saddened to hear of his death, and assumed, obviously, that meant the lecture was off." Beaumont cast a glance at Eden, standing in the doorway to his right. She stood still and straight, her face rigid against any emotions.

"But, just two weeks ago, at the eleventh hour if you will, his daughter, Eden Black, volunteered to lecture in his place. If the media interest in Miss Black's recent escapades are anything to go by, I think we're in for a very illuminating afternoon." Professor Beaumont retired from the lectern and joined his colleagues in the front row.

Eden climbed slowly on to the stage. She looked out at the waiting audience. Every eye focused on her. She swallowed hard, feeling the first prickle of sweat on her neck.

The leading security guard slid the aluminium briefcase on to a table.

Eden entered a code into the briefcase's digital locking system. The lock disengaged and the lid snapped open.

Hundreds of people took a united intake of breath.

Eden approached the lectern and began.

"My father believed in something. He believed that we, the citizens of this planet, deserve to know the truth." Eden scanned the audience again. Hundreds of people stared back, entranced. Millions more watched around the world.

For a moment Eden felt a flurry of anxiety. A fissure of worry that she wasn't able to do it, that she couldn't do it. She swallowed and gripped the lectern.

She glanced at the professors in the front row, men who

had spent their whole lives in preparation for a discovery like this.

As Eden watched, Professor Beaumont pulled a tiny chain from the pocket of his waist coat. He held it up and Eden saw, in the bright lights of the auditorium, a tiny silver symbol. The Key to the Nile. However big the task ahead, Eden wasn't doing it alone.

"Several weeks ago, I made a discovery which will allow us to rewrite history."

Eden pulled on a pair of white cotton gloves. She crossed to the case and lifted out one of the stone tablets. A collective gasp rose from the audience.

"Professor Beaumont and his team are currently working on translating these stone tablets. They contain the diary of a woman named Aloma, who lived over five thousand years ago. They are the only living record of one of our planet's most defining moments, the Great Deluge. With this record, and the solutions it is already giving us, we can start to answer some of humankind's greatest questions."

Eden paused and looked directly down the lens of the camera at the front of the crowd. Although every single person in the hall, and several million more watching around the world, looked on, Eden felt as if she were speaking to one person only. And strangely, in that moment, Eden could have sworn that he was watching too.

"And I promise you," she said to her father, "I will do whatever it takes to answer those questions."

THE MAN KNOWN ONLY as Helios clicked off the screen and climbed out of his chair. He had just watched a presentation live from Cambridge University in which a young woman had revealed her discovery of a set of tablets. What the tablets meant, still wasn't understood.

Helios knew, however, that if Eden Black followed the clues hidden within those tablets, they would lead her straight to him, and ultimately, to The Council of the Selene.

Helios strode through the doors and out on to the Balonia's back deck. Uninterrupted water surrounded the yacht on all sides. The warmth of the day was fading, and stars had started to appear above. This far away from land, the stars covered every inch of the heavens in an unrivalled display of light and dark.

The tablets would detail a secret Council, set up at the very birth of this age. A Council that had, over the centuries, controlled the flow of finance, the outbreak and resolution of conflict, the invention of new technologies, even the development of medicine. A Council that was carefully controlled by Helios, the seven councilors, and their predecessors.

Of course, over time the people serving as The Councilors, and even Helios himself, had changed — they were only human — but the roles and their duty had remained the same. Keep humankind on the trajectory of progress.

Helios gazed out at the horizon now as the last strokes of light faded from the sky. Maybe now, he thought, it was time to give humankind a chance to govern itself.

THE GIZA PROTOCOL

Eden returns in The Giza Protocol - OUT NOW!

THE POWER TO RULE THE WORLD OR SET US ALL FREE.

WHEN AN UNDISCOVERED TEMPLE emerges from the waters of a drought-stricken lake, the world of archeology starts to pay attention.

On the discovery of a set of hieroglyphs suggesting the location of an ancient power source so abundant it could boil the world's oceans dry, a lot more people start to listen.

Enter EDEN BLACK.

With forest fires, droughts, and famine worldwide, Eden and her band of unlikely heroes must move quickly to make sure this lifeline for humankind doesn't become another asset for the super-rich.

From Lake Nasser to the labyrinthine tunnels beneath the Giza Plateau, Eden will find herself trapped in the crosshairs of a tycoon on the make, an enigmatic secret society, and a foe who's closer to home than she could ever imagine.

Read The Giza Protocol TODAY!

AUTHOR'S NOTE

Thank you for reading The Ark Files.

I hope you've enjoyed meeting Eden. I've loved writing about her. It's been my privilege to entertain you for the last few hours!

Now that we've reached the end of this part of the story, I have a confession to make with you.

The story you've just read is based on true people and real events.

Or at least, the person who came to me with the story, has some extremely compelling evidence to suggest that it is true.

Let me digress for a moment. As a writer, stories come to me from all sorts of places and in all manner of ways. The story for my book Riga came to me while I was reading about the history of Latvia, Istanbul came to me after a conversation with a man in a pub, and many others I uncovered while I was writing.

But the story you've just finished came to me in a completely different form. One evening I was cycling home in the rain and my phone rang. I pulled over beneath a tree and answered. It was a friend I've known for several years, but who shall remain anonymous here. I was surprised by the call as we've spoken many times over that period, but never really in depth.

"I've just had a thought. I don't know why I didn't think of this before," he started, in an unusually excited tone. "I've got a story that needs telling. You'll love it."

Over the next hour, and several subsequent meetups, he told me an amazing story of hidden manuscripts, secret societies, and millennia-old conspiracies.

Whilst Eden and her RV in the woods is a product of my imagination, almost everything else in this story is real. I have changed some names for readability, but some of them even remain the same.

The story started for my friend at the age of thirteen when he was given a manuscript to read. Titled 'Seola' and published in 1878, the manuscript was a diary of a woman from before and during The Great Flood. It's since been rewritten and published under the title 'The Diary of Aloma' – yes, it's a real book. I have a copy on my shelf!

After reading the manuscript my friend was asked a simple question – is it fact or fiction? He answered assuredly that it was fiction. It had to be, right?

In research for this book, I read 'The Diary of Aloma,' and would have absolutely thought the same if I didn't know the background.

It was only years later, when researching another subject, that he realized he had come across the same information before. That led him to revisit "Seola". Things slowly started to make sense. Looking back at "Seola", he realized that it wasn't quite as fictional as he'd first thought.

I'm not going to be too specific here, as that's to come in Eden's next adventure.

He's since spent decades checking the etymology and researching the historical details in *'Seola.'* Strangely, *'Seola'* makes several claims that weren't historically known when it was written in the 1870s, and one particular detail which wasn't discovered until the 1990s!

There is also a big question mark over the author as well. The book is credited as being written by Ann Eliza Brainerd using the pen name Mrs. J G Smith. My friend has a very different theory for who the author of *'Seola'* might be – we will come to that in a minute!

In 1924, *'Seola'* was revised by Charles Taze Russell and published as *'Angels & Women.'* Then in 2001 it was revised for a third time by theologian and historian, Alexander Winslow – that's right, he's a real person. Now titled *'Diary of Aloma,'* Winslow spent over two decades revising *'Seola'* in collaboration, with other historians, theologians, and translators. Alexander Winslow published books and articles for many years and died in 2021.

In the 1977 book, 'Secrets of the Lost Races,' Rene Noorbergen suggests there is strong evidence *'Seola'* was translated from ancient documents. Such documents were discussed in letters regarding a manuscript called *'Amoela's Diary,'* which was the focus of an Oriental Archaeological Research Expedition in 1950.

Whether the diary did, or does exist, though, that's up to you to decide. What is unrefusable however, is the fascinating work of the archeologists who discovered thousands of tablets throughout the Middle East in the 19th and 20th centuries.

These men are no strangers to thriller writers. Even the queen of mysteries, Agatha Christie, based a few of her novels on the exploits of these men. That's no surprise when you consider that as well as being some of the most successful archaeologists of all time, they were also spying for the Crown in the Ottoman Empire.

Four of the most prominent archeologists of the period were: George Smith, Hormuzd Rassam, Sir Austen Henry Layard (Assyriologists) and Sir Henry Rawlinson, the "Father of Assyriology."

Now we come to 'Seola's' original author.

In 1876 George Smith died in Syria. One of the few people in the world at that time with the ability to translate cuneiform, this was a dire blow to the archeological community. However, two years later, an anonymous manuscript was sent from America to Mrs J G Smith – the supposed author of the original 'Seola.' Furthermore, the manuscript was delivered to the home address of Hormuzd Rassam in England!

Is it impossible to suggest that George Smith escaped death in Syria and fled to the States, where he set about translating this life-changing manuscript?

We know he had contacts there, namely another George, George Goodspeed.

George Smith and George Goodspeed's CVs are so similar I decided to merge these characters into the fictional George Godspeed.

George Smith, alongside Hormuzd Rassam are most noted for discovering and translating the Epic of Gilgamesh.

Hormuzd Rassam (you may recognize him, although I tweaked his first name to Horsam in this book) is actually buried in Brighton. He died in 1910, as one of the leading archaeologists of his time.

British Museum curator, Wallis Budge accused Rassam of not declaring all the tablets that they had discovered.

Deeply hurt, Rassam sued Budge in 1893 for libel and won. But the resulting publicity left Rassam's reputation in tatters.

I wonder if there are any secrets buried in and around his tomb in Brighton?

I did make the choice to present this book in the present day, which means we didn't get to meet these characters in person. But learning about them, as Eden does, was fascinating for me.

This topic and has some interesting theories about where the original diary may be, only one of which I've explored in this book.

Why is the diary so important?

Its existence means that there was a living witness on the ground who covered all the fine details of what went on during and after The Great Flood. A news reporter live on the ground, if you will. Proof of this would mean that many ancient sites in the fertile crescent and Egypt would fall in an earlier epoch. Something many Geologists have been telling Egyptologists they have got wrong for a long time!

That would just be the start of re-writing history.

You'll have to follow Eden on her future adventures to learn more as she uncovers the truth.

As for the person who provided me the story, he prefers his anonymity. He's working on something in the background, but until he gets the physical evidence that is just another theory.

Thank you again for joining me on this adventure!

Luke

September 2022

CAN A PRICELESS PAINTING VANISH INTO THIN AIR?

Eden Black meets Ernest Dempsey's Adriana Villa

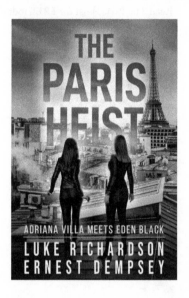

Ten years ago, Bernard Moreau baffled police by stealing a Picasso from the Modern Art Museum. He was arrested and imprisoned, but the painting was never found.

Now, back on the streets, all eyes are on Moreau. But he's a skilled thief and isn't going to make it easy.

EDEN BLACK can't stand corruption and the theft of priceless art. This case reeks of them both. Heading to Paris, she vows to return the Picasso to its rightful home as soon as possible.

ADRIANA VILLA works alone, always, that's the rule. So, when she sees another woman following her mark, things get heated.

To find the painting before a dirty police inspector with a score to settle, the pair must put their egos aside and work together. What they discover shows that nothing is as simple as it first seems.

THE PARIS HEIST is an up-tempo novella which will keep you pinned to the pages until the very end. If you like the sound of a race against the clock, action packed, adventure thriller, set amongst the blissful Parisian streets, you'll love THE PARIS HEIST.

Read The Paris Heist for FREE today!

ABOUT THE AUTHOR

First of all, thanks so much for taking an interest in my writing. My books are the culmination of years of travelling, dreaming and writing. I'm so excited to share them with you.

My journey towards writing, like most, wasn't straight-forward. I've always loved stories, but it wasn't until my thirties that I actually put pen to paper. I think I needed to see and experience the world a bit before writing about it.

I grew up in the South of England, near Hastings, and moved to Nottingham for university. After that I worked as a nightclub DJ for a few years - I still do from time to time.

In 2013 I trained to be an English teacher. Helping young people realize and enjoy their creativity was wonderful. But, as many teachers will testify, it's not a job that sits well with other hobbies and interests. So, in 2020 I made the decision to leave the classroom and focus on my writing, travel, and spend time with friends and family.

My stories are part adventure, part mystery, and always rely heavily on the places I go and the people I meet.

Where do you want to go now?

BOOK REVIEWS

If you've enjoyed this book I would appreciate a review.

Reviews are essential for three reasons. Firstly, they encourage people to take a chance on an author they've never heard of. Secondly, bookselling websites use them to decide what books to recommend through their search engine. And third, I love to hear what you think!

Having good reviews really can make a massive difference to new authors like me.

It'll take you no longer than two minutes, and will mean the world to me.

www.lukerichardsonauthor.com/reviews

Thank you.

OTHER SERIES BY LUKE RICHARDSON

International Detectives

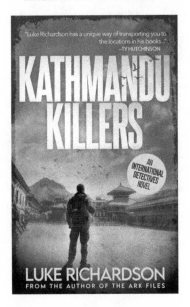

You visit a restaurant in a far-away city, only to find you're on the menu.

Leo Keane is sent abroad to track down Allissa, a politician's daughter who vanished two years ago in Kathmandu. But with a storm on the horizon and intrigue at every turn, Leo's mission may be more dangerous than he bargained for... A propulsive international thriller!

READ FREE TODAY

https://www.lukerichardsonauthor.com/kathmandu

Kickass Vigilantes

Justice is her beat

Her name is Kayla Stone

She is 'The Liberator'

The Liberator Series is a ferocious new collaboration between Luke Richardson and Steven Moore.

If you like Clive Cussler, Nick Thacker, Ernest Dempsey and Russel Blake, then you'll love this explosive series!

READ TODAY

Printed in the USA
CPSIA information can be obtained
at www.ICGtesting.com
LVHW041518090923
757264LV00005B/889